SHUT DOWN

A Story of Economic Collapse and Hope

W. R. FLYNN

Copyright © 2011 W. R. Flynn
All rights reserved.

ISBN: 1460969413
ISBN-13: 9781460969410

This book is a work of fiction. Names, characters, places, and incidents either are products of the author's imagination or are used fictitiously. Any resemblance to actual events or locales or persons, living or dead, is entirely coincidental.

First Edition

Correspondence for the author should be addressed to: wrflynn54@gmail.com

Manufactured in the United States of America
CreateSpace, Charleston, SC

The vast and fathomless seas
Will eventually dry up.
The earth, sun, and moon
Will all perish in due time.
Not one thing in the world
Can escape impermanence.

Shakyamuni Buddha
The Sutra on Impermanence

Acknowledgements

The list of those who contributed to make this project a reality is a long one. I hope I haven't missed anyone.

First, I want to thank my dear wife, Deborah, who kindly offered her proofreading skills and patience. Without her help, writing this novel would have been impossible.

My sister, Patricia, performed the last editing making the work publishable.

Next, I must thank my daughter, Alison, who painstakingly edited punctuation and grammar from start to finish.

My daughter, Kelly, suggested the title and corrected numerous typographical errors as the work progressed.

My son, Casey, who proofread early drafts and kindly edited several critical points, deserves special thanks.

My friend, Jerry Kalapus, proofread this work and offered priceless suggestions and encouragement. The advice he provided was critical to the successful completion of this novel.

I have to give thanks also to my good friend, Pete Roth, who offered vital technical suggestions in many areas. Furthermore, he provided a guided tour of the scene of the final battles.

Thanks also must be given to my other good friends who contributed: Jeff Fauth, who provided much needed economics advice;

Corey Anderson, who created the Black American Dialect dialogues; Chris Saunders, who assisted in building several key scenes; Scott Pritchard … well, I can't tell anyone how he helped but he certainly did; John Henderson, who early on kindly steered this work in the proper direction; Kevin Sakai, who kindly offered his priceless firearms-related expertise; Bob Bents, who encouraged me right from the start; the fantastic Troutdale Police Department for keeping the people of that fine city safe every minute of the day, and all the other good people who helped make this work a reality: you know who you are and I thank you.

TRIPLE ESPRESSO

Chapter One

After stepping out of her train car and briskly walking two blocks from the First Avenue MAX platform, Kelly Lee opened the Starbucks front door and quickly got the place ready for business. It was 5:58 a.m. and the first thirsty, caffeine starved customers would be arriving any second. She hoped Tina, the other barista, would show up for work. Tina called in sick about every other Monday but Kelly had opened the place alone before and knew she could do it again. The customers really enjoyed Kelly's cheerful manner and occasional jokes, plus she was tall and beautiful making her a fun person to drop in and visit with each morning. Her boss, Mark would be showing up for work in 45 minutes and since he never missed a day of work or showed up late she knew almost to the minute when he would walk in the door. Kelly was an unusually fast and efficient worker, but she would definitely need his help when the morning got busier, as it always did.

At 6:37 Kelly made a triple espresso to go for one of her regular customers. He ordered the same drink each morning, almost like clockwork.

"That will be $3.25."

The man handed Kelly his green bankcard issued by Oregon State Bank.

As she gracefully slid the three-quarters filled tiny paper cup across the counter with one hand, she deftly swiped his debit card through the card reader slot with the other.

'Error,' it read.

Nearly all her customers paid with a bankcard. She had been successfully swiping debit and credit cards through the slot all morning, exactly as she had been doing for months so she sent it through once more: 'Error,' the tiny screen again displayed.

"I'm sorry sir, do you have a different card?"

"No. Here's a five, my card should be working just fine. How annoying. I don't know what's wrong with it. I'll call the bank when it opens and find out what's wrong with my account. Oh, keep the change, Kelly."

The same thing happened with the next customer. Then the following four customers' cards failed. It was time to text Mark and let him know that the card reader was no longer working.

For Mark, it was a normal warm summer commute. The traffic along I-5 was crawling along as it usually does as tens of thousands of commuters headed to their jobs in the core of the city. There was nothing particularly out of the ordinary on the radio at 6:15 a.m. as Mark Edmunds slowly moved north at 35 mph toward the downtown Portland exit. He enjoyed listening to his favorite talk show host chat with the many listeners calling in complaining about the nation's political and economic situation much as they had each morning during the past twelve years of his monotonous daily drive to work as the manager of a busy downtown Starbucks. Today the host was talking about bank closures which bored Mark so he turned off his radio, cranked down his window, and enjoyed the cool morning breeze.

He was a bit sleepy this morning because, as with each Monday morning for the past few months, he woke up early to join an hour-long wait in line for gas. The daily lines started forming early in the year and were happening across the USA. It was considered a minor annoyance to most and was reminiscent to older drivers of the long gas lines in 1973 and 1979, each of which thankfully lasted only a few months.

Mark, like millions of others waiting for gas this morning, didn't mind it that much. He was used to it by now and used the free time to sip his morning coffee while eating a bagel. He also busied himself by reading the daily news, texting a few friends, and otherwise getting his day started happily tapping away the minutes on the screen of his new phone while he slowly crept toward the pump. At exactly 6:00 a.m., the motorcyclists who had exclusive pump use for the previous hour were finished and by 6:15 after a one-hour wait, Mark was now at the head of the line. The time in line went quickly this morning and as he pulled out of the gas station in his four year old Yaris he smiled to himself, knowing it was a chore he wouldn't need to deal with for another week. At 37 mpg he could make each of the $8.25 gallons of gasoline last longer than most drivers.

As he neared his exit, his senior barista, Kelly Lee, sent him an urgent text message: "Most of the customers' debit cards are no longer working and they're not very happy about it." She didn't know it at the time, but it would be the last text message she would ever send because the nation's cell phones would soon quit working.

Like he had for the previous 15 years, Mark quickly wound through the one way downtown streets and at 6:45 found a place for his car in his favorite parking garage. He got out of his car and began his daily brisk six-block walk to his corner coffee shop. He enjoyed starting off the day with some nice healthy exercise. At an unusually handsome 5'8" and 150 lbs, he was trim and fit for a 42-year-old man and he wanted to stay that way.

As he walked he noticed the sidewalks were starting to fill with the usual assortment of early rising foot traffic including office workers, bums, and uniformed delivery drivers. It started out as a perfectly normal day until he turned up Second Avenue and saw a line of about a half-dozen Portland Police Bureau officers standing in front of the Oregon State Bank Building with their cars parked bumper to bumper along the curb in front. Standing among them were about a dozen stern-faced men wearing dark t-shirts with an assortment of large yellow letters on the back of them. He recognized a few of the three-letter combinations, such as 'FBI' and 'DOJ,' but the others were unfamiliar to him. It was no doubt a federal raid of some sort. Something important was happening at the Oregon State Bank headquarters, which Mark knew was the largest bank in the state.

They must be preparing to search someone's office or maybe arrest someone important, Mark thought to himself as he walked by. He walked another half block and into work thinking nothing more of it.

Chapter Two

Late Sunday night, while Kelly, Mark and most other Americans slept, the FDIC was busy processing the paperwork needed to declare Oregon State Bank and 623 other US banks insolvent. The wave of bank failures had been accelerating for several years. The pace of bank failures accelerated with an additional 417 failing the previous year. However, this stunning and unprecedented one-day move left countless city, county, and state governments as well as 85 million Americans unable to access their bank accounts including those attempting their usual morning debit card ritual at Mark's Starbucks.

Under normal circumstances, when the FDIC ordered a bank closed, a competing bank was quickly lined up in advance ready and able to seamlessly assume operations. Unfortunately for the coffee drinkers and millions of other Americans on this otherwise fine summer morning, the number of dollars deposited in banks shut down by the overnight wave of bank closures was $1.6 trillion. It far exceeded the FDIC's Deposit Insurance Fund, which only contained $22 billion when the weekend began. The FDIC had the authority to borrow an additional $500 billion from the Treasury Department, but that back-up funding did not exist. Therefore, the banks would remain closed until Congress or the recently weakened Federal Reserve acted. The lines of police officers and assorted federal agents standing guard in front of many of the thousands of closed bank branches across the USA were there to ensure that their bank doors remained locked to the public while bank officers and federal officials prepared the final documents related to the closures. But as the morning rolled by the situation changed and most of the police were dispatched to guard property elsewhere, leaving the majority of the nation's banks protected only by vertical sheets of thin glass.

The morning surge of bank closures triggered an economic shock wave when the news broke at 9:30 a.m. in Washington, DC. When the equity trading markets opened in New York, stock market chaos was correctly predicted by nearly everyone. At 9:30 a.m. EDT the three major US stock markets, which had grown increasingly volatile since January, opened for trading. The Dow immediately fell over 5,500 points, blasting through all three circuit breakers within seconds causing the market to immediately close for the remainder of the day. The expected major market correction had found its feared trigger event. Its devastating impact was quickly felt across the entire USA.

Monday was payday for Chicago city employees, and the bank handling their payroll was on the closed list. This left 42,000 Chicago city employees to join hundreds of thousands of city, county and state government employees along with millions of other private sector Americans whose paychecks would not be accessible. The news media eagerly reported every frightening detail as the financial disaster spread and deepened.

In Oregon, as hundreds of thousands of hungry public assistance recipients queued up in the early morning for their usual first-day-of-the-month grocery shopping ritual, they found that their Oregon Trail Cards no longer worked. Over one million Oregonians dependent on food stamps would be unable to get food. Word spread fast, and as the warm summer sun rose, large increasingly agitated crowds soon formed at stores throughout the state. As supermarkets across Oregon opened for business, purchases were conducted in cash only, but few customers had cash. 'The Shut-Down Event,' as the reporters soon called it, was now well underway and spreading deeper each minute into the quickly unraveling financial and social fabric of the nation.

All remaining banks opened as usual Monday, offering an initial sense of stability and calm. No one had expected such a massive wave of bank failures. The USA had not experienced any bank-runs for many generations and it was the last thing on most people's minds. Faith in the power of the government to sort things out still ran high. As the morning progressed, however, long queues of customers formed as people across the USA emptied their safe deposit boxes and withdrew their money in case their banks were next to close. By mid-morning on the West Coast most banks ran out of dispensable cash reserves. At 1:15 p.m. EDT the Federal Reserve Board of Governors met via teleconference hoping to find a solution to the growing crisis and forged a tentative plan, but their proposal required a presidential emergency declaration. It should have occurred immediately, but events would prove they moved too late. The newly elected president was voted in based partially on his principled stand against federal intervention in the economy. The Federal Reserve Board Chairman called a press conference for 3:30 p.m. in New York, but it would take more than mere words to quell this crisis and rapidly unfolding events would lead to a cancellation of the conference and a cancellation of their plan, which was never revealed but undoubtedly would have involved printing even more money. However, by 1:30 p.m. EDT, looting and rioting were well underway in most US cities.

As fear spread across the USA, supermarkets everywhere were besieged by mobs. Prior to the New Year's Day attack on Iran, many supermarkets and big-box stores were open 24 hours a day, but by March, as the financial crisis progressed, nearly all had cut back on their hours and opened no earlier than seven a.m.

Today, the lines of hungry Americans were forming well before then, as they did on the first of every month. On the first day of every month, an estimated 92 million people in the United States had next to no food in their homes. As usual on this first day of the month tens of millions of hungry Americans, along with a few million non-Americans, were queuing up in supermarkets and big box stores across the United States expecting to restock their refrigerators and pantries using federally funded and state-managed public assistance debit cards used by an astounding 31% of the U.S. population. The growing crowds soon discovered that their cards no longer worked.

As the morning wore on, fewer and fewer let that stop them from filling up shopping carts and simply loading their haul into their vehicles or pushing the heaping carts home without paying. For most, it was their very first looting experience. Employees began to flee for their lives and as the morning moved forward, widespread, panicked looting settled in across the USA.

Gas lines grew much longer than usual as frightened motorists lined up to top off their gas tanks. Tempers flared as the morning warmed and angry motorists were forced to pay rapidly rising gasoline prices. At 8:15 a.m. in Los Angeles, a well-organized street gang controlling a large section of south central LA seized every gas station in that part of the city and began charging $15.00 per gallon, cash only: no limit. By early afternoon their newly conquered filling stations had run dry.

As looting became widespread, National Guard troops were activated in 44 states. However, organizing the units was proving difficult and slow since so many guard units were partially depleted with large numbers serving duty in an assortment of overseas police actions and combat assignments including 40,000 recently deployed into western Pakistan, tens of thousands more sent once again into Iraq, 15,000 into the United Arab Emirates, 12,000 into Libya and 12,000 deployed into Yemen.

With the majority of police units initially assigned guarding banks, citizens were largely left to protect themselves and 911 calls in most major cities went unanswered. In fact, if people wanted to place any calls on their cell phones, they were unable to do so because by mid-morning on the West Coast few cell phones systems anywhere in the USA remained operational.

After January, as the economic crisis began to deepen further, most major carriers had to lay off large numbers of technical staff to remain profitable. Critical maintenance was put off. Making matters worse, only 15% of residences still had landlines and many carriers were no longer offering them. Since the start of the year cell phone users throughout the U.S. were complaining more and more that it was getting tough to get a signal: much like in the mid-'90s, but worse. Furthermore, the various cellular systems had become unbelievably complicated and interconnected. A major malfunction in one area could cause havoc throughout the entire system. As the hours ticked by on Monday matters became much worse. A technical expert interviewed at 11:05 a.m. EDT on CNN calmly explained the situation, "The operating systems in most cities have suddenly become overloaded. It is much worse than during 9/11 and people are working very hard to get the system operational and back online." But the reality was that the highly skilled technical staff required to make the system operational again were as frightened as anyone else and were simply no longer available.

By 10:15 in the morning nervous customers had been besieging the Portland Bullion Exchange for over an hour. It was located across 3rd Avenue from Mark's Starbucks and had been enjoying a growing business since the recent unsuccessful Israeli air attack on Iran's nuclear infrastructure. Five men with rifles were inside guarding the bullion business. Normally on a Monday morning Mark would be busy serving a bewildering array of coffee drinks to hundreds of customers and all morning the 21 seats inside this Starbucks would be filled, but by 10:30 a.m. only three nervous customers were sipping coffee at his Starbucks.

Fewer cars passed down this usually busy downtown Portland street. By 10:30 a.m. most downtown workers increasingly fearful of the growing emergency, headed home early much like they would if a surprise snowstorm had hit. Most businesses closed early. Downtown Portland was closing down. Mark took great pride in never missing a single day of work in over ten years and he wasn't about to ruin his stellar attendance record by closing his Starbucks early. So he stayed.

Chapter Three

At 10:45, Kelly, his attractive and intelligent senior barista, who was starting her fourth month in this high-turnover position, wiped the counter for the hundredth time that morning. She glanced once more at the clock and looked at Mark, "Hey Mark, would you mind if I went home a little early today? I get off in about an hour anyhow and … well, since the place is so quiet … I was just wondering…"

The downtown area was emptying out fast and Mark knew it. Something very unusual was going on and he was getting nervous about it. So was Kelly. Normally she got off work at noon, but mindful of the growing panic and concerned about her safety, Mark replied, "Rather than risk a MAX train ride to Gresham, why don't you stick around and see how things are in an hour. Besides, if you left, I'd be stuck here all alone. Jill is due at noon … maybe you could wait 'til then."

Kelly desperately wanted to go home.

"No problem, Mark. I'll stick around and keep you safe," she laughed.

The radio offered no real news about the sudden bank closures and the various talk shows Mark flicked back and forth to mentioned little about what caused the FDIC to close so many banks at once.

Since there was little else to do, Mark turned to Kelly, who was dressed in her trademark black cargo pants and loose fitting safari shirt, "Miss Lee," he called her that all the time, "why don't you spend some time on your laptop and see if you can find out what's going on. This whole thing is starting to get a little creepy."

"Sure Mark." Kelly happily replied.

Like most Americans, Mark was unaware that almost each Friday the FDIC closed a few banks. There was no legal mandate to close them on Fridays, but the FDIC preferred to do it at the close of business Friday to allow a few days to transition accounts from the closed bank to the bank assuming the accounts. They then quietly and calmly announced that all depositors were insured, and advised the customers that another bank had taken over their old one's business. It was considered no big deal and just one of a thousand business news reports covered by the media and generally ignored by most of the public. The previous Friday went by without any bank closures, which was not uncommon.

This time things were different, Kelly quickly found out. It was impossible to submit all the required documents and perform all the paperwork on so many banks by Friday, so the FDIC chose to wait until 9:30 a.m. EDT Monday to make the announcements.

She quickly skimmed through a few old news reports and discovered that the new Congress, under increasing and relentless pressure from constituents, underwater homeowners, bond holders, and most importantly, China, had just last May passed a series of extraordinarily complex laws requiring all FDIC insured banks to submit to the US Treasury Department quarterly statements demonstrating their financial solvency. Strict provisions and severe criminal penalties were clearly spelled out. The FDIC was already authorized to declare banks insolvent when they determined the bank was critically undercapitalized, but Congress demanded stronger FDIC oversight and they got it. The FDIC could no longer operate independently. Fraudulent banking practices would no longer be tolerated. The Congress and the American people had lost their patience with business as usual. The first of these reports were submitted last Wednesday. Action would be required no later than Monday morning, July first.

Kelly read on and told Mark that the legislation gave the Treasury Department 72 hours to review the reports and advise the FDIC if any of the banks failed to pass. In other words, the Treasury Department had to let the FDIC know which banks they had determined to be insolvent and the FDIC had 24 hours to explain why they should remain open, or shut them down immediately. Critics of the legislation including powerful voices within the banking and insurance industry argued forcefully but unsuccessfully against this legislation they referred to as dangerous. America's nervous trading partners and a weary public demanded full transparency in the banking industry and an end to the era of phantom balance sheets. The sponsors of the legislation knew the time was ripe for a house cleaning and if the nation could weed out the fiscally insolvent banks over three or four quarters the nation would emerge stronger. In an effort to quell rising inflation fears, and to regain control of the nation's currency, the legislation contained a provision severely limiting the power of the Federal Reserve. There would be no more quantitative easing.

However, no one expected such a large number of banks to be declared insolvent and ordered closed. It was apparent that the FDIC had in the past allowed hundreds of critically underfunded banks to remain open. By early Sunday morning the length of the closure list shocked even the most optimistic among the five FDIC directors: 624 banks were to be shuttered including 611 small and mid-sized regional banks and, what terrified them the most, 13 large banks including Bank of America. Nevertheless, the orders were quietly generated and prepared by early Sunday afternoon. By late afternoon on this otherwise typical summer Sunday only a handful of high-ranking Homeland Security officials had been briefed and few considered it their area of concern.

A few panicked mid-level Treasury Department officials made frantic calls to key senators and congressional representatives. Unfortunately, summer break was in full force and by late afternoon it was apparent that government action to forestall or reduce the size of the wave of closures would not occur.

As news of the first closures spread few were concerned because the FDIC had in the past arranged a smooth transition when banks were declared insolvent. After all, 37 banks were closed on the last Friday in May and the Treasury Department not only guaranteed a 127 billion dollar emergency loan to the FDIC Deposit Insurance Fund, but they quickly provided an additional 40 billion to replenish its reserves. But this could not go on forever and the new Congress was in no mood for any more trillion-dollar bailouts so by late Monday morning, the USA had suddenly entered the greatest financial crisis in its history.

The FDIC and the Treasury Department knew this wave of bank failures would be very different from the others: the accounts would not be covered.

"It's all about the bank news, Mark." Kelly said as she stared at her computer screen. "Over 600 banks were closed this morning and everyone's freaked out that their bank might be next. A few people on the news are saying bank accounts can't be guaranteed because there isn't enough money. It's too big. People are starting to panic. The banks that are still open … people are lined up outside of them. It's just like the pictures in the history books. For some reason bankcards aren't working. Anywhere. It's all the news is talking about."

Mark tipped his head back a bit, pointed his right index finger directly at Kelly and a bit louder than usual replied, "Well, I'm with Oregon State, and they can't possibly close. No way. They're the biggest bank in Oregon. Plus, all my money is there. How would I pay my hairstylist? My Nordstrom account? My bills?"

Kelly smiled and just shook her head at her excitable boss. Financial matters were on Kelly's mind as well. She had just graduated last winter from the University of Oregon with a BS in Biology and was eager to get home and work on another of her many applications for veterinary school. Her lifelong dream was to become a veterinarian and she was living with her parents in Troutdale while working at Starbucks to help pay her tuition. Her brilliant older sister, Alison, who had recently finished her Doctorate in Physics, had just returned home for a month-long visit a few days earlier and Kelly was eager to spend some time with her.

As she began to read the local news it was looking more and more like she wouldn't be riding the MAX train home. Channel 4 News had just reported that members of street gangs were openly robbing people all along the east side MAX train system. People were being attacked and robbed both on the various boarding platforms and inside the moving train cars throughout the East County lines.

At 10:15 a.m. six passengers in succession had been shot after being robbed on the 162nd Avenue MAX platform. Two were dead. The wounded staggered away bleeding, seeking help at a nearby senior care facility. The Sur Trece Califas street gang, or 'Trece,' as they were popularly known, was known to be an active presence at that station and by mid morning they appeared on and around the boarding platform in large numbers. Police responded but were driven back by gunfire and as of 10:45 a.m. the Trece still controlled the station and the bodies remained where they fell.

Kelly took MAX to work and back nearly each workday. She parked her prized 150cc Vespa scooter at the Cleveland MAX station, which was two miles from her home. At 10:47 a.m. TRIMET announced that the Red, Blue and Green MAX lines east of downtown had been closed due to the developing emergency, so she was stuck downtown.

"Mark, MAX is shut down. The trains are too dangerous to ride and they just shut them all down. I can't get home." Kelly blurted out as she read the news about MAX.

"You should always ride your scooter downtown and park it in the Smart Park garage." Bouncing his right index finger at Kelly, Mark cocked his head a bit and continued, "Besides, I always told you to never take MAX. No one takes MAX anymore! It's way too crowded and people are always getting beaten up and robbed. I haven't taken MAX in ten years. Never will again either."

"I'm trying to be serious, Mark. I'm stuck downtown!"

"Don't be silly, dear. You know I'll drive you home. But you'll have to stay 'til four … that's when I get off today." Mark looked at the three customers sitting quietly in different corners of his Starbucks, "but if it gets any quieter, we may leave early … wait … I gotta be here when Stevie and his crew show up at four. We'll have to stay. You can work if you like. Molly and Danke didn't show up at nine like they were supposed to so it'd be nice if you stuck around." Normally there were four or five baristas including Mark working the morning shift. Today it was just the two of them.

"Sure boss." Kelly tapped on her keyboard some more, "I'll be happy to."

She found herself worrying about her scooter, which her father had just bought her as a graduation present. As Kelly thought about her scooter, Mark was looking out the window at a battered sub-compact that had just crept by his Starbucks for the third time in the last two minutes.

Chapter Four

Directly across the street from Mark's Starbucks sat the Portland Bullion Exchange, Oregon's largest bullion dealer stocking hundreds of gold, platinum, and silver coins and bars. At 8:00 a.m. when it opened for business a long queue of customers were waiting. By 10:30, in spite of a sudden rise in gold from $3,850/oz to $5,631/oz, all the gold coins were sold. At 11:00 the flow of customers slowed to a trickle as downtown began to empty early much like it did when a surprise snowstorm struck. All of the silver and platinum bullion was sold out and there was absolutely nothing remaining in stock other than ten unsold PAMP Suisse kilo gold bars and the $822,960 in cash the two-hour long morning sales frenzy had generated.

Daniel, the owner, always came to work wearing one of his many flashy-looking and loose-fitting Hawaiian-style shirts along with dark slacks and white running shoes. His shirt for today was a bright and cheerful orange short-sleeved Reyn Spooner design featuring an array of fist-sized green palm trees. He rarely smiled and had few kind words for anyone, but his reputation in the bullion market was rock solid and people trusted him. His precious metals business was the largest in the Pacific Northwest and he was proud of his accomplishment. He never accepted credit cards or personal checks. Although he had in the past gladly accepted money orders and bank drafts, this morning, after the huge number of bank closures, it would be cash only.

After a badly botched robbery attempt two years earlier, he had a nasty-looking scar on his left ear from being struck by a stray bullet. The armed robber amazingly fired once after being shot in the center of his chest by Eugene LePage, one of the beefy security guards. Although one would never know it by his expression, as the morning wore on Daniel was very happy to have called Eugene and his other trusted guards to help him guard the few remaining gold bars and his huge pile of currency.

Normally, two heavily armed men were on hand guarding the business. Today he started out with Joe and Bill. But shortly after opening at 8:00 a.m. Daniel prudently called in Gene and two others telling them to bring their handguns and rifles. By late-morning the guards were getting increasingly cautious after local news reports described the widespread looting and the often-violent robberies, which had broken out in numerous locations throughout the city and suburbs as well as across the nation.

They were also nervous about the thought of transporting all that cash to the bank. Daniel, having never planned for a day quite like this, wasn't sure if he should leave the cash in his safe, transport it 16 blocks to his 10th floor Pearl District condo as he had done many times in the past, or walk it four blocks to the nearby Bank of the Northwest branch office. At 2:25 p.m. EDT, a Presidential Proclamation would help him decide what to do.

Chapter Five

In the meantime, Daniel grabbed the Exchange's land phone and called the Starbucks across the street, ordering a round of coffee and an early lunch for his guards. "Is this Kelly? Hi, Kelly. This is Daniel, across the street. I'm just fine, thanks, how are you? Great! Hey, listen sweetheart, we have six of us here and the boys can't make up their minds, as usual, so I'm just gonna order for them: six triple espressos and another half-dozen of those cinnamon rolls the guys like." He thought a second, "… oh, and toss in another six desserts … you just pick 'em for us, okay? You know my guards, these guys'll eat anything."

Kelly laughed. She was used to Daniel's rough style of talking and found it hilarious. "Sure thing. It'll all be ready in five minutes. But don't send Joe. He's too cute and no one can work when he's here."

"Okay, I'll send Joe over."

Five minutes later, Daniel shouted at Joe, "Hey," he asked Joe, by far his biggest guard, "Could you run across the street and get our coffee? I called Kelly a few minutes ago and it should be ready by now."

Joe, 31 years old and with 245 pounds of chiseled muscle on his 6'2" frame, who had between deployments, been guarding Daniel's business for nine years, turned his shaved head toward Daniel and smiled at the opportunity to visit with Kelly.

"You got it, boss," replied Joe as he quickly but gently leaned his personally owned AR-15 rifle against the back of a glass top display case near the front door. He then sprinted across 3rd Avenue taking a quick glance to his right noticing three scruffy-looking young men getting out of a beat-up looking old compact car parked a few spaces north.

Bill Hartigan, another of Daniel's trusted close-knit group of guards, closed the Bullion Exchange door behind him.

At 6' and 200 lb, Bill, 52, was a former competitive weight-lifter who had recently backed off the heavy lifting due to his sore shoulders. To avoid gym fees and remain fit at his age he did daily calisthenics for 20 minutes and became an avid bicyclist. He grew up in nearby Corbett not far from Joe and was a long-time family friend. Always looking out for his buddy, Bill joined the other three guards keeping a close eye on the sidewalks and street outside and in particular on the three young men nervously walking toward the Starbucks front door. Although Bill could understand some spoken Spanish, the three dark haired men were talking softly and were too far away to be clearly understood, especially with his poor hearing. But what they had in mind was becoming increasingly clear.

Bill, Joe and the other guards knew very well that their duty as guards was clearly spelled out both by Daniel and by the law: they were hired by Daniel to protect the Portland Bullion Exchange, period. But it was growing clear from the morning news reports that the rules they had lived by all their lives were rapidly dissolving. At this moment all Bill thought about was protecting Joe.

Joe, who carried a fully loaded and concealed high-capacity Glock Model 17 nine-millimeter handgun under his oversized t-shirt, opened the Starbucks front door offering his big country-style trademark smile and in his deep voice quietly said a friendly hello to his new female friend Kelly.

Like many young and attractive women before her, she had developed a growing fondness for Joe affectionately calling him 'Joe-Joe,' but kept her attraction toward Joe mostly to herself. Only her sister knew, although Joe had been more and more mentioning her name to his parents and a few friends. She had the $44.75 to-go order packed neatly in a handy cardboard carry-tray ready and waiting for Joe on the front 'pick-up' counter. Joe handed Kelly a fifty telling her to keep the change. Kelly smiled at him as he gently picked up the large carry-tray in his left hand. Joe always kept his right hand free, an old habit he had picked up during his three tours in Afghanistan.

Kelly saw him take the box in his left hand and suggested, "Hey Joe-Joe, why don't you carry that box with both hands? You're gonna spill!"

Joe smiled once more, "Thanks Kelly. It's easier to get the door this way. Hey, nice to see you again, Kelly. Drop by across the street some time and buy a few Eagles." Joe joked. "They're only $5,500 apiece today."

Kelly laughed, "Sure Joe-Joe. I'll stop over and buy a few rolls right after work." She paused a second and stared at Joe, "Hey, nice to see you too, Joe. I'm staying late today. Drop by around four and I'll fix you a free espresso."

"I'll be back at four." Joe smiled. Few things in life made Joe happier than free coffee. And free coffee from Kelly was even better. He turned toward the door just as the largest of the three men he had seen moments earlier quickly pushed open the Starbucks door with his shoulder, followed closely by his two short friends who turned to enter behind him.

Meanwhile, from across the street, Bill saw the sawed-off shotgun emerge from under the baggy black sweatshirt of the first of the three men moments after Joe walked into the Starbucks. "We got a little problem guys," he calmly said to the other guards, as the black handguns appeared from under the t-shirts of the other two.

Bill slightly cracked open the front door of the Bullion Exchange and held it open three inches with the outside of his left foot. At the same time he instantly lined up the crosshairs of his old Colt 4X scope, which was secured to the top of his AR-15, on the throat of the largest of the young threesome as all three slowly approached the Starbucks door.

The smaller two trailing behind almost tripped over their low-hanging baggy pants as they approached the Starbucks with the tops of their boxer shorts showing. None of them even bothered to look across the street. To Bill this meant these three were beginners, but beginners luck wasn't on their side today. It wasn't the first time Bill had placed someone in his crosshairs, and he was perfectly calm as his finger began to gently press against the trigger. As the larger man cautiously neared the tinted glass door of the Starbucks, Bill estimated he was 60 feet from him. But the view from the compact 4X scope made it appear he was only 15 feet away. It made his neck look so big that Bill could read the black gothic-style cursive tattoo on it, which read, 'Jose.' He lined the center of his scope's crosshairs on the letter 'e' as he prepared to fire.

Bill was a retired Oakland, California police officer and had been involved in exactly 11 shootings during his 19-year police career. Four of the men he had shot were taken into custody zipped into large plastic bags. Two were much luckier and, after serving their prison time, spent the rest of their lives in wheelchairs. The other five fully recovered, but did their daily walking in assorted cell blocks and tax-funded exercise yards.

During this time, Bill had been shot exactly one time and although his right arm had been in a sling for 16 weeks, his deep gruesome shoulder wound had eventually healed. Push-ups were no longer difficult nor did holding a rifle firmly against it cause pain.

The large young man holding a shotgun had just stepped off the sidewalk and through the open front doorway, but before he could announce his felonious intentions to Kelly and Mark two sharp explosions rang out a fraction of a second after his neck blew apart.

The inside of the Starbucks was immediately covered with an asymmetrical fan-shaped, pink-colored spray, which gently descended through the few remaining rays of morning sunlight finally settling on nearby tables, chairs, and the shiny dark green floor tiles. A split second later, as Kelly and Mark began a panicked dive for cover, the glass front doors shattered as each of the man's two friends, gripping what were later determined to be black air pistols, had their throats and upper chests perforated by two additional very loud and perfectly placed double-taps from Bill's scoped assault rifle.

"Whoa," Joe quietly whispered to himself.

He was a former U.S. Navy Seal who never said a single word to anyone about his tours of duty in Afghanistan or about his other military assignments. He was very familiar with violence and stood silently and motionless by the pick-up counter and faced the door. He had the convenient carry-tray balanced in his left hand while his handgun suddenly appeared in his right as he stoically waited the approximately three seconds it took for the sudden one-sided battle to end. Before the familiar strange looking mist had fully settled, Joe saw Bill running across the street with his rifle carefully aimed at the bloody carnage now displayed at the Starbucks front door.

Joe, who hadn't spilled a single drop of anyone's coffee, calmly set the carry tray back down on the pick-up counter and walked toward the door with his handgun aimed at the fallen men. He quickly inspected the three who had dropped straight down and were now lying motionless alongside their weapons. Joe silently kicked their weapons far away from them in the direction of the main counter. He then turned to the few remaining customers who had been seated apart from one another, silently sipping what would be their last Starbucks coffee, and quietly but firmly ordered them to leave. "Everyone out. This Starbucks is now closed for the day. Get moving." He calmly told them.

They offered no argument, immediately running out the door and heading out in different directions.

He returned to the counter, and peeked over at Kelly and Mark. They were crouched low. Mark was terrified and visibly trembling while Kelly crouched next to him.

Kelly, who appeared surprisingly calm, had never witnessed a shooting before and was crouching low and motionless alongside Mark with her right hand deep in her purse. She looked up and asked, "Is it over, Joe?"

He leaned over the counter, smiled at them, and in his soft deep voice said, "Yup. For now it is. But I think the city is falling apart." Joe, happy neither of them was injured, paused a second to smile at Kelly before he continued, "Get your things and come with us. This Starbucks is closed."

Joe first spoke briefly with Bill near the front door while waiting for Kelly and Mark to gather their things, "It's too dangerous to hang around here. You hear all those gunshots in the distance? We need to get the hell out of downtown, like right now."

"Boy howdy, you're right, Joe. Well we can't just leave Kelly and her boss here. Let's take 'em across the street and then we'll figure out what to do with 'em," Bill replied.

"Good plan," Joe said.

Mark had never experienced such violence in his life, and he was curled up on the floor behind the counter trembling violently with his eyes closed tightly. In fact, Mark's Starbucks had never even been robbed.

"Are they gone?" He opened his eyes and managed to whisper to Kelly. "Is it safe? Can I get up now?"

Kelly looked down at her boss, "Yes, it's safe now, Mark. Joe and Bill are here and everything's fine. But we gotta go now."

They didn't know it yet, but life was about to change for all of them in ways they couldn't possibly have predicted when they woke up on that warm summer morning.

Chapter Six

While Bill's .223 bullets were doing their unhappy work at exactly 11:25 a.m. on the West Coast, so was the President. He was signing an emergency Presidential Proclamation declaring a seven-day bank holiday. The intent of this desperate action was to try to prevent a wholesale collapse of the entire US banking system.

The early morning's shocking closure of 624 insolvent banks represented approximately 20% of the entire US banking industry, but an unbelievable 42% of the nation's checking accounts. This meant that as this particular July sunrise made its continuous sunny pass over the continental United States, most of the money Americans had on deposit was by law still protected. However, the FDIC officials had no choice: the insolvent banks had to close and shocking the banking system to its very core was the announcement that bank depositors, whose accounts were insured up to $250,000, would wait indefinitely for reimbursement. Any bank deposit amounts over $250,000, which had in the past been fully reimbursed by the FDIC, could for now be written off as tax-deductible losses. However, top-level Treasury Department officials remained optimistic. They firmly believed that the remaining 80% of the nation's banking industry would quickly absorb the remains of the hundreds of insolvent banks and after a rocky period things would sort themselves out as they always had in the past.

However the event moved too fast. By 9:25 a.m. on the East Coast, the banks that were not subject to the mass-closure were overwhelmed by card transactions, which now constituted 85% of the nation's routine purchases. They experienced a complete breakdown of their debit card transaction verification systems, which, for technical reasons that were most likely due to the sudden crush of debit card requests, soon spread to all bankcards. For the first time ever, the nation's ritual use of plastic debit and credit cards suddenly ceased. This meant that if anyone wanted to buy coffee, gas, bread, or gold, they had to fork over cold, hard cash, and cash was soon going to get harder to find. With the nation's banks about to be closed for seven days, for most, cash would be almost impossible to get.

Americans whose money was deposited in that still-solvent 80% of the banks panicked and the panic struck like lightning. They quickly began a stunning and historically unprecedented bank run shocking not only the nation but sending panic throughout the entire world as it soon depleted virtually all the dispensable cash the nation's remaining bank branches had on hand.

Initial desperate pleas by banking officials to horrified US Treasury Department bureaucrats drew promises and guarantees of additional cash. The banks were told more cash would be delivered within 24 hours, and the Bureau of Engraving and Printing was ordered to quadruple its production of the newly redesigned $100 bills immediately. By 1:00 p.m. EDT, the order was changed to increase production of the just-released high-tech Franklin note by tenfold.

After several hours of furious printing an unanticipated technical flaw was discovered. It streaked a blank horizontal line approximately one mm in width across the entire note running through Franklin's eyes on approximately 12% of the bills. The flawed notes were randomly distributed among the millions of notes printed. In order to salvage the print-run, each note had to be inspected by hand and by the human eye, which would result in at least a ten-day delay in critically needed currency distributions. Plus, the Bureau of Engraving and Printing had no idea what was causing the freakish line and were completely baffled that it impacted only 12% of printed notes. Solving this mystery would take time. Meanwhile, they focused on the production of $50 notes and the printing presses went at it full blast, but it was too little and too late. Making matters worse, a critical delivery of special security ink was expected, but with the nation's transportation infrastructure grinding to a halt, it never arrived and by late evening all printing ceased.

The morning bank run was so complete and thorough that by 11:00 a.m. PDT there wasn't a single bank in the USA with any disbursable cash on hand. Minutes after that they closed after receiving news of what was called The Presidential Bank Holiday Proclamation.

But the growing crowds of terrified and panicked bank customers would not give up their frantic quest for cash so easily. Many took matters into their own hands. The police, a growing number of whom had decided that guarding their families and communities was far more important than guarding closed banks and looted supermarkets, were spread out thin. There was nothing stopping the mobs of angry bank customers from smashing their way into the closed banks and ransacking them.

And ransack they did. From coast to coast managers of many of the closed banks, who had shown up for work to facilitate the FDIC-ordered shutdown, were forced to open their vaults. Many of the nation's safe deposit boxes were noisily ripped apart and emptied by men wielding hand tools and crowbars. Many others were carefully drilled open by more sophisticated thieves while some were expertly broken into by terrified locksmiths held at gunpoint.

Across America, most of the banks that had opened that Monday morning had their vaults looted of all remaining reserve cash. The nation's frenzy of looting and pillaging had struck hard at the very core of the one single industry that had, for countless generations, kept the American empire humming along by guarding and dispensing money.

Across the USA, an army of unprotected cash machines was silently standing by waiting to perform its daily duty by spitting out twenties by the billions to help feed America's endless craving to consume. By noon Eastern this steel and plastic army of cash machines was under deadly attack. Few were spared. They were assaulted by bare hands, crowbars, steel chains and pulleys latched to the bumpers of gasoline-hungry pick-up trucks, and an assortment of small explosive devices all battling together to render this army of greenback dispensers thoroughly defeated by early evening.

The people who were most valiant in this fanatically fought war soon found out that their newly filled pockets of cash couldn't buy much because by late afternoon the nation's stores and malls were also under attack. For the first time in the history of the USA nearly everything that was once for sale had overnight become free for the taking. Although by mid-afternoon the festival of looting and burning would be apocalyptic, the early battles in the war for America's self-destruction were just getting underway as Joe led Mark and Kelly across 3rd Avenue to the relative safety of the Portland Bullion Exchange. The final battles, which would be fought in the coming days, would feature horrors far beyond anyone's imagination.

Chapter Seven

Bill, who had sprinted into the Starbucks with his rifle aimed low, saw no point in securing or cleaning up the grizzly mess sprayed across the Starbucks. But as soon as he saw that Mark, Kelly and Joe had safely arrived at the Bullion Exchange, he casually dragged the three bodies a short distance away from the coffee house and across the sidewalk, laying them side by side in the gutter alongside their beat-up parked car. He walked back to the Starbucks, found a piece of paper and scribbled a brief note for the police, "Shot while trying to rob Starbucks." He signed it, "Concerned Citizen," and folded it up tightly. He then placed it in a small paper espresso cup, which he crumpled in his powerful fist. He then walked over and stuffed the crumpled cup into the mouth of the largest of the three dead men with his pen and left it poking out. He returned to the Bullion Exchange with his rifle, their shotgun, and the two air pistols, happily announcing to all, "Hey! It's time for my late morning espresso." Before allowing himself a sip, he gently raised the tiny paper cup to his nose and smiled at Kelly, savoring the wonderful flavor of the perfectly made hot espresso Kelly had just prepared.

"I'm glad you like it." replied Kelly. She was seated on the floor near the front door of the Exchange, as some locals called it, trying to get her shaking fingers to cooperate as she turned on her laptop. She was suddenly hungry for more news about the event. Even though she had earned a full academic scholarship gaining a 3.9 GPA at the University of Oregon, she felt a bit lost and in the dark about the economic and political state of the world and wished she had followed the news and current events more closely during college. But studies came first, which was fully understandable.

She silently whispered, "How could this happen?" Her world had been so safe and secure living peacefully with her wonderful and supportive parents in a quiet suburb along the Sandy River. She tried to call her father but could not get a signal. She went online and started reading.

She did know a few things, of course. Last year her father, a retired federal agent, devout Buddhist and local community volunteer, bought her a new S 150 Vespa rather than a small car as a graduation present because he told her gasoline was soon going to get too expensive to burn in cars. For several years he had been telling her, and anyone else who would listen, that the age of cheap oil was ending. Few listened. However, as regular gas crept past $7.00 a gallon it appeared he was right. In fact, he told her just yesterday that people would soon wish for ten dollar per gallon of gas, and in California most gas stations were now selling it for over $8.00.

She knew little about the growing bank crisis, which was occasionally mentioned by her father. She remembered that unemployment had jumped to an official 16% since Christmas, but the real unemployment rate was believed to be closer to 35%. It was probably why she had so much trouble finding a job nearer to home. It was also why she had to ride MAX downtown each weekday.

She preferred to commute on her scooter, but didn't like the risk of parking it in a busy downtown parking garage and paying the costly fee. She also didn't like paying $8.25 a gallon for premium and waiting several hours to do it, but in February, Multnomah County, like countless jurisdictions across the country, started requiring all gas stations to reserve their first hour of operation for motorcycles only which made the wait much easier for her. Most gas stations did this from five to six in the morning and the obvious reason was to get people out of cars and into better mileage transportation. There was never a long wait during the motorcycle-only hour, and everyone noticed more scooters and motorcycles on the road.

As Kelly sat and read, she grew increasingly nervous. She knew it all started after last Christmas when Israel surprised and shocked the world by sending 97 US made F-16I Sufa fighter jets on a mission to seriously damage or destroy Iran's nuclear infrastructure and larger oil facilities. The Israelis had been threatening to do this for years and with recent intelligence suggesting an Iranian nuclear explosives test was imminent, they took clear preemptive action. The F-16Is, from the 107th Fighter squadron, began leaving Hatzerim Airbase at 9:50 p.m. Tel Aviv time on New Year's Eve. They flew south toward Aqaba and headed toward Tabuk in northwest Saudi Arabia. It took each fighter about 90 seconds to fly over the small corner of Jordanian territory. As they flew they communicated in perfect English identifying themselves as Americans. By the time Jordanian Armed Forces started investigating the fighters were long gone. The Saudis were expecting them. Within 90 minutes they started landing at the Saudi Arabian Air Force base at Hafar Al-Batin to refuel and arm for their mission.

The F-16Is were designed to fly within a combat radius of 340 miles when fully loaded. This range could be extended considerably with external fuel tanks or lighter payloads. Each fighter jet was quickly prepared for its mission depending on its target and distance. Most targets were over 500 miles away so most fighters carried less than their maximum payload, but with nearly one hundred fighters involved, they had full confidence in the success of the mission.

Iran's Ministry of Intelligence and National Security (MISIRI) had long feared such a move. Leaked diplomatic discussions between high ranking American and Saudi officials revealed that the King of Saudi Arabia was strongly and secretly encouraging the Israelis to attack Iran's nuclear facilities eagerly offering to provide any help they needed. These leaks did not surprise Iranian officials. It merely confirmed what they already knew. The Iranians had long expected such an attack and believed they were adequately prepared.

Ali Rohjantalab, a senior intelligence officer in MISIRI, was performing routine duties in his office in Tehran on New Year's Eve. His job as the senior officer on duty was to supervise the many duty agents listening in on selected communications into and out of the Islamic Republic. His work area was packed full with serious-looking men and the most advanced communications equipment.

He was also responsible for personally receiving dispatches from a handful of agents working in other nations: field agents, otherwise known as spies. At 11:30 p.m. local time in Tehran, Intelligence Officer Rohjantalab received a cell phone call on his secure line from one of his field agents. Only twelve people knew that phone number. One was an agent who had been working as a janitor for three years at the Royal Saudi Air Force base near Hafar Al-Batin. It was located in the northeast Saudi desert. Senior Intelligence Officer Rohjantalab knew exactly whom it was when he saw the number appear and his staff would record the phone call. He answered and without a word began to listen carefully.

"It is so hot tonight in the desert, mother," the nameless janitor said.

The janitor immediately hung up and smashed his phone into tiny bits with a hammer. He took the crushed parts and burned them behind his work shed in a small metal can. This took two minutes. He then sprinkled the burnt remains on the rocky ground not far from his shed and kicked them into the sand in a process he had practiced several times during training. He took a few deep breaths, walked to his filthy wheeled garbage can and resumed his usual mundane janitorial duties.

Senior Intelligence Officer Rohjantalab knew exactly what to do next. He had rehearsed his response dozens of times.

"Director, I just received a call from our agent in Hafar Al-Batin. The Israelis are coming. We are about to be attacked. One hundred Israeli fighter jets, probably F-16s, are arming and fueling there as we speak."

"Thank you," The director said.

The director quickly made a call. "General Salehi. We will be under attack in moments. One hundred Israeli fighters are fueling and arming at Hafar Al-Batin as we speak."

The Armed Forces of the Islamic Republic of Iran went into full alert. The Israeli fighters were soon airborne. The Three Hour War was about to begin. It would not be a surprise attack.

Six fighters were ordered to attack the Persian Star refinery at Assalouyeh. They succeeded and utterly destroyed the facility causing severe damage to Iran's economy.

However, in a shocking and tragic underestimation of Iranian defense capabilities, the 21 Israeli fighters that were sent to destroy the Hormuz refinery and tanker terminal at Bandar Abbas never got close. They were all shot down over the Persian Gulf near the port city of Bushehr by a shower of Iran's newly acquired S-300 missiles. The remaining 70 Sufas scattered across Iranian airspace toward a number of pre-designated nuclear targets.

The Israeli attack failed miserably. Iranian fighter jets were no match for the Israeli F-16s and remained on the ground, but S-300 missiles and traditional anti-air defenses destroyed 34 Israeli fighter jets as they flew northeast across the western slopes of the Zagros Mountains. Four fighters flying wing to wing became disoriented in a severe winter storm and crashed simultaneously into the same mountain range near the town of Estahan while the remaining fighters found their targets hitting sites near Arak, Qom, and Natanz.

Sixteen were shot down as they headed back to Hafar Al-Batin and the remaining 33 Sufas made it back safely to Saudi soil. Iranian officials later claimed and international observers confirmed that damage to the secure, concrete encased underground nuclear facilities was minimal. Afterward, Israel had little to celebrate. Seven Israeli pilots who had safely ejected from their doomed jets over Iranian airspace were tried, convicted and publically hanged for murder and terrorism in a one-day public trial held in Tehran three days later on January 4th.

As Iran had repeatedly threatened during the preceding months, they swiftly retaliated sending twenty Sejil 2 missiles at the Saudi Ras Tanura offshore oil export terminal. All twenty found their targets, completely destroying the facility along with three waiting supertankers in a spectacular fireball easily visible to the naked eye from the International Space Station. The price of oil immediately rocketed from $144 per barrel to $210 per barrel. Fortunes were made and lost as it made further climbs. By early February it had settled in a narrow band ranging from $220 to $245 per barrel and $235 was where it settled as June came to a close.

The exchange of firepower stopped as quickly as it began as nations and their diplomats from oil hungry nations the world over rose together demanding a cease-fire. Israel wisely decided against continuing the attack. Iran saved its few remaining S-300s. The USA sat by quietly. None of the combatants approached or threatened US ships or bases. The US military, fearing an uncontrollable escalation of hostilities and further increases in the price of oil, ordered the Saudis in clear terms not to strike back at Iran. The Saudis, fearing a further weakening of their already shaky kingdom, complied. The US president, aware of the planned Israeli attack, ordered the sizeable US forces stationed on land and at sea to not fire unless fired upon. The Iranians knew about this, and stayed well clear of US warships. An uneasy truce was somehow managed and hostilities ceased as quickly as they had started.

Violence flared elsewhere in the wake of the short war. Civil war ignited once again in Iraq. The Iranians were quick to exploit the growing unrest supplying the Shiite Iraqi minority with cash, small arms, and other badly needed supplies fueling the growing insurgency. Fifty thousand additional NATO peacekeeping soldiers, 48,000 of whom were flown in from the USA, quickly supplemented the 50,000 US non-combatant military advisers stationed near Baghdad. The House of Saud, which had been a long-time military ally of the USA, found itself under siege internally. Unable to cope with and stop the domestic unrest fueled by the collapse in oil revenue, the Saudi government requested American assistance. The U.S. quickly agreed to provide military forces. Within weeks, 55,000 US combat soldiers were moved into Saudi Arabia to assist in anti-terror efforts and to help guard undamaged oil facilities, but the real reason suspected by most was to protect the Saud family's weakening grip on power. NATO soon provided an additional 35,000 troops and the Muslim minorities throughout Europe immediately began to protest what they called 'crusades' against Islam.

But the economic damage was done. The Ras Tanura facility would need to be completely reconstructed from scratch. Rebuilding the sprawling port complex would take several years. The sudden spike in oil prices had devastated the already-fragile economies of oil-importing nations. Repeatedly promised increases in oil production by other OPEC nations did not occur: it was simply not possible to produce more oil from their depleted oilfields.

Chapter Eight

The price of gasoline doubled almost overnight. On the West Coast, gas lines started forming in mid-January. By the first of February motorists across the entire country waited in long lines to fill up. Deadly fights in the gas lines and at the pump were commonplace. Long gas lines snaked across intersections and zigzagged through neighborhoods. The police could barely keep the peace in many cities as queue cutters and those trying to stop them were regularly beaten, stabbed or shot.

Yesterday in Houston, for example, a man whose car was nearly out of gas had waited patiently in line at a gas station in the 95-degree heat for nearly three hours. At 3:15 p.m. he finally reached the pump. Witnesses reported that the attendant told him the single-island gas station was closed and that he could try again the next day. Normally, the attendant would walk down the gas line and place a magnet-held 'Last Car' sign on the back of the final car as had become the custom across the country. That day he forgot.

The motorist begged and pleaded with the attendant to allow him to fill up, but his pleadings went unheeded. When the attendant finally ordered the man to leave, the man pulled a knife out of his pocket and stabbed the attendant thirteen times. The badly bleeding attendant staggered toward his office falling unconscious near the front door. The angry motorist then fished the pump keys out of the bleeding man's pocket and restarted the station's gas pump. He filled up his car and drove off. Other cars followed behind ignoring the unconscious attendant while filling up their cars. Dozens of motorists continued filling their tanks for 45 minutes before police arrived and closed the station for the day. No one got a license plate number and descriptions of the man and his vehicle varied. Video footage was fuzzy and of very little help.

Kelly continued reading. She found out that the official unemployment rate in the US had just climbed to 16%. In Oregon where she lived it stood at an official 19%, but no one believed the official numbers. Elsewhere it was worse. By May, unemployment in Spain had reached 35% while in Japan it grew to a historically unprecedented official 18%. In China, it was recently reported that 100 million people were unemployed and fully reliant upon government handouts for food. A drought and the worsening water crisis would force China to import enough food to feed 25% of their population this year or enough to feed the entire USA.

The economic strain was felt everywhere. As the price of oil rose, so did the price of food and basic goods. A regular, tall Starbucks coffee, for example, was now $3.25. A standard size loaf of bread was over $6.00. Bank lending ground to a near-halt as few stepped into car dealerships while housing construction fell to historic lows. The CPI for May showed a 9% increase over the previous May. Interest rates rose. Government revenue plummeted while expenditures grew wildly. By May, all government revenue income had declined to roughly one-third of federal government expenditures. As spring approached, the new fiscally conservative Congress decided that repeated efforts at quantitative easing had failed. Printing and spending the nation's way out of its economic quagmire was not going to happen: it was time to allow the market to correct this situation even though it was going to be very harsh on many.

The sovereign debt crisis became unsustainable throughout the industrialized world, as nation after nation fearing social disorder tried to spend and print their way out of the growing financial crisis. The British security agency MI5 had for years warned that advanced societies were four meals away from complete anarchy and in country after country this would soon prove true. Many European nations fearing the potential unrest and chaos that might result refused to tighten their belts sufficiently. A few tried to keep their finances in order, but all suffered. Moves toward isolationism became more and more popular throughout Europe. As a result, Germany, the economic powerhouse of the EU, prepared for a return of the Deutschmark and an end to their participation in the Euro.

It appeared that the European Union itself would soon disintegrate, when the wealthier nations, who had grown tired of continuously bailing out the weaker ones, refused to comply with repeated demands for additional financial assistance. Moody's sovereign debt rating for all four of the worst-hit countries, Ireland, Spain, Greece, and Portugal, was at Ca, meaning it could not get any lower. After the bitter failure of QE4, even the USA was just last April downgraded by Moody's to B2, otherwise known as 'Junk' grade.

The US banking industry was teetering badly and Kelly started to understand that the situation was looking very, very bleak. She started to cry. She suddenly wanted to go home.

A BLACK HUMMER

Chapter Nine

By now Daniel, like just about everyone else, was well aware that the nation's banks had closed. So rather than leave his cash and gold bars in the store safe, he decided to take the mountain of cash and his unsold gold to his condo where he could keep an eye on it.

"Let's pack it up and get ready to roll, boys."

News reports focused entirely on the growing chaos. Although constant gunfire was heard in the distance, downtown was fairly quiet for the moment. But to be safe he asked his guards to escort him to his Pearl District condo. "Would you all mind driving me home? I'm gonna close up shop early today." They would need two vehicles.

After finishing his espresso, Bill jogged a block south to the Smart Park garage, started Daniel's white Escalade, and drove it to the front of the Bullion Exchange, parking it in a no parking zone. As soon as Bill returned, Joe, who couldn't run quite as fast, then jogged to the same parking garage and drove back with his prized black Hummer H2, parking it right behind the Escalade. This took ten minutes.

Daniel then looked at Kelly and Mark and growled, "You two wanna come along, or what?"

Rather than go with them or be left downtown alone, Mark chose to take his chances and head back to Lake Oswego. "I'm going to get my car and drive home," Mark announced nervously. "If Steve gets home and no one's there he'll completely freak out." He said goodbye to everyone and was last seen sprinting north on 3rd heading to the same parking garage. Kelly didn't know it at the time, but it was the last time she would say goodbye to her boss.

Kelly had no choice. As a burst of gunfire blasted away not far up Washington Street, she spoke up. "I would like to come with you guys, if that's okay."

She would ride in the Hummer with Joe and Bill. It was time for everyone to get moving. The guards grabbed their weapons and moved toward the door. Kelly closed her laptop, stood up, and walked a few steps toward the front door where she waited.

At 11:40 Daniel took his heavy leather gold and cash-filled bag and stood by the door next to Kelly. Joe and Bill went out first and stood with their rifles ready between the mean-looking front bumper of the Hummer and the rear of the pristine Escalade. Kelly, Daniel, and the other three guards followed them outside. Daniel turned and locked the front door. One of the guards got in the driver's seat of the Escalade and started its engine. Another stood by while the third opened the Escalade's right rear door, allowing Daniel to quickly slide into the back seat with his large bag of cash and gold bars. As the four took their seats in the Escalade, Joe and Bill climbed up into the front seat of the Hummer and Kelly climbed in back next to a large old black canvas bag Bill had just flung over his seat. Everyone was silent as the two vehicles then moved out fast heading west on SW Washington before taking a right on NW 12th.

When they reached Burnside the light was red. Even so, they blasted straight through it after a brief check for traffic. The downtown streets were eerily quiet for late Monday morning. They only had 10 blocks to go before reaching their destination near 11th and

NW Lovejoy. They drove fast, reaching Daniel's condo building in about two minutes.

As they drove, Kelly peered out the tinted back window. She noticed that the scene along the street appeared quiet but in some ways normal. If not for the periodic gunfire echoing from the northeast and the cops standing in front of the branch office of the ransacked Bank of the Northwest on her left, it could have passed for a typical sunny weekday morning. A woman was walking her two small nicely trimmed dogs. A group of three young women were jogging close together. A dozen or so well-dressed men and women were sitting in the shade at a cluster of outdoor tables eating lunch. How could such an otherwise normal street scene take place so close to mindless looting and chaos? It was like a very bizarre dream.

At 11:44 a.m., the two cars pulled into the secure underground parking garage that served the wealthy residents of Daniel's luxury high-rise.

The guards grabbed their weapons and, along with Kelly, followed Daniel into the stairwell. They knew the drill. Daniel never took elevators so the group dutifully began the ten-story climb.

When they reached the tenth and top floor, Daniel opened the stairway door to his hallway and peeked around the corner. Seeing no one, he walked briskly toward his front door. With everyone following close behind, he stopped at his door, opened it, and went inside, dropping the bag of cash and gold on a small table near his front door. Kelly and the five guards followed Daniel in while Joe closed and locked the door.

Kelly, never the shy one and strikingly fit and beautiful at 5' 10", flung her straight black hair over her left shoulder, looked around the room with her stunning almond-shaped brown eyes, and asked no one in particular, "Now what do we do?"

Chapter Ten

Daniel, not too happy about having a helpless young female to deal with, told her, "Don't worry your sweet head about it. Just sit back and see what you can find out on your little laptop." In the meantime, he and the five guards crowded around his 60" flat screen TV hoping to make some sense out the day's events.

Kelly smiled to herself, not offended in the least by the condescending remark. Only her immediate family and a handful of her closest friends knew that she and her sister Alison were both second-degree black belts in kajukenbo-style kung fu. They had practiced this art for 15 years under the guidance of one of the world's best martial artists, Sifu Rick Cropper. He was an internationally recognized Grand Master and an eighth-degree black belt who operated a highly exclusive and wildly popular dojo on Stark Street: one of the few in the country with a long waiting list for membership.

Kelly was, in fact, a very confident young woman fully capable of taking care of herself in almost any mean situation as one particular young black male in Eugene could testify. In fact, he did testify to that effect. The first time was when he was wheeled into his arraignment charged with aggravated assault and attempted armed robbery. The second time was at his trial four months later.

Last September third, at 07:35 a.m., as Kelly was walking along the shaded sidewalk near her studio apartment heading to her first morning class at the nearby University of Oregon campus, she was accosted by the 6' 4", 260 lb man who placed a knife near her chin, telling her to hand over her purse or get stabbed in the face. What the man didn't know was that Kelly had a Walther PPS handgun in her cross-slung purse that she didn't want stolen. It was a gift from her father, who had been deeply concerned about her safety while she was away living alone and going to school so far from home.

Within three-quarters of a second, the blade of the knife was buried deep in the man's neck, piercing his adam's apple in half but barely missing his spinal cord. To make matters worse for him, a half-second later he was struck with such incredible force by Kelly's right foot that he would never father children. He crumpled to the sidewalk, losing consciousness in a growing pool of blood. Kelly screamed for help and the police arrived fast. After interviewing her for 45 minutes the police let her go. She only missed half of her first morning class that day, and before the day was done she had become a folk hero among her classmates. The unsympathetic judge, who later sentenced her attacker to fifteen years in prison, didn't take the man's injuries into consideration, noting that in prison it would be impossible for him to father children anyhow.

Her well-hidden self-defense and fighting skills did not stop there. Before heading off to college, her father had arranged for her to become familiar with his 9mm Walther handgun, which he had inherited from his father. He asked a close family friend, Chris McClanahan – an Army Ranger, highly trained weapons expert, and Washington State police academy firearms instructor – if he would train her in firearms safety and target shooting, as well as in police-style combat shooting as he had done for Kelly's older sister four years earlier. Chris immediately agreed, saying he would be honored. He repeatedly refused payment, and after outfitting Kelly in a pair of Danner Model 400G Acadia boots, black 511 tactical gear, several different holsters, plus all the proper safety equipment (which Kelly's father gladly paid for) she immediately began training.

They met three times a week for the next eight weeks for four hours of intense training in the hot afternoon sun. After 2,400 spent rounds and countless cuts and scrapes, Chris told her she was in his opinion an expert combat shooter. He warned her, however, that she would need to practice monthly in order to maintain her skill level. He also suggested she periodically attend his advanced combat firearms course, which she gladly did each year.

The day she left for college her father told her that the Walther was hers and to never tell anyone about it or let it out of her reach.

Chapter Eleven

Kelly thought carefully about what her father had said and about what she had learned from Chris as she read the news and tapped away quickly on the keys of her laptop. As she read more, she grew increasingly sad. It looked like the world was coming to an end. She quickly found out that the crisis unfolding before her had been accurately predicted many years ago, but few wanted to listen.

The six men comically turned to aim twelve eyes in unison at her as she shifted her position on the dark bamboo floor while stretching out gracefully on her tummy in front of her laptop. She read things she had never before considered. The economic warning signs of a financial meltdown were unmistakable. The economy in general had long faced a series of fast-approaching converging catastrophes, any one of which could have easily triggered a financial and social disaster. For example, world oil production had peaked in 2005. Many so-called 'experts' expressed initial doubts, but by last Christmas it was indisputable, as world oil production had steadily fallen from 87 to 82 million barrels per day. Some still clung to the belief that the decline was due to falling demand, but the two went hand-in-hand. The Saudis continued to claim that they could ramp up oil production to 12 million barrels per day whenever they wanted. Few believed this any longer and with their main export terminal in ruins they now produced only 3.5 million barrels per day and after domestic consumption this allowed little for export through their smaller Red Sea terminal. All OPEC nations ignored their self-imposed production limits and were pumping oil out as fast as they could, as were non-OPEC producers, but oil production refused to increase. Since the developed economies of the world had again slowed due to the previous fall's second credit crisis, demand for oil had weakened and shortages had yet to appear.

Ominously, Saudi Arabia's oil production had been falling and falling fast. By the first of the year it was less than 7.6 million barrels per day. Their ever-growing domestic consumption was 2.5 million barrels per day, meaning prior to the attack they had only 5.1 million available for export. Oil production at the super giant Ghawar oil field, which once produced 5.7 million barrels per day and 6% of the entire world's oil, was down to 3.7 million barrels per day and declined more each month prior to the Iranian attack. Likewise, production at the Safaniya offshore oil field, which in 2007 was the world's third largest, had now fallen off drastically. Oil production at other Saudi oil fields, most of which had been in production for decades, was likewise either dropping or flat. The once spectacular Saudi Arabian miracle was now well into its twilight.

Persistent high fuel prices that had put the brakes on economic recovery in the wake of the 2008 market crash were again, by the end of last year, being blamed by many for the second and most recent financial crisis as well.

The whole world knew that in the aftermath of the New Year's Day attack, nearly all of Saudi Arabia's oil exports were offline indefinitely. The Persian Gulf closed down tanker traffic completely for five weeks while safety and insurance details could be arranged. The USA and China, who had each imported about one million barrels per day of Saudi oil, started tapping into their strategic petroleum reserves. When tanker shipments again started sailing through the Strait of Hormuz in early February, the International Energy Agency reported that with Saudi and Iranian losses combined, 7.5 million fewer barrels per day were passing through. The amount of oil available for export throughout the world had just dropped by about one-third and nearly all of it was claimed by pre-existing trade agreements.

But that was not all. Worldwide grain reserves had been declining for many years, and after last summer's shocking Russian wheat crop failure, Kelly's dad's favorite multi-grain bread, Jailhouse Brand, was now selling for $9.50 a loaf. And with over 60% of the US corn crop now being turned into vehicle fuel, the US and world's grain supply situation was getting bleaker all the time.

Kelly had started reading on about the rapidly developing shortages of rare earth metals, potassium, uranium, and lithium. She read about aquifer depletion. She had no idea how interconnected it all was to transportation, industrial production and farming. In particular, she read that a growing water crisis was forcing once self-sufficient China to import more and more of its food as millions of once-fertile acres of farmland stretching across northern China were rapidly turning into desert.

She read that higher interest rates and the worsening balance of trade deficit brought on by higher oil prices were putting severe economic pressure on the nation. The USA had been importing 9 to 10 million barrels of oil each and every day prior to the disastrous Israeli attack on Iran. Now it was down to 5 or 6 million, but each barrel cost 2.5 times what it did a year earlier. As the USA weakened, so did the dollar. Interest rates rose dramatically. The percent of federal tax revenue being diverted to financing the interest on the national debt was at a staggering 75%. For the first time since the nation's founding, the US government was approaching bankruptcy. An increasing number of people began to plan on a general collapse and initiated a wide range of well thought-out survival preparations, most of which would prove futile.

Just then, her train of thought was quietly interrupted as the six men who had for the past 15 minutes been staring silently in shocked disbelief at Daniel's television, started discussing what they should do next. It did not take long for them to reach a decision.

Chapter Twelve

Bill turned to Joe and whispered, "Hey bro, you hear all that gunfire? We gotta get moving. Like, right now. This town is falling apart boy howdy quick and if we wait much longer it'll be too late."

Joe nodded in agreement making a mental note to one day ask Bill, who constantly listened to country music, what 'boy howdy' meant. He then leaned toward Daniel. "You got a map handy?"

Daniel, who rarely left town looked at Joe with a puzzled expression. "What are you talking about?"

"I mean, a street map of Multnomah County. I need one. A paper one. You got one handy?"

"Oh. Somewhere, I think." Daniel dug through a large antique wooden cabinet, found an old paper street map he probably hadn't looked at in years, and spread it out on his dining table.

As the six men stared at the map, they occasionally pointed at certain parts, whispering back and forth. It was something important. Since Kelly couldn't quite understand what they were saying, she closed her laptop, jumped to her feet, walked over to the table and stood alongside the men. She listened a moment as they continued their discussion. While Kelly was reading on her laptop, the group decided to split up.

"Hey girl, good news. Bill and I are taking you home. We're leaving in a few minutes," Joe said.

"Thank you," replied Kelly. "You know, Joe," she continued, speaking in a soft, quiet voice, "I think maybe the whole world is falling apart. I'm really starting to get kinda scared. What's happening out there might be something big. I mean something REALLY big." Kelly looked genuinely frightened. "I'm going to email my mom and dad right now, let them know I'm okay and that I'm coming home."

Joe and Bill were both born and raised in Corbett. They regularly commuted together, taking the same freeway route each time. He gently placed his massive hand on her shoulder and tried to comfort her, "It can't be that bad, Kelly. Things always get brighter. You know that."

Joe's face turned serious a second, then he smiled, "I've seen some really horrible things in the military. But no matter how bad it got, the next day everyone's out shopping like nothing happened. You'll see. Things will be back to normal in a few days at most. Bill and I will get you home safely and everything will be fine." Joe stood beside Kelly another minute or so then joined in with the others. He felt a bit guilty because he didn't believe a word he just said ... and he could tell she didn't either.

The three other guards, who lived just west of the Pearl District, were going to stay with Daniel, who had enough food in a hall closet to keep the four of them well fed for more than a month if needed. And if it came to that, he also had plenty of ammunition stored in his condo: 3,000 rounds of .223 ammunition and another 2,000 rounds of 9mm.

Joe, staring intently at the map, tapped his finger on the paper and told Bill, "We can't take I-84 because it's closed at 205 due to multiple accidents." He stared at the map another few seconds, "Burnside east is out too. It's far too dangerous." In fact, Joe noted that all of the primary east/west urban surface streets were too risky to take.

Bill drew his finger across the map, “Hey, maybe we could take Marine Drive straight to Troutdale. Getting to Marine could be a trick, though. Whadda ya think?” He knew getting to Marine Drive meant crossing straight through a crime-ridden and dangerous part of northeast Portland.

Joe pondered this a moment.

“Fine,” Joe said.

Bill nodded in agreement. “We could take Lovejoy across the Broadway Bridge, then go north on I-5. Then we get off on Marine Drive. Simple. Safest route out of downtown too.” Bill glanced over at Kelly a second, “Then we take it east along the south bank of the Columbia River all the way to Troutdale. Hopefully there’ll be no stops.”

Joe smiled, “Okay, let’s make it happen.”

But they had one big problem: “I need to get some gas first.” Joe’s Hummer was almost out of gas.

Chapter Thirteen

Joe and Bill drove into Portland early that morning thinking they would stop and get gas on the way home later that afternoon. But the news was reporting that no gas stations remained open in the entire Portland and Vancouver metropolitan area.

Joe slowly walked toward Daniel's front door, "I think I know where there's plenty of gas." He stared at the door with his back to the others, "Bill, you wanna give me a hand?"

Bill shook his head in disbelief. "How embarrassing. No problem, buddy, let's make it happen."

As he started toward the door he muttered under his breath, "Maybe next time he'll listen to me and get a ride with better mileage."

At 12:30 p.m. they both went out Daniel's front door and quietly down the stairs to the spacious and well lighted parking garage. His Hummer had a 32-gallon gas tank, but at 8 mpg, it went fast.

This wasn't the first time Joe had run really low on fuel and just about each time Bill was there. One thing about Joe: other than constantly running out of gas, he was generally well prepared. At this moment, however, he was quite embarrassed. Without saying a word, Joe opened the rear door of his shiny, new-looking black Hummer and pulled out a four-foot long, well-used crowbar and a dark orange plastic five-gallon gas container. He handed both to Bill. He leaned back in and dug through a deep pile of clutter. He found what he was looking for: an old and stained six-foot length of three-eighths inch garden hose. Digging deeper into the pile, he found an unopened half-liter bottle of water and stuck it in his right rear pocket. He then gently closed the rear hatch as he and Bill wordlessly gazed across the well-lit parking garage.

It was about half full of vehicles. Joe spotted the one he believed most likely to have a full tank parked in a darker corner and walked quickly toward it: a beautiful spotless white new BMW 335is convertible. Its gas cap cover was located about eight inches above the right-rear wheel well. Joe jammed the unbent sharpened straight end of his crowbar into the gap on the right side of the cover and sprung it open without scratching the side panel too badly. He then flipped the crowbar over and used the bent portion to quickly pry off the locked gas cap, which left a nasty-looking dent.

Bill knew the drill. He silently set the five-gallon gas container on the garage floor alongside the BMW's right rear tire. Without taking a sip, he cracked open the water bottle which Joe had just handed him. He then loosely re-tightened the small water bottle and placed it next to his feet on the cool concrete garage floor. They both glanced around the garage one more time and Bill, looking a bit bummed, stared painfully at the gas can, "It's my turn, ain't it?"

Joe smiled, "Yup."

Bill quickly snaked about three feet of the slender green garden hose deep into the BMW's gas tank and mumbled under his breath, "Fine. I'll do it then."

Grabbing the other end of the hose in his left hand, he then took a few quick breaths and whispered to himself, "Here we go." He blew his air out and placed the hose into his mouth and sucked hard.

It didn't take long before a nasty-tasting but precious flow of 10% ethanol blended regular grade gasoline began to gush past his lips. As soon as he tasted the fuel, Bill quickly pulled the hose out of his mouth and stuck the now flowing end of the hose into the gas container. A stream of fuel splashed across his shirt. He spit a few times and scowled playfully at Joe, "Hey, muscle head, you owe me a t-shirt."

"We'll take your car next time," Joe quietly laughed back. It was an inside joke. Bill's finances were in such terrible disarray, he didn't own a car: he couldn't afford gas, insurance, any of it. For transportation, all he had was a bicycle.

Bill then quickly rinsed out his mouth with water while they both silently stood by as the gas container filled. When the gas container was full, Bill yanked the hose out of the BMW's gas tank and stopped the flow while Joe picked up the full gas container, walked it over to his Hummer, and emptied it into his tank. Bill and Joe repeated this process five more times in the silent garage: once more on the shiny new white BMW, and, in a stroke of surprisingly good luck they often joked about in later years, four times in a row on a black GMC Yukon bearing US Government license plates starting with the letters, 'DHS,' before Joe's Hummer had a full tank.

Afterward, Joe quickly shook out the hose and placed it and his gas container in the back of his heavily tinted Hummer while whistling a country tune. "Hey, Bill. You like writing people notes all the time. You gonna write the guys in the Yukon a nice thank you note?"

Bill trailed a nasty smell of gasoline as he walked across the garage. "I left my pen at Starbucks ... in that dead Mexican's mouth. Maybe next time." He opened up the door to the stairs and jogged with Joe up the ten flights to Daniel's condo.

When they were about halfway up Joe remarked, "Hey, Bill. Does this stairway smell like gasoline to you?"

Chapter Fourteen

As soon as they entered, Bill, always quick and to the point, looked at Kelly. "Grab your stuff. It's time to go."

"Sounds good." She stood up from the floor and gathered up her things. "Hey. One of you two really smells like gas. Is that you, Bill?"

"You knuckleheads be careful and don't do anything stupid," said Bill as he looked across the room at the other three guards.

"You mean like pour gasoline all over myself?" joked LePage. "How embarrassing."

Bill ignored the remark and with a rare display of emotion gave Daniel a big hug, "Be careful. Stay indoors until the 'storm' passes. If any of your apes over there tell you to do something," he nodded playfully toward the three guards, "do the exact opposite."

Joe shook Daniel's hand firmly in both of his, then walked over and gave each of the three guards a punch in the chest, as he liked to do when he said goodbye. "See you guys in a few days." He didn't know it at the time, but he would never see any of them or Daniel again.

While Bill and Joe were getting gas, Daniel had prepared a send off present to help them in the coming days: a large heavy manila envelope for each. "Here. Take this. Bring back what you don't spend. Remember, I'm keeping accurate records."

Without looking inside, they each stuffed them into the front of their denim jeans and covered them with their t-shirts. They then picked up their rifles. Joe smiled and looked at the guys staying behind while he pulled playfully on Bill's t-shirt, "Hey guys, one more thing. Homeland Security agents are somewhere in the building. If you happen to see them, thank them for the gas."

Kelly had no idea what Joe was joking about, but even Daniel laughed. Joe thought it was the first time he had ever seen Daniel laugh.

"Hey, check it out. Daniel just laughed," Joe said to the others.

"If you tell anyone, you're fired!" Daniel sternly warned Joe.

"Yes, boss. No one. Hey, I'll see you guys soon."

Bill, Joe and Kelly then left Daniel's condo and jogged quickly down the 10 flights of stairs to the underground parking lot. They piled into the same seats they had before, and at 12:50 p.m., Joe started his gas-guzzling 6.2-liter engine. As they were nearing the garage exit, they noticed four thirty-something men casually dressed in baggy, loose-fitting dark clothes: one black, one Asian carrying a large black leather briefcase, and two white, walking toward the black Yukon. Bill cranked up a big crooked tooth smile and waved at them through the lowered front passenger window. "Heck of a day, huh, fellas? Man, I'd sure hate to be outside walkin' the streets today."

The friendly feds all smiled and without a word a few nodded in agreement as the Hummer pulled out of the garage and into the bright July sun. Joe didn't want these four guys chasing after him on foot, so after tossing Bill a quick hard look he punched his foot on the gas a little harder than usual, which accomplished very little, as usual, and sped east toward the Willamette.

Chapter Fifteen

As they were crossing the Broadway Bridge, Bill lifted up the front of his t-shirt and pulled out the large envelope, hefting it up and down in his left hand.

"Let me take a little peek here." He winked conspiratorially at Joe and then unwound the little red flap string, opened the manila flap, squinted a bit and peeked inside. "Nice. Next year's pay." It contained a one-inch thick packet of $100 bills and several dozen assorted gold and silver coins. He cracked it open and smiled showing Joe what was inside. "Yo. Take a look stud muffin. Sweet!"

"Nice, but dude, you still smell like gas."

Joe dug his right hand into the front of his pants. "Here." He pulled out his hand. "Do something with this."

Joe handed Bill his envelope.

Bill took it, quickly peeked inside, nodded once and quickly turned back to let Kelly peek inside.

"Whoa!" Kelly said, borrowing one of Joe's favorite exclamations. She had never seen so much cash at once, which spoke volumes about her family's working class roots.

Bill placed both envelopes in the glove box.

"'Whoa,' indeed. I don't think Daniel expects us back for quite awhile," said Bill.

As they neared I-5, the news was reporting that a terrible accident had occurred on the old I-5 interstate bridge and it was closed. "Great. This is just wonderful. A parking lot." Joe said. It was clear they picked the wrong route. Traffic on the freeway was completely stopped, so they continued east along Broadway and turned left on NE Martin Luther King, Jr. Road, which was the next most direct path to Marine Drive.

As Joe started driving north on MLK, Bill unfastened his seatbelt, turned and reached into the canvas bag on the back seat behind Joe and next to Kelly. He pulled out four full 30-round magazines for the two rifles. He winked at Kelly, "These are for the rifles. We may need them. They're called magazines, but they're not the kind ya read."

Unbeknownst to the two men, Kelly had her grandfather's Walther 9mm in her purse. In the few years she had carried it only her sister Alison knew about it and Alison told no one. It was quite different from the Walther James Bond used in his movies. Her handgun held a full six-round magazine and another round in the chamber. In her purse, she also had four extra magazines in case of an emergency.

As they neared NE Holman Street, she saw a large scary-looking mob cheering wildly near a burning building. To her right, just past Holman, she could see dozens of looters running into and out of another large building. While staring at the crowd, she started breathing deeply through her nose over and over again while repeating to herself a silent calming chant her kung fu master had taught her.

Chapter Sixteen

Up and down MLK and as far down side streets, crowds of people were milling about; some standing in small groups, some scurrying down the sidewalk carrying boxes, some pushing full shopping carts down the street, and others simply running this way and that. Smoke and flames were rising in all directions and gunfire was everywhere. Here and there along the road a body rotted in the hot sun. To Joe, it looked like a war zone and was just like old times. He was in his zone and on full alert. His synapses were firing full-blast showering his brain with primeval signals designed and locked solid into his DNA, bred over thousands of generations of hunters and warriors for pure survival. To Kelly, it was her first experience witnessing what her father had for years been warning her about: unless people soon started respecting the environment, consuming and spending less and began following the path of peace, the eventual breakdown of society was inevitable.

Joe suddenly hit the brakes and stopped near the middle of the intersection of NE Rosa Parks Way and MLK. "Whoa," he said, and backhanded Bill hard on his left shoulder, "Get your rifle ready."

Bill raised his rifle to window height and poked the barrel a few inches out.

Kelly placed her right hand deep in her purse and gripped her Walther. She leaned over and fully lowered the deeply tinted driver's side rear passenger power window.

In the west side of the intersection, about 30 feet from where Joe had stopped, a group of six young black males dressed similarly in oversized t-shirts and low-hung baggy pants was grouped near a small, stranded south-bound KIA sedan. One of them grinned widely as he screamed out an odd loud noise while jumping up and down waving his arms wildly. He then shouted something totally unintelligible at the driver followed by, " … we kill you white boys. Mutha fukkahs, we kill you. We kill you now. We kill you all!"

The driver, an older white male, was crouched near the wide-open driver's door with his arms covering his bloody face as the young men took turns kicking and punching him.

Joe grabbed his rifle and sprinted at the attackers without a word. As one of them was about to kick the cowering man in the face again, the punk smiled and glanced toward Joe while at the same instant two bullets from Joe's rifle made fatal entry into his chest at 2,350 feet per second. The other five thugs scattered while the beaten man immediately stood up in front of Joe on the hot pavement, "I have to get home. My wife needs me now." The stunned and bleeding man then sat in the driver's seat of his blood-spattered white car, closed his door, and sped away south on MLK without offering a word of thanks or looking back.

While Joe turned and glanced south at the car as it sped away, Kelly, out of the corner of her eye, saw another man peek out from behind a shaded doorway about 50 feet north of the intersection along the west side of MLK. She saw him raise one arm up gripping a sideways-held handgun. He aimed it directly at Joe. Kelly, holding her handgun with both hands just as she had learned from Chris, instantly twisted to her left over to the driver's side of the backseat, and stuck her handgun out of the open back window, gently resting the bottom of her left forearm on the center of the window sill, "JOE! WATCH OUT!" She shouted.

Joe looked both directions at once as he crouched down low scanning in all directions with his rifle. He saw the man with the gun just as he suddenly crumpled and fell to the pavement.

She instantly lined up her front and rear sights on the very center of the young man's chest, and without hesitation pulled her trigger twice, just as her father's good friend had taught her. Sight alignment. Trigger pull. The 124-grain Hydra-Shok hollow-point 9mm bullets, which her father had recommended she always use, passed ten feet west of Joe's head and struck the man at 1,120 feet per second an inch lower than where she had aimed and a half-inch below his sternum in a nice and tight two-inch group.

One round ripped right through his body, while the other lodged in his spine. They sent him crumbling to the ground where he spent the final ten minutes of his sorry life lying fully paralyzed yet conscious and open-eyed on the hot summer sidewalk six inches away from, yet unable to reach, his prized stolen handgun. As he was rapidly bleeding out on the sidewalk, a pedestrian in an expensive, light tan business suit casually paused a few feet from him and stared a moment. "Hey bro. Nice iron." He bent over, grabbed the handgun, wiped a few blood splatters off on the paralyzed man's pant-leg and stood up. He stuck it under his belt and covered it with the flap of his suit jacket. "Aw right mah man, see you 'round, homie," and he continued on his way.

The dying man had no idea where the bullets came from and neither did Joe or Bill. The reports from Kelly's Walther rang loud in Bill's ears but it initially didn't register at all to him that they could possibly have come from cute Miss Lee sitting in the back seat. They must have come from Joe, he thought, but Joe was standing farther away. It didn't make sense. He shouted, "Kelly! Where did those shots come from?"

Kelly was too busy looking outside for additional threats to respond properly and instead blurted out, "What shots?"

Joe quickly looked around everywhere completely dumfounded and unable to figure out who had shot the man as he returned backward to his Hummer. It couldn't have been Bill, who was focusing all his attention straight ahead, plus an AR-15 sounds totally different from the sudden loud sharp cracks. It never occurred to him that it could've come from Kelly: the beautiful and friendly Starbucks barista who in her deep, sweet voice always affectionately called him Joe-Joe.

Kelly, who he then saw scanning back and forth out the left rear window in a standard police-style high-search position seeking possible additional threats, shouted at Joe, still crouched in the street, "JOE! Get back here! MOVE NOW!"

Joe, after recovering from the momentary shock of seeing Kelly so expertly handling a firearm, did as he was told.

As he put his transmission into Drive, he asked, "Kelly? Was that you?" Within seconds they were once again moving north up MLK.

Kelly spoke briefly, "I think I should explain, but can it wait until later? She waited a few seconds, "Okay, I've fired weapons before. It's my handgun and I have a concealed weapons permit."

Kelly wanted to explain to these guys all about her dad and Chris … and about her older sister, Alison, who encouraged her to train hard for any emergency, but that could wait. Instead, she smacked Joe hard on his rock-solid shoulder slightly spraining her hand and shouted, "Joe! Dammit, Joe-Joe … ah, crap, now my hand hurts … Joe, can't you drive this thing any faster?"

Joe, who barely felt the strike to his right shoulder replied, "It's floored." The Hummer weighed something like ten tons and like its Humvee cousin it was slow to get moving.

Joe was a bit bewildered. Not from the short sudden battle, but because Kelly had just saved his life. He glanced briefly over his shoulder and stared a short second into Kelly's eyes. His words to her were brief and to the point, "You just saved my life."

He turned back to watch the road and his eyes started to moisten, "I will never forget what you just did, Kelly. Never. That's a promise."

Bill looked at his buddy as he started to tear up and quietly muttered under his breath as he slowly shook his head, "How embarrassing."

"Shut up Bill."

"Yeah, Bill. Let him cry if he wants," Kelly said as she leaned forward and gently rubbed the solid back and sides of Joe's 19-inch neck.

Bill looked at each of them and smiled, "Fine. Cry. Joe always cries after a fight. You'll see."

The Hummer continued north through the growing chaos and mayhem along MLK. As they neared NE Morgan Street, a group of several dozen people stood in the middle of the intersection and from a distance they could see the group was stopping and robbing the occupants of the vehicles. Joe slowed from 45 to 30 mph and stopped crying, suddenly flipping back to warrior-mode.

He saw that several men were armed. "Get ready," he said to Bill and Kelly.

They were members of a black social club that went by the name, Columbia Villa Crips, but Bill and Joe didn't know that or care. Control over the streets along MLK went back and forth between the Hoovers Crips and their rivals the Columbia Villa Crips. This week it was the CVC's turn to control the action along the busy avenue. Two of the bandanna-wearing, muscular black men dangled dark handguns loosely at their sides as the Hummer steadily approached. A dozen or more pair of dark brown eyes glared menacingly toward the Hummer and they grew larger with the passing of each second.

Bill once again poked the barrel of his rifle out his window and gently rested it on Joe's right side mirror, "I promise you, Joe, I will NOT scratch your chrome this time."

"Thanks, Bill."

Bill reached over and gently patted Joe's right shoulder, "Hey, that's what friends are for."

"Would you two knock it off? Those men have guns!"

Joe sped up a bit driving directly at the two with weapons and smacked Bill's shoulder, "Whoa, dude. You stink of gas big time. You need to do something about that."

One of them raised his handgun up sideways toward the approaching Hummer but before he could shoot, Bill fired once. The man fell straight down, bleeding and severely wounded, while his gun hit the pavement and slid several feet away. Another man quickly stooped down and reached for it and as soon as he touched the gun, Joe hit a small bump in the road and, upsetting his aim, the stooping man took one of Bill's rounds in his upper chest instead of in the center of his face where Bill was aiming. The rest of the noisy unruly crowd scattered shouting and screaming as the black Hummer blasted through the intersection and headed toward Marine Drive.

Chapter Seventeen

They had no further trouble as they crossed the Columbia Slough and headed north. When they approached NE Walker, Bill tapped Joe's massive right arm with his much smaller left, "Turn right here. It's a shortcut. You always like my shortcuts, don't you? This'll get us to Marine Drive faster." Joe tearlessly made the turn and without further conversation they reached Marine Drive by 1:00 p.m.

As they headed east along Marine Drive, they listened to the radio. The local news repeated the now-familiar stories of spreading unrest throughout much of the Portland metro area. Occasional gunfire boomed in the distance and many dark columns of smoke rose in all directions. Bill turned to Kelly and asked her, "What did you learn about the national situation, I mean while you were on your laptop at Daniel's condo?"

For the next 10 minutes as they slowly made the drive along Marine Drive past Portland International Airport toward I-205, Kelly, who remained unbuckled, stuck her head between the men and told them what she had learned. "The entire US banking system is collapsed. But what's sad is that many saw it coming. Many powerful people knew it was about to fall apart, yet nothing was done. Government and industrial leaders also did nothing." She continued, recalling what she read from assorted popular market news websites, "The Republicans called any government action 'interference in the marketplace', and the new Republican majority in both houses had the votes to back up that philosophy. The Democrats were no better. Fearing the financial instability government action might cause, and fiercely yet wrongly blamed by nearly everyone for the ruinous recent epidemic of market tinkering, Democrats in Congress quietly went along."

Bill clarified, "So in other words, everyone running the show knew it was coming, is that about right?"

"That's one way of putting it," Kelly replied.

She continued, "Many predicted that putting a tighter leash on the Fed and placing greater restrictions on banks would cause a shakeup of the banking industry and cause instability in the financial markets."

They were comfortable with that and firmly believed, as one Congressman from Texas said, "The marketplace would sort things out in short order." But what they did not foresee was Monday morning's wave of bank failures and the total collapse of the nation's financial system.

The websites told her much more, but instead of sharing all the details, she allowed the guys to just drive and quietly ponder the new situation. And so did she.

She had learned plenty. Earlier in the year after what is now called, 'The Three-Hour War' and after the Saudi and Iranian oil had been removed from the market, the rising cost of oil led to strong inflationary pressures. Several poor nations could no longer afford to import any fuel. By March, there wasn't a gallon of fuel available for purchase in the entire country of Zimbabwe and in six other sub-Saharan African nations only the military had fuel. Uruguay, which imported 100% of its fuel, began strict fuel rationing allowing, at $12.00 per gallon, two gallons per month per vehicle. Singapore, another oil-import dependant nation, curtailed all Saturday and Sunday driving and imposed a $5.00 per gallon surcharge to force less consumption. Japan and Taiwan did the same in order to avoid unpopular rationing. Across Western Europe, where nearly all fuel was imported, petrol had recently been selling for between $14.00 and $16.00 per gallon.

Mexico, which had exported oil to the US for decades, saw its oil fields accelerate their terminal decline. Their oil production had just fallen to below 2.1 million barrels per day meaning Mexico had become a net oil importer, as the energy analysts would say. Despite applying the latest technologies and with near-heroic steps taken by PEMEX scientists and other experts, even $250 per barrel oil could not encourage their depleted and aged oil fields to produce more. Making things worse, they could not afford increasingly costly, imported oil. Therefore, long gasoline queues, higher prices and brutal fuel rationing had become the norm across Mexico. The Mexican government, which had relied on oil revenue for about half its national budget, was severely weakened from the revenue loss while the drug cartels were strengthened by the loss of government control. The gangsters became the de facto rulers across much of that nation.

The USA responded to the northward crush of humanity by positioning 50,000 US Army soldiers along its southern border in an effort to prevent a wholesale migration of increasingly desperate and hungry Mexicans and other Latin Americans from illegally entering. The USA could no longer offer sanctuary for the starving 'huddled masses yearning to breathe free' and took strong and decisive steps to implement a new restrictive policy. Congress had, over the winter, voted by a close margin to implement a controversial five-year immigration moratorium limiting net immigration to 100,000 people per year. It favored the highly educated and uniquely skilled and essentially eliminated all other categories of immigrants, including family members, asylum-seekers and refugees.

In January, the landlocked nation Paraguay banned non-farm private consumption of gasoline and diesel, completely restricting its use for buses, police, military, and emergency vehicles. Deadly rioting in that small land-locked nation broke out immediately. After a five-day orgy of looting and widespread social unrest, order was restored by the army, which shortly afterward dissolved both houses of the National Congress and declared martial law. Argentina, Uruguay, Peru, Bolivia, Venezuela, Honduras, Guatemala and Panama quickly followed suit, declaring martial law while rolling back basic civil liberties. The 20th century era of the military dictator appeared to have suddenly returned across much of South and Central America.

The economic crisis forced entire industries to shut down. Unemployment grew worse and among US construction workers it reached 60%. Boeing closed all its manufacturing facilities as thousands of airplane orders were cancelled. Housing and auto sales plummeted.

Many gas stations across the USA started offering an hour a day of motorcycles-only fueling. In response, scooter and small displacement motorcycle sales skyrocketed, but other than an increase in firearms sales, it was the only bright spot across the increasingly dreary economic landscape. Auto factories in the USA and abroad shut down forcing millions of formerly relatively well-paid autoworkers out on the streets.

Imports of washers, dryers, refrigerators, computers, televisions, cell phones, and a vast and bewildering array of other costly consumer goods slowed to a trickle across North America and Europe. As a result, tens of millions of Chinese and other Southeast Asian factory workers suddenly found themselves out on the streets in desperate search of employment. Without the social safety net of unemployment insurance, most soon grew hungry and more than a few starved. Social and political instability was starting to raise its ugly head across much of Asia. As industry after industry shut down, their economies were creeping toward the very brink of collapse and anarchy.

Tourism and business travel ground to a halt. Several smaller airlines went bankrupt and remained closed. A rapid consolidation of the airline industry had, by June, left the continental US with only three major airlines, and the few remaining regional carriers were in their final death throes as June came to a close. Fares shot up. Thousands of commercial airplanes were grounded and parked in long rows lying mothballed on a few vast airplane parking lots in Arizona, Southern California, and Texas.

Across Oregon, many city and county governments had already or were preparing to stop functioning altogether. Coos and Curry counties closed down completely. They were forced to lay off all their employees including deputies, and had no money remaining for basic essential services. At least a dozen other Oregon counties were likewise preparing to shut down as July approached.

The Coos and Curry county jails closed. Inmates charged with the most serious crimes were temporarily moved to neighboring counties. Those charged with lesser offenses were freed. Citizens were advised to arm and protect themselves. A loose assortment of civilian militia groups, many on horseback, formed almost overnight in that sparsely-populated corner of the state offering a vigilante force of law providing some sense of safety and protection. However, as summer was getting underway, a quiet yet underlying sense of impending doom was beginning to be felt by all.

Some counties in Oregon fared better and were able to continue functioning, but all suffered shocking reductions in services. Multnomah County laid off 355 out of 850 sworn deputies as county law enforcement services were reduced. All patrols east of the Sandy River were eliminated and the number of staff assigned to the Inverness facility was cut by 40%. The jail's kitchen vault often contained only enough food to feed the inmates for one day.

Chapter Eighteen

By June, as schools across the USA closed for summer vacation, the fuse was ready and about to be lit. A rapidly growing army numbering in the tens of millions of unemployed men and women was growing increasingly desperate and hungry. All it would take was a tiny spark to set them off.

After reading to herself, Kelly spoke up, "It's hard to believe all this is happening. The situation in Portland and near my parent's house in Troutdale seemed fairly normal up until this morning."

But things were no longer normal, and as they approached the airport they noticed that there were no take-offs or landings. Generally there would be a plane taking off or landing every few minutes, but now there were none. A few cars and trucks could be seen heading into and out of the airport, but other than that it was as if someone had pulled the plug on the entire sky.

As they continued east on Marine Drive and under I-205 they saw that traffic on the I-205 interstate bridge was very light heading into and out of Washington. A long convoy of military vehicles could be seen slowly heading over the bridge into Oregon, and Joe thought it was possibly heading toward the airport. It was the last National Guard force they saw.

Listening to the local news on Joe's radio, it was reported that hundreds of semi-trucks were parked stranded on and along NE Frontage Road near the huge Troutdale truck stop waiting for fuel. The road from Marine Drive to Troutdale was impassible. They would head south on 223rd and take it to NE Glisan instead. This would take them through more neighborhoods, which was something they wanted to avoid, but they had no choice.

Surprisingly, the drive down 223rd to Glisan was uneventful. With the exception of a few dozen people silently pushing shopping carts filled with boxes and un-bagged grocery items along 223rd, it was much like any other hot summer afternoon. However, traffic was exceptionally light. A large group of people could be seen standing near the northeast corner of the intersection, but they weren't bothering anyone. More than a few bicyclists could be seen, but they rode by in small groups: rarely alone.

They turned east on Glisan and could see, looking left, that the large Fred Meyer store and the other businesses in the small shopping area were being looted. Mobs of people were busily ransacking the large Kohl's as well. The drug store and pharmacy across the street on the south side of Glisan was completely smashed apart and smoke could be seen drifting through broken windows. It was probably the first business to go. People often went for drugs and alcohol even before food. Garbage and debris could be seen scattered across the parking lot and into the nearly traffic-free streets.

"This is where we do our shopping." Kelly pointed across Glisan, "Look at Kohl's, you guys! It's on fire! I just bought a spring jacket there yesterday. I went with my mom and sister. They had a big clearance sale. Everything was super-cheap. The jacket was on sale for $11.00! Do you think they knew this was coming?"

Her question went unanswered.

People were loading their looted goods into the backs of pickups and into car trunks. There were no police to be seen so it was a free for all. They didn't know it, but this would be their last shopping day forever.

Interestingly, it was as though a happy, festive, almost carnival-like atmosphere prevailed as the mobs tore the unguarded stores apart. People laughed. Kids chased each other and played in the parking lot. Strangely, the McDonalds on the corner was open with a few cars and well-behaved people queuing up as usual, placing their lunch requests in a peculiarly well-ordered manner.

They drove on and when they reached 242nd they could see that the town's Safeway was temporarily closed yet unransacked for now. It was guarded by two Troutdale police officers assisted by four or five armed men wearing street clothes. Kelly looked out her side window. These men couldn't stand there forever. In time even Safeway, the store her mother often shopped at, would be looted clean and closed.

The Albertson's a mile away was not so lucky. As the morning progressed the store was besieged by a growing mob of people, many of whom quickly found out their Oregon Trail Cards, which 1.2 million Oregonians expected to have been refilled with another month's worth of free cash, no longer worked. By 10:30 a.m. shoplifting became widespread. Employees could no longer control the theft of beer, wine, and groceries and by 10:55, fearful of the growing angry mob outside, most fled. By 11:00 out of control open looting began. At 11:02 three Troutdale police cars arrived, stopping on Stark Street as the surreal scene unfolded before them. At 11:04, outnumbered by hundreds to one, they drove off and continued their patrol. They didn't know it at the time, but these three police cars were burning their last tanks of gas. When they ran out of fuel they would remain where they stopped until they oxidized into dust.

The mobs had taken over not only in east Multnomah County, but nearly the entire nation was now suffering a complete breakdown of law and order. The Troutdale Police Department had to lay off five of their 19 sworn police officers last spring. The city relied heavily on income from property taxes and state shared revenue, both of which had fallen like a rock, shattering the city budget. Lodging fees, which in earlier years offered a steady stream of tax revenue into the city's coffers, fell to 25% of what it was earlier in the decade. Property tax revenue flowed in slowly as more and more delayed their tax payments or skipped them entirely. The citywide budget cuts hit like a sledgehammer. Troutdale was forced to lay-off all their parks staff and all but three of their city hall staff. The city manager was terminated. The mayor assumed the duties of supervising the skeleton staff but wasn't compensated for his effort.

Troutdale fared better than many Multnomah County cities. Nearby Gresham was forced to close city hall completely and layoff 40% of their police officers while nearby Fairview closed down its police department entirely. Eugene had to eliminate its ten-officer traffic patrol division and cut police salaries in half promising to pay the other half in a city-backed IOU.

Elsewhere, even The New York City Police Department, which two years earlier had 39,000 regular and auxiliary, was now trying to keep the streets safe with 28,000 officers, all of whom had to take a morale crushing 20% pay cut in order to help bridge the city's budget gap. But on this day they couldn't keep control. By noon, every pharmacy in the city was raided while by early afternoon every store shelf in the city was emptied of liquor, beer, wine, food, toilet paper and everything else they once sold.

The shelves would remain empty forever as fruits and vegetables quickly rotted in tens of thousands of hot big rigs parked at truck stops and along the nation's freeways. Trucks carrying non-perishable packaged food were broken into and looted. In Troutdale, the truck stop was safe for now, but by Tuesday afternoon it was under attack by the hungry populace. The police did not respond and no papers covered this story.

The uncontrollable frenzy continued across the USA for several days. Then part way through Wednesday the looting suddenly stopped and the store fires began to die out. The supermarkets were emptied and there was little remaining to loot across the country. All that could be heard along the interstate freeway system was silence stretching from coast to coast. As soon as the looting of stores stopped, the nation turned on itself. A plague of home invasions featuring murder, rape, robbery and arson swept across the nation like a deadly incurable new strain of bird flu. By Thursday morning the entire nation was infected. In a month or so it would completely run its course and very few would survive.

Around noon, Monday, the Troutdale Albertson's was completely emptied of merchandise and ablaze. The Gresham Fire Department didn't bother responding since their remaining on-duty firefighters were triaged, ordered to save lives instead of putting out the many property fires that had broken out in eastern Multnomah county.

At 1:24 p.m. they drove by Kelly's old high school, Reynolds. She wondered what it would be like to go to school there now and she told the guys, "This is my old high school. I should have known something was wrong when they made all those cuts a few years ago. Then the really crazy cuts last spring made things even worse."

Reynolds High School had suffered severe budget cuts since 2008. Much worse cuts were inflicted during the early 2010s. The performing arts building was closed and shuttered. Physical education was discontinued. All sports had been cancelled. Fifty-one full-time teachers were laid off. Class sizes averaged 52 students and the school focused only on the most basic and core academic subjects, but with classes that large, most students were learning little. Even busing had been discontinued. The local papers had reported that teacher salaries statewide had just been slashed to 70% of what they were the previous year, but even those smaller paychecks did not arrive today. At 1:25 as the Hummer was turning north on 257th, the three could see several black columns of smoke rising to the south, but strangely, no sirens. They slowly turned into Kelly's neighborhood.

HOME, SWEET HOME

Chapter Nineteen

As they drove the final two blocks toward Kelly's house, Kelly noticed that unlike most warm summer days, there were no children playing in the street. It made her think of her childhood when she spent her summer days riding her bike or roller-blading up and down these very same streets. Kelly was suddenly reminded of her Vespa, and she wanted to get her scooter immediately.

"Hey, guys," she said, "would you two mind taking me to the Cleveland MAX station so I can get my scooter? I wanna get it right now." Not only was it her only transportation, it was a gift from her dad!

Bill and Joe just looked at each other and shook their heads. "Are you crazy? This town is a war-zone. It's way too dangerous to go right now."

"I'm not joking guys. I need to get my scooter and I need to go now before someone steals it or wrecks it," Kelly said as the Hummer prepared to stop in front of her house, "It's okay if you two think it's too dangerous. I totally understand. I'll just ask my sister Alison to drive me. She'll gladly do it."

After the incident on MLK Bill and Joe knew Kelly could take care of herself. However, they doubted her scooter was still there and in one piece. After all, the MAX stations had all been hit hard by violence and it was probably stolen or destroyed by now. Bill and Joe were tough men, but they weren't reckless. On the other hand, they were somewhat offended by the minor assault on their manhood.

"Kelly," Joe turned to look back at her, "Bill and I'll be happy to take you. But we should leave now before things get worse. Okay?"

Bill looked at Joe like he was completely insane, and as everyone paused a second to listen to the sound of gunfire in the distance, he added, "We'll be happy to do it for you, Kelly. But let's get going … like, right now."

Chapter Twenty

Noticing the unfamiliar car parking in front of their house, Alison, Kelly's 5' 7" 24-year-old sister, warily peeked through a narrow crack in the blinds covering Kelly's slightly open upstairs bedroom window. Her mother was in the back yard tending her lush vegetable garden while her dad, armed with his revolver, was peering at the strange black vehicle through a dark shaded crack in his side-yard gate. Slung from a green canvas shoulder strap, Alison held her father's favorite rifle: a Chinese-made semi-automatic AK-47, loaded with a full 30-round magazine. She held it lowered at a 45-degree angle, ready to stop any threat on her family. She had an additional loaded magazine in each of the side pockets of her fashionably baggy dark green cargo pants. Alison and her father, Jimmy, also had 20 additional pre-loaded magazines scattered throughout the house as a precaution. They didn't want to hurt anyone, but guarding the family was paramount and wouldn't be compromised.

Many years ago Alison's father had told her, "Bad karma is generated when you harm people, even in self-defense, but far worse karma is generated when you do nothing and allow violence to fall on your family. If attacked, you must minimize the bad karma. Always use the very least amount of force needed." Alison always smiled and was comforted when she thought of this and considered it very solid advice.

Like her sister Kelly, Alison was a second-degree black belt in kung-fu style karate, and she was well aware that karate and its martial arts forerunners had their roots in Buddhism. Stopping a threat and protecting yourself and loved ones with minimum force was the primary rule. Alison liked the thought of defending her family that way, but she had to be realistic knowing that the thin blue line, which could have been summoned with a single phone call, had effectively dissolved on this day. 911 no longer existed. The police would no longer come to their aid and if necessary perform the violence for them as they would have in the past. Like her father told her that morning, "It appears as though we'll be defending ourselves for quite awhile. We'll stand guard and sleep in shifts." She thought about that while she remained vigilant sitting by the upstairs window.

Chapter Twenty-One

"Hey guys, would you mind waiting by the Hummer a few seconds? My parents and my sister don't know you and they want to see if I'm safe," Kelly told Bill and Joe.

She walked to the center of the yard, turned her head toward an upstairs window and yelled, "Alison, you can relax! These two guys are the good guys! They just saved my life and then drove me home from work. Come down here a sec and meet them."

Meanwhile, her father peeked around the side of the house out of Kelly's view and aimed his revolver toward Bill and Joe. "You two step away from the truck. No weapons. Let me see your hands."

"Yes, sir." Joe and Bill assumed it was Kelly's father and understood his concern.

"Lift your shirts so I can see what's under."

Bill and Joe lifted their shirts revealing their holstered handguns.

"Okay, now remove your weapons, but leave them in their holsters. Place them on the hood of your car and step away from it."

After placing their holstered handguns on the hood of the truck, they walked ten feet away from the Hummer and stood waiting.

Kelly thought she heard her dad's voice and saw Bill and Joe walking away from the Hummer. She walked toward the corner of the house and saw her dad. "Daddy!"

She smiled and ran toward him with her purse bouncing on her right hip and the strap slung over her left shoulder as his friend Chris had taught her. "Daddy! Bill and Joe are friends of mine! They drove me home. I couldn't have made it without them."

Jimmy holstered his old Smith and Wesson revolver and stepped around the corner of the house greeting Kelly and to meet the two men.

"I am so glad you are home safe and sound, Kelly," her father said as he gave her a big hug.

"I'm fine, dad. This is Joe and he's Bill. They drove me home. Oh dad, it was the scariest drive I ever had. Where's mom?"

"She's working on the garden in the back yard. In fact, we both were," her dad replied. "Hey guys, sorry about pointing my gun at you. We're a bit tense here. A few homes were robbed today and everyone's really nervous."

"No problem, sir. You must be Mr. Lee." Joe smiled. "My name is Joe Hancock. I work across the street from your daughter. My friend Bill and I guard the Bullion Exchange and we drove her home. The city is a mess right now. We barely made it here."

"I've heard your name before. Call me Jimmy," and with a big smile stuck out his right hand to shake Joe's.

Bill walked around and offered Jimmy his hand, "Mr. Lee. Bill Hartigan. Everyone just calls me Bill. I'm very pleased to meet you, sir. This is quite an impressive daughter you have here. She saved Joe's life on the way home. Maybe mine too."

"Nice to meet you, Bill," replied Jimmy. "We are very proud of her and her sister, Alison. Kelly has spoken of you guys a few times. Guards? Must be a tense job at times. I can't wait to hear the details. In fact, I want to hear any news you have. Maybe we can talk over lunch."

Seeing this gathering in the yard, Alison meanwhile quickly ran downstairs to greet Kelly.

"Hi Kelly. I am so glad to see you home," Alison said as she hugged her sister.

After their quick sister-to-sister hug, Kelly turned toward Joe and Bill, "Alison, these are my friends from across the street from Starbucks. This is Bill."

Alison shook Bill's hand, "Happy to meet you. I'm Alison. Kelly's sister."

"And this is Joe." Kelly said as she smiled.

"Hi, I'm Alison." Alison shook Joe's huge hand and looked at Kelly briefly, "Kelly has mentioned your name to me once or twice."

Kelly looked a bit embarrassed. "Alison, do you mind?"

Alison giggled briefly, but said nothing more. Kelly often spoke affectionately to her mother about her new guard friend who worked across from Starbucks at the Bullion Exchange. Her father had done some business there over the years and trusted the owner.

Taking turns, the three arrivals excitedly told Alison and her dad the very short version of their terrifying drive home from downtown.

"Hold on a second, everyone. STOP!" Kelly waved her arms over her head suddenly interrupting everyone. "Alison. Bill and Joe just volunteered to drive me to the MAX station so I can get my scooter. You wanna come too?"

"It's in the garage, Kelly." Alison said. "In fact, it's plugged into the trickle-charger. Dad and I got it this morning when we heard what was happening on the news. We kept calling the Starbucks and there was no answer. We even emailed you."

Her dad had a spare key and had driven Alison to the MAX station earlier in the morning when they found out the trains were stopped. At first they figured they could pick Kelly up when she called. Then everything started falling apart including the phones, so they just waited for her to email.

"It was easy to find. The first place we looked was the motorcycle-only spaces near the platform, and there it was." Her dad said, "No one touched it. I rode it home myself. Sweet ride, Kelly."

Kelly loved her scooter and gave her dad a great big thank you hug and a great big traditional Irish-style loving kiss on his forehead. Her father completely adored his two daughters and his eyes watered up slightly as Kelly leaned back and smiled at him, "Thanks, daddy! I love you."

But making Kelly smile even more was the wonderful sight of her mom. She heard the commotion in the front yard, but finished tending to one of the family vegetable beds before she walked out front to see what it was all about. The Lee family had a lush, well-tended vegetable garden. It was supplemented by a half-dozen assorted fruit trees, the fruit from which would be finding its way into jars of home-made jam and pies in a month or two. Plus, they grew five kinds of berries to offer a tasty variety to the harvest. Some, such as the strawberries and blueberries, were already getting picked. Her mom walked through the gate with a smile that could calm anyone. "Hi, Kelly. Hey, what's going on? Are we having a party?"

"Mommy!" Kelly hugged her mom. "Mom, these are my friends from downtown. They drove me home – saved my life, too!" Kelly introduced her mom.

"Deborah Lee," She said, as she shook each of their hands. "But please call me Deborah."

Deborah stayed in the front yard a few minutes while she joined everyone excitedly discussing the terrible situation they faced.

"I bet you guys could use some freshening up. Why don't I go fix some lunch while you guys finish talking." She said. "Maybe I'll fix some lemon tea for everyone."

Sadly, tomorrow would be the last time any of them would ever taste lemon tea.

Chapter Twenty-Two

"I gotta go back upstairs. It's my turn to watch the street from up there." Alison announced. "Nice to meet you guys." She went back upstairs to watch the street from Kelly's upstairs bedroom window.

After first peeking in on her scooter, Kelly went into the kitchen and helped her mom prepare a nice vegetarian snack for everyone. If Bill and Joe wanted hamburgers or chicken or any other meat they would have to go somewhere else because both Deborah and Jimmy were devout Buddhists and never allowed meat of any kind in their home. Kelly mentioned this to their two guests commenting that she 'almost' never ate meat either and, of course, never when she stayed at home.

But Deborah was a master in the kitchen as well as in the garden. With Kelly's help she quickly whipped together a fantastic vegetarian lunch nearly all of which came from their tiny garden. It included slices of whole grain bread and a fantastic vegetarian tofu salad. For dessert the group would soon sip ice-cold strawberry smoothies made from strawberries she picked from the garden that morning. The two of them had it all displayed on the kitchen counter and it looked to Deborah like a nirvana-inspired feast.

She was proud of the fact that because of their tiny yet lush garden, the family didn't buy any fruit or vegetables from about mid-June until late October each year. A portion of the crop from their suburban micro-farm, as Jimmy jokingly called it, was stored in the garage freezer. It was nowhere near enough for the family to live on, but it was a wonderful supplement to supermarket food.

The Lees were careful about their garden. They didn't add any chemical fertilizers and no insecticides were used either. They occasionally added chicken manure and coffee grounds to the garden soil and composted all of their kitchen scraps. Their garden soil was rich and full of nutrients. Although they didn't test the soil and were admittedly very unscientific about managing it, after fifteen years the wide variety and large quantities of berries and vegetables it continued to produce was hard to believe.

The Lee garden produced so much fresh produce they were able to give away small gift bags of vegetables to neighbors and friends all summer, and well into fall. Caring for the garden took surprisingly little time and the Lees often commented how it was so strange that very few of their neighbors had food gardens of their own.

Chapter Twenty-Three

As Deborah finished preparing lunch, she allowed herself to daydream a minute about how tenuous their lives had become. She and her husband of 25 years, who was active in local politics and served on several important city committees, kept up on current events. They were both getting deeply concerned about the general state of the world's economy and over the past few years had moved most of their money out of the bank and converted it into American Eagle gold and silver coins. They kept a small amount of cash on hand, but after a recent scooter purchase, there was very little cash in the house.

She thought about how the US economy was more and more like a very unsteady house of cards, and how the world's economy was even worse. All it would take was a gentle breeze and it could all fold in upon itself in a flash. She followed that train of thought as she stared into the green belt behind their house. She remembered learning that when a house of cards collapsed, it fell into a two-dimensional form and was no longer three-dimensional meaning it was no longer part of our three-dimensional existence. All forms in our world needed to be three-dimensional in order to exist. Was it possible that a house of cards that fell vanished completely and no longer existed at all? That gentle breeze the country feared had definitely drifted in this morning, causing the nation's entire economic house of cards to collapse in a blinding flash. It appeared to be disappearing too.

The house of cards analogy faded and she drifted in her brief little daydream into exploring the economic situation. Her thoughts changed a bit, as daydreams can, and she now pictured the economy dangling by a very tiny linked chain. Everyone lived a life supported by this slenderest of chains. Their neighborhood was 100% reliant upon a small handful of nearby and a few not-so-nearby big-box stores. These stores were 100% reliant upon a thousands-of-miles-long and extraordinarily complex chain of just-in-time trucked-in deliveries. The truck drivers were 100% reliant upon a complex and interconnected system of cash cards constantly verifying and authorizing each fuel purchase they made. The trucks were 100% dependent upon a steady supply of increasingly scarce yet increasingly needed diesel fuel and if any link in the chain broke it all crashed down.

She thought back to what she and Jimmy had discussed over the past few years imagining a few of the links as they started to fatigue. The first link in this chain to weaken was the fuel link. Across North America, truckers had since January been waiting for hours for fuel in long lines. The price of diesel had just increased from about $4.50 per gallon to over $8.50 per gallon since the New Year's Day Three Hour War. This meant a typical semi-truck now burned about a thousand dollars worth of increasingly difficult to find diesel fuel just driving from Portland to San Jose, California.

Recent news reports told repeated stories of truckers across the nation's freeway system waiting several days for diesel shipments to reach some truck stops. It caused miles-long queues of trucks parked along freeways snaking across the cornfields and deserts silently waiting their chance to fill up. Perishables rotted in the heat as air conditioning units in trailers failed. Some big rigs were abandoned with poorly paid truckers simply walking away from their loads. The news media gleefully broadcast these bizarre images to all.

Fuel was getting scarcer and scarcer and would never be readily or cheaply available again. The world's one-time-only endowment of oil was finite and it was more than half gone. By 2005 a major milestone had been reached: about half of the world's oil had been burned according to the International Energy Agency. The world was well into the second half of this increasingly precious liquid and the desperate thirst for more was reflected in the ever more dangerous and costly places where it was being drilled and produced. The easy to get oil was nearly all burned. Plus, the quality of the oil produced was getting lower and lower. The once-fringe concept of peak oil, or a point where the world enters a permanent decline in oil production, had by now become common knowledge. The largest oil exporter of them all, Russia, had in the past two years seen its once-massive oil production settle into a frightening cliff-like terminal decline and fall by 8% each year.

The sudden decline in oil available for export was forcing prices higher and higher in all international energy markets and was wreaking utter havoc on economies all across the globe. And unless a cheap source of liquid energy was soon discovered ... well, very few politicians and business leaders would ever publically discuss that question. However, the inevitability of the coming geologic-driven resource collapse was slowly searing its way into everyone's consciousness.

The second link in the chain to weaken was the banks. When the first wave of layoffs struck last winter, a common sense of impending doom swept across the USA. Auto sales plummeted and the housing industry, already weakened by the 2008 financial crisis, simply froze up. Millions were laid off. As the so-called, 'quantitative easing' experiments and other money-printing gimmicks failed one after another there was a growing sense that the nation's economy would never recover. The money printing schemes were much like an addictive drug. They would allow the economy to briefly recover, but afterward the economy would demand an even larger dose to regain that artificial burst of satisfaction. All it served to do was grow the nation's sovereign debt, which by now was clearly unserviceable. If another wave of money printing were allowed to occur, the annual interest payments alone on the national debt would surpass annual federal revenue. That was link two. The financial markets and the banking industry were teetering on the very razor's edge of collapse.

The third fatiguing link was food itself. As cheap energy swept across the globe during the 20th century, the world's population grew like bacteria in a very nourishing petri dish swelling from one billion to seven billion in four generations. The sudden, historically unprecedented and completely unsustainable surge in the human population was fully reliant upon an ever-growing supply of cheap oil.

Many theorized that if oil were to deplete so would the population, but, to put it mildly, such discussion was considered impolite and in the rarified air of government officialdom and academia it was rarely mentioned. Fossil fuel based fertilizers had nourished the world's long-depleted farm soils for decades. Oil powered the plows, the fertilizer trucks, the insecticide spraying machinery, the harvesters, the processing factories, the food delivery trucks, and without cheap and steady oil deliveries the farms and the food they produced would cease to exist. That was link three. The world's ability to produce enough food to feed seven billion people was coming to a close and there was only one question remaining: when oil and fossil fuel-based products could no longer reach farms, how would the world's population return to one billion? Would the inevitable decline in population occur over many decades or, as more than a few predicted, would the decline occur very quickly? The answer to that question would be known in a matter of weeks.

Kelly saw her mother silently staring out the kitchen window and off into the greenbelt behind their home. She smiled and snapped her fingers, "Hey, mom. Earth to mommy."

Kelly produced another loud 'snap'. "Having a nice trip?" she joked.

Her mother instantly awoke from her brief daydream, slowly nodded her head and smiled back at her daughter.

"I guess I was daydreaming."

"Yes, Mom. But it's okay."

"Would you mind getting everyone to the table and start passing out the plates?"

"Sure, mom," Kelly replied.

She stepped around the corner of the kitchen. "Hey everyone, lunch time."

Chapter Twenty-Four

"Kelly, dear?" Jimmy asked, "Could you please log onto your laptop and see if you can find out any new information?"

"Sure, dad," Kelly replied. She was always ready to help her parents.

While Kelly tapped away, Deborah and the three men talked about what they should do next.

"Protecting the neighborhood and house is most important," Jimmy said. "We can hold out here until things get back to normal."

Bill looked a little concerned. "I agree, but if the neighborhood watch falls apart you're sunk. We don't have enough ammunition to keep all of East County away," he coldly joked. "I'm not so sure we'll ever see normal again, Jimmy. This mess is really getting bad fast."

"Oh, Jimmy. And Bill," Deborah said. "Things always have a way of fixing themselves. Even this crisis will be resolved somehow. I think we can still keep an optimistic attitude about things."

Joe avoided the conversation and focused on his lunch. He had to somehow contact his parents. Like most people, the Lee family no longer had a home phone. And since none of their cell phones were working, Joe first asked Kelly, "Hey, can I shoot off a quick email to my parents in Corbett?"

"Of course," Kelly replied, "let me get it started while you eat. What's their email address?"

Joe, who couldn't operate a computer keyboard if his life depended on it, asked Kelly. "Could you just say I'm fine, at a friend's house in Troutdale, and ask them to reply as soon as they can?" Joe watched in amazement as Kelly wrote it all out in a few seconds. "Could you check now and then to find out if they replied?"

"Sure, Joe-Joe."

Kelly's dad smiled slyly at his daughter. "Joe-Joe?"

She glanced over at her dad without saying a word. Her dad was still smiling.

As they sat at the table, Deborah saw a pause developing and moved to sit down in the empty chair nestled between Bill and Joe. "Well, guys. Tell us a little about yourselves."

"Sure." Joe was more than happy to talk about his family. "We own a berry farm." That comment opened a floodgate and between bites he told his family history while finishing his lunch. It was not a pioneer family, but the Hancock family had lived in Corbett since long before WW II. He still lived with his parents on their small blueberry farm about a mile west of Corbett High School, where he graduated 13 years ago. For decades, they hired temporary summer help to harvest berries from among the older high school kids out on their summer vacation.

Joe's dad was 62, the same age as Kelly's father, Jimmy, and had recently retired from his 35 years as a maintenance worker at the high school. His dad liked the job at the school because it gave him each summer off allowing him to fully focus his attention to the farm during the summer harvest.

"Starting in mid-July," Joe continued, "I take a few months off from my job guarding the Exchange and work 12-hour days picking and packing berries on the family farm as my father and his father before that had always done. Bill helps too. The locals call it

"The berry farm," but its official name is Hancock's Happy Berry Farm, named after my family."

Bill didn't like talking about himself because he felt his personal life was a mess. He was right. After working all his life, often earning well over a hundred thousand dollars a year, he had no 401k, no IRA, no savings, and had, through poor investment decisions and two failed marriages, managed to amass a personal debt in excess of $200,000 by age 52. His early-retirement pension was adequate, but half was seized for back child support payments and the garnishment was ordered to continue for six more years. He was flat broke. Daniel was concerned about paying Bill with a normal payroll check, so he paid him under the table in gold: one ounce every five shifts. Bill dutifully placed all of them in an ever-growing pile of coins safely stashed in a small plastic box buried under his house.

"I was born and raised in Corbett. Now I live alone in a so-called tiny home, a 200-square-foot efficiency home I built myself two years ago for $24,000." He secretly saved the cash for this cute little house by working for Daniel at the Bullion Exchange. "It sits on a small rocky lot full of weeds near Corbett High and I own it free and clear. I live the life of a simple bachelor."

His well insulated little home was only two years old and in perfect condition. It was ideal for him since he owned so few possessions. It was all he could afford but he was happy with what he had.

A few personal details he kept to himself. His two boys were now adults, but he hadn't seen or heard from them for many years after an unhappy divorce left them 2,000 miles away. "I work part-time at the Bullion Exchange with Joe, and I get a small pension from my years as a police officer. The monthly checks are automatically deposited into my checking account at Oregon State Bank. The bank is closed, but my account is empty now so it doesn't matter to me anyhow. I ride my bike a lot. Once a week I pedal to the top of Larch Mountain. I'm really happy living in Corbett."

He didn't tell her that half his pension check went to him and half went to pay his immense child support debt. If not for the envelope Daniel had handed him he would be flat broke. He didn't have an IRA or a 401k or any other retirement account. His entire salary from the Exchange was paid to him in gold, but only Daniel and Joe knew this. Bill was a little sensitive about his personal financial mess, and didn't like to talk about it.

"I live about a mile from the berry farm," Bill went on, "I usually helped out during summer vacations when I was a high school student in Corbett. Corbett High School has changed a lot since then. I can't believe it, the school operates year-round now!" This was due to a recent increase in enrollment, which was brought on by its spectacular top-ten national ranking. As a result of the switch to year-round schooling, many of the local small farmers hired far fewer high school kids. Although Joe's family farm continued to hire only locals, many of the other Corbett area farms cut costs by hiring mostly low-wage illegal aliens: mostly from Mexico, but this trend would soon come to a close.

Although Bill had been around farming much of his life, for the past 19 years he was in California dealing with street crime and hadn't had his hands muddy in ages. Although nearly his entire working career was spent in law enforcement, Bill had his fill of crime while working in Oakland and wanted nothing more to do with law enforcement. However, he would soon get very intimately reacquainted with farming and with muddy hands.

Chapter Twenty-Five

As they were finishing their delicious cold strawberry smoothies, Kelly, who was now seated at the dining room table, kicked Joe's ankle. "I have an incoming email from 'corbettcowboy.' You know anything about that?"

"It's my dad," Joe said.

Kelly slid her laptop over so he could open it. He quickly read it to himself. "My parents say they're safe, and that other than the cell phones no longer working the situation in Corbett was completely normal."

"My dad wants to know when me and Bill will be heading up the hill. He says to not hurry because the situation where we live is unusually quiet and calm." Joe's dad, always the comic, finished the brief and to-the-point message by adding, 'there are no rampaging mobs and no fires burning,' a comment that he jokingly followed with a tiny happy face and 'lol.'

His dad, who everyone called Joseph, also knew, but saw no reason to bother explaining in the email to his son, that Corbett's small general store, which sold gasoline from an ancient one-pump island, had closed that morning at 9:30. He was happy that other than the store being closed for a while, the small town remained unaffected by the day's surprising disaster. In fact, the Corbett

Market, which his long-time friend Luke Mershon owned, had just received a large morning food delivery. Additionally, a fuel tanker had topped off his 5,000-gallon underground tank with an 87 octane, 10% ethanol fuel blend two days earlier, and after the typically busy Saturday sales, the market still had 2,800 gallons of gasoline remaining. But the market was no longer selling any because Luke had closed the store.

The owner had told Joseph he was considering rationing the remaining fuel for use in farm machinery only. Some of the local townspeople wouldn't like his plan, but it was his market and he had pretty much made up his mind to stop selling any more gas for personal use. Until he had more time to think about it, the pumps would remain locked and guarded. Joseph told him he fully agreed with that idea and would totally support him. At 6'4" and built just like his son, people listened to Joseph, and Luke was thankful for his support. In fact, last September at Luke's 50th birthday party, Joseph had jokingly given Luke a white t-shirt, the front of which, in block-style black letters, read, 'You Mess With Me and You Mess With Joe Hancock.'

Joseph often laughed to himself about that goofy t-shirt and this morning as he walked around his berry farm he was grinning off and on as the thought of that shirt for some reason kept crossing his mind. But he and the others in Corbett knew that the situation was getting serious. Usually at this time of year, the constant sounds of internal combustion engines softly rumbled in the distance and crisscrossed from hill to hill throughout this rural part of Multnomah County. But today it was as quiet as it must have been back before the 19th century settlers arrived.

The people living in this close-knit community suspected it could be a long time before they would get more gas. For that reason they had already started either walking or riding bikes if they needed to contact anyone. Those who had walked or bicycled to Luke's store today were courteously turned away. After

Luke explained why, few of them complained. Corbett's only store remained fairly well stocked and was being guarded by a handful of trusted, and just in case of trouble, well-armed local young men. This was rural Corbett after all, and few boys and even fewer girls reached 18 years of age without their fathers or mothers teaching them how to shoot. This also meant the men guarding the stores would remain on duty and vigilant.

Joe knew that as the hours wore on, the danger his new friend Kelly and her family would be facing would only grow worse. For that reason, he quickly made a decision and he wouldn't allow anyone to change his mind.

Chapter Twenty-Six

Joe slowly stood up at the table and stretched, "Thanks for the awesome lunch, Deborah."

It was nearly 90 degrees outside and since the Lees didn't have air conditioning it was getting warm in the house. Joe sucked in the last few drops of his smoothie, set the glass back down on the table, and smiled at Deborah. "Whoa. That was the best dessert I've ever had. Perfect for a hot day like today. Thank you, Deborah."

Joe would have preferred a couple of ice-cold beers, but he remembered Kelly mentioning to him many weeks ago that her parents didn't drink at all, so he kept that thought to himself. In fact, as he glanced around the table, it dawned on him that he was surrounded by a bunch of non-drinkers. Weird. Bill hadn't touched a drink since he was 27, and neither Kelly nor her sister Alison, who was still upstairs, cared for drinking or for drinkers, for that matter. Joe rarely drank, but his dad was a bit of a boozer, and he was getting concerned that his occasional craving for a cold beer was something he inherited from his dad.

Joe wisely kept his sudden craving for beer to himself and asked Jimmy, "May I please use the restroom?"

As Jimmy was giving directions to the downstairs bathroom, Bill turned toward Kelly. "Do you think you and your family will be safe staying in Troutdale?" As he paused a few seconds while awaiting her reply they could both hear gunshots.

Kelly just stared at Bill a few seconds and his question went unanswered. It was as if the gunfire itself was her reply.

Kelly was completely confident that her family was capable and fully prepared to defend themselves. The family philosophy about self-defense was simple and based on their Buddhist beliefs: when people were under attack and called the police, as they regularly did prior to that morning, they were asking someone else: the police or the government, to possibly perform deadly violence on their behalf. The Lee philosophy saw no difference between asking the police to kill on your behalf or, in self-defense, killing an attacker yourself. Bad karma was generated by either action and one should avoid it at all costs unless there was absolutely no other choice.

There had never been a 911 police call made from the Lee house, but it was partly because they lived in an unusually safe neighborhood. But they all could sense that terrible danger was approaching and as people got hungrier and more desperate there would be no telling what they might do.

Deborah overheard Bill's question and spoke up, "We will do what we can, but unless the government stepped in and did something soon, we might consider leaving Troutdale until the storm passes." She continued, "We have close family friends who live on a 25-acre hay farm in the sticks near Sweet Home. They have several times in the past few months offered an open invitation for us to head down and stay with them if any kind of catastrophe ever struck."

Jimmy replied, but what he said was an understatement, "Sweet Home is over 100 miles away and getting all of us there safely and in one piece will be very difficult with the current situation."

Deborah then silently shrugged and held out her upraised hands as if to say she had no idea what they would do except deal with the situation hour by hour.

About that time, Joe walked back to the table, stopped in front of it and said he had an announcement to make.

Bill chuckled. "Did you finally decide to go back to college?"

Deborah looked at Joe quizzically, "You're going to college?"

Joe smiled at Deborah and ignored Bill's ridiculous remark. "I have an announcement to make." Joe said. Everyone listened. "Bill and I've decided that we'd like to stay the night to help safeguard your neighborhood and home."

Joe then looked straight at Jimmy and reminded him, "Kelly saved my life on MLK today and we just can't drive off home."

A bit surprised by getting suddenly drafted to guard the Lee family and taken aback by the surprise announcement, Bill glared straight at Joe with an unusually serious expression.

Joe glared right back.

Bill's expression slowly changed into an easy smile as he turned to face Jimmy and Deborah. "I agree with Joe. It's what we want to do. Would it be okay?"

Chapter Twenty-Seven

Jimmy and Alison gave Joe and Bill a quick tour of Strawberry Park introducing them to as many residents as possible. If the two newcomers were going to be in the area it was important they were seen by as many as possible as friends. Afterward, they showed them around the Lee's small property. Meanwhile, Kelly went up to begin her turn standing guard at her upstairs bedroom window.

From a strategic perspective the Lee house was very well positioned. The upstairs windows offered a 180-degree view of the front of the house and of the street to the south. The house was snuggled between two other similar homes each built 20 feet apart with a fence running through the middle of each property line. The back yard had no fence, but the small lot was safely protected from the north, as was the entire north side of the neighborhood, by a wicked green belt featuring a 100-foot deep and impenetrable thick field of thorn wielding blackberry vines. It was so dense and prickly even dogs and cats never went back there. Only an occasional pack of coyotes risked the brutal thorns. No paths cut through it. It was like a perimeter of concertina wire. Bill and Joe knew no one was getting through that.

As they went on their tour, Kelly took her two-hour turn at window duty. She didn't intend to use her laptop during her watch, but it was another special gift from her father and she felt compelled for some reason to never let it out of her sight for long. Kelly walked across her room and adjusted the blinds so they were cracked open a few millimeters: just enough for her to observe while not allowing those outside to see into her darkened room. She then sat on a high wooden stool, the same one Alison had just sat on, and peered up and down the street listening to the occasional gunfire and noticing the many columns of smoke rising here and there off in the distance.

By now it was almost 3:00 p.m., and the sun was no longer shining through the window. She continued to sit patiently. After a little while, her mom walked upstairs, came into the room, sat on the edge of Kelly's bed and started softly crying. Kelly made a brief glance up and down the street, abandoned her window duty, and sat on the bed next to her mom quietly holding her in her arms for a time.

Chapter Twenty-Eight

Deborah spoke to Kelly. “I am so proud of you and your sister Alison.” She went silent a moment “I couldn’t even begin to explain how happy I am to be a part of this wonderful American family that your father and I have raised.” Her life was an amazing and fascinating journey filled with unexpected adventures, harsh suffering, and a deep love for her family.

Deborah was born in the Peoples Republic of China back in 1965. She grew up during a period of unbelievable social turmoil and economic instability. She knew extreme hardship. As a little girl she clearly remembered owning only one dress and one pair of shoes. She remembered when her home farming village near Wuhan ran out of food for several months when she was nine years old. She saw many of her neighbors slowly starve to death. Her mom and dad recently told her this happens every other generation and it was now overdue.

“I feel in my heart that another period of unspeakable hardship and suffering is coming.” She told Kelly.

“This is why I am now very much afraid: not for me, but for you and Alison, as well as for Jimmy.” Deborah spoke further, “I met your father while I was a student at the University of Washington. As you know, he was raised in an unusually harsh US-style poverty served only to those who lived in east Oakland. Few escaped from the grip of such hardship. However, your father is very bright and pushed hard with all his blue-collar background could offer in his battle to get out of poverty."

"He worked full-time in a steel foundry to pay his rent as well as pay for his higher education. He had to skip classes every third week because in the steel mill the men worked rotating shifts." Deborah explained. "I deeply admire his strength and relentless efforts in climbing out of such severe poverty and hardship. I remember telling him we have much in common even though we come from such different backgrounds."

She told Kelly her story: a story she told her daughters years ago. "I made the long, and for a simple girl from rural China, frightening journey to America where I studied economics on a full scholarship. During the late 1980s there were very few students from China studying at UW and we were easy to spot. Our monthly allowances barely kept us fed and clothed. I remember the strange looks I got from other students because my clothes were so old and out of date. Like the handful of other students from China, I rarely left campus and completely avoided the college social life while focusing all my energy on studies. When other students were spending their weekends having fun at the ocean or skiing, I was in the library studying. When others were out visiting nightclubs or cafes I was in my dorm preparing for the following week's lessons."

She told Kelly that she had made only one good friend outside her small circle of Chinese students. It was Kelly's dad, Jimmy Lee, her American friend who took an immediate liking for Deborah after meeting in an American government class. However, the extent of their deepening friendship was limited by their ever-changing schedules to regular yet eagerly awaited lunches or frequent quick chats between classes.

Deborah did well in her studies and graduated with honors earning a BS in Economics, a field in which she continued to maintain a keen interest. Shortly afterward, she landed a well-paid job under the H1B visiting foreign worker program with United Airlines and her first assignment was in Oakland. Jimmy, who was by now her adoring boyfriend, landed a job with the U. S. State Department, and although it allowed him to be based in San Francisco, it required him to travel often.

His first travel experience was to a government law enforcement academy in Georgia where he trained daily for four months. He was then ordered to train seven days a week, 12 hours a day, for eight weeks at another government-run facility in the desert 30 miles north of Tucson, Arizona, but he never mentioned a single word about it. The six-month separation was difficult to endure and cruel for the new lovers and within a week after he returned to San Francisco, the two quietly married. Nine months later Alison was born. Three years after that, baby Kelly joined the family. Over time, the continuing separations required by Jimmy's frequent overseas travelling became less traumatic for the family and, thankfully, they soon became routine.

Jimmy never spoke a word to anyone about the details of his government job. None of his few buddies or even Deborah knew any details of his many trips to various parts of the world. After 19 years of service, he grew tired of his work with the State Department and having saved more than enough to support his family and finance his retirement, in 2007 he unexpectedly arranged for an early retirement. Although he never regretted working for the government, Jimmy often felt as though 19 years of his life had simply vanished without a trace. It was almost as if his life had started fresh all over again when he retired.

They then decided to move to a quieter place and shortly afterward, Deborah arranged for a transfer to Portland. The family bought a house in Troutdale near the Columbia River gorge where they live today. Deborah continued working for United until they went bankrupt two months ago.

"No matter how harsh things may appear, anyone can survive if they have the will," Deborah said. But Deborah suspected that the will of her family to survive this disaster would be severely tested in the coming months.

Kelly moved back to her window duty while her mother reclined to rest on her bed for a few minutes. "Rest here with me awhile, mom."

Deborah closed her eyes. Life was filled with one hardship after another. Her parents had often told her about the periodic crop failures that brought starvation to her part of rural China. She understood very well that all life involves suffering and that everything is impermanent, which were both basic tenets of her Buddhist beliefs, but it sometimes seemed as though she had experienced more than her fair share of both. She quickly stopped that train of thought. Exploring her sadness further would get her family nowhere. Deborah suddenly smiled, opened her eyes and sat up. She knew exactly what to do to if her family was to survive: the family must work very hard, avoid negative thoughts, and most important of all they must remain together. For now, that meant saying goodbye to Kelly and heading back downstairs to clean up after lunch. She sat up on the bed. "I'll rest later."

Chapter Twenty-Nine

When she got to the kitchen, she realized Jimmy had already taken care of the kitchen, as he often did. Jimmy, Alison and the two guests were back in the dining room talking about their security.

"Hey guys. In a few minutes our neighbor Don and I are scheduled to guard the footpath connecting Strawberry Park with 257th Avenue. We'll stay there until 8:00 p.m. Only residents and accompanied guests were to be allowed in," Jimmy said.

Bill and Joe offered to join them and Jimmy, knowing his daughters could safely keep the house safe, was more than happy to have the solid support.

At 4:00 p.m. the four men met at the beginning of the dirt foot trail next to the Lee's neighbor's house. Bill and Joe had already met Don and took a liking to him. Bill liked the idea of a lone, hidden back-up man, and spoke up. "Hey guys, I'll be the first back-up. If it's okay with you guys, I'll hide out behind that fence near the blackberry bushes. If there's any sign of trouble, I'll be watching your backs."

"Great idea," said Don, "we'll trade off every hour."

Meanwhile, Alison and Kelly stayed behind guarding the house, while Deborah went in the backyard to work on her garden. They didn't expect serious trouble, but while fewer and fewer vehicles could be heard, the dark smoke and intermittent gunfire piercing the newly forming quiet told them to prepare for the worst.

Chapter Thirty

As mid-afternoon turned into late afternoon, fewer vehicles and pedestrians were being turned away from the main entrance into Strawberry Park. Most residents with cars or trucks had returned home as dinnertime rolled around. Getting and affording gas was already a major problem so there was no more casual driving anyhow. Occasionally drivers pulled up to the entrance. Many appeared lost and disoriented and were offered water and directions. Some brought news from around town. It was mostly bad. Others appeared more than a little suspicious and were immediately told to leave. Quite a few people rode by on bicycles. Some were simply out getting exercise. Others were just inspecting the town. A few pedestrians passing by were obviously looters. Some walked by carrying TV's and other stolen items, while others pushed shopping carts filled with groceries and household goods. Since they weren't asking to enter Strawberry Park, they were simply ignored.

Standing guard at the main street entrance at 5:48 p.m. was Big Don, an energetic, charismatic and strapping 6' 1", 190 lb, 72-year-old, and tough-as-nails retired railroad worker. He wore faded jeans and a long-sleeved flannel shirt and because he hated guns and because he didn't own one he was unarmed. Plus, he thought some of his neighbors were getting a bit hysterical and in his opinion, which was shared by more than a few of his neighbors, the whole idea of posting guards was probably overdoing things a bit.

On the other hand, an emergency neighborhood meeting was held late that morning and as they stood in Vince's yard and voted, it was overwhelmingly agreed: Everyone who could would share security duty, period. About half the residents showed up at the hastily arranged meeting, and a few who missed eagerly put their names on the watch schedule as soon as they found out. Vince, who lived across the street from Big Don, volunteered to oversee and coordinate the schedule. Big Don lived right on the corner by the entrance and always wanted to be helpful so he asked to perform the first street entrance sentry duty, which he began right away.

Joining him that Monday afternoon was Vince, a 5' 10", 225 lb, crew-cut, laid-off truck driver, who at age 44 with 21 continuous years of seat time under his belt was in serious need of a fitness program. He had his old .38 revolver stuck under the front of his belt, well concealed by a faded old un-tucked white dress shirt.

Another man, Adam Bergin, served as their backup. Adam was a counselor at the nearby state juvenile detention facility and an avid hunter and outdoorsman. He knew how to shoot. He had a perfect view of the entrance and of the other two men. He was patiently waiting for the signal he hoped would never come while lying flat on his tummy with his powerful German-made Heckler and Koch .308 caliber rifle. He was safely positioned unseen behind the peak of his roofline about 120 feet north of the other two. Through his $600 20-power Leupold scope he could, if he was so inclined, easily determine that Don's eye color was deep blue. He could also have easily placed the sharp intersection of its crosshairs on old Don's cute chin mole from this distance. Seated into his lower receiver was a 30-round magazine containing 27 military surplus rounds. Each of the two cargo pockets of his well-worn black BDU pants held two more magazines each filled the same.

Unfortunately, Adam was too far away to hear what his two neighbors were saying to anyone approaching the entrance. This meant he might miss a deadly threat. Therefore the guards had agreed on a final signal. As their fail-safe backup, the signal Adam patiently awaited was simple: if either Vince or Big Don removed his sunglasses and hung them on his head Adam would kill whomever they were talking to.

Chapter Thirty-One

The rest of the evening went quietly. As 9:00 p.m. rolled by and as the day darkened, the scheduled shift changes occurred. Jimmy, Bill, and Joe were relieved by two other neighbors and went back home. The men guarding the footpath and the street entrance noticed, other than the occasional police officer stopping by for a very brief and friendly chat, that traffic was next to nonexistent. It was eerily quiet and although the ugly smell of smoke remained, the fires around them had died down. Jimmy, Bill and Joe were scheduled to guard the path again at 7:00 a.m. and they needed rest.

The Lee family decided they should maintain a continuous lookout from the upstairs window overnight. They weren't the only family doing it, but were one of few. The neighborhood was well guarded, but one never knew for sure what might happen. Three-hour shifts would work best thereby allowing each of them to get some sleep. It had been a long, tiring day for all. Joe and Bill volunteered to walk the neighborhood now and then and otherwise wait in the Lee's side yard just in case anyone uninvited wandered by. It didn't surprise Jimmy in the least when told by Deborah that the two men from Corbett would be outside all night.

At 9:10 p.m., two men, who would perform the next six-hour shift, replaced Don and Vince. Adam went home and no one replaced him on the roof. As darkness fell on Strawberry Park it strangely appeared as though the whole world fell silent. Other than the lingering smell of smoke and the occasional gunshots in the distance, it was a perfect summer evening and the entire night went by without a problem.

Chapter Thirty-Two

The next morning came and went without incident. The nation's stock markets and all banks remained closed. The only businesses that opened were those in isolated small rural towns. At 6:00 a.m., the Lee family and their two guests had breakfast. After a three-hour nap, Bill and Joe joined in sharing lookout duty along with many others in the neighborhood. Bill with his rock-solid demeanor and Joe with his friendly, easy going, yet powerful presence had quickly earned their trust and had quickly become well liked among the Lee's neighbors. It was an easy decision for them to make: they decided to stay another night.

By late Tuesday afternoon, Jimmy spoke privately to the two men about a serious problem he saw developing. "Several families have already started running out of a few basics. The Morgans ran out of bread and old man Morgan, as the kids called him, had dropped by the Lee's home asking if he could borrow a few slices. Rosa Ramirez was going door-to-door asking if anyone had any baby formula for her eight-month-old baby son. There was none. A walk to Safeway is far too dangerous and out of the question. You guys have any ideas?"

Joe had seen first hand what happened in Third World towns when the food had completely run out. "It's going to get very, very ugly in a few days. I think we might be good for a few hours, maybe days, but after that…"

Bill nodded in agreement.

"Okay," Jimmy concluded, "we'll see how the afternoon goes and then play it hour by hour. I don't want to upset or needlessly frighten anyone just yet."

As the rest of the day passed, more and more people dropped by the Lee's trying to borrow or trade essential items. About 120 or 130 people lived in Strawberry Park, and few had participated in the looting. Even if they had, the food and essentials in all the homes wouldn't last long. The Lee family had always prudently stored enough to last them a month, they believed. A few others did too, but it was becoming sadly apparent that most didn't have enough to last more than a few days. Most were already running out of basics such as bread, milk and meat. Joe had a small 12 pack of high-energy protein bars, which he generally carried in his Hummer, but he and Bill could go through them in a few days.

If Strawberry Park was running low on food, so were other neighborhoods including the 322 unit low-income housing project located down the hill a few hundred yards north. Seven hundred hard working and mostly decent low-income people called the well-maintained Columbia Heights development home. Each apartment was no doubt quickly running out of food. If the nearby stores weren't re-opened and, more importantly, replenished soon, the people would get desperate, as would the other 14,000 people calling Troutdale home. They did not know this, but in a very short time hunger and desperation would spread like a plague across Oregon, the entire nation and far beyond.

Chapter Thirty-Three

At 4:49 p.m. it was still 87 degrees outside and the sun was still shining bright. While Bill, Joe, and Jimmy were guarding the east side footpath they noticed a large flatbed truck stop on 257th, just to the north of them. It appeared to have a dozen or so bodies stacked on its bed. They saw two men wearing blue jeans and short-sleeved white shirts with large red crosses on the backs and fronts. They jumped out and placed the decaying bodies of the three looters shot the day before on the growing stack and slowly drove on.

As this was happening, four young men approached the south side Strawberry Park street entrance on foot. They were white and appeared to be in their early 20s. Three wore dark hooded sweat-shirts with the hoods pulled over their heads. One of the three hooded men carried a bulky backpack. The larger and taller of the four smiled in a crudely exaggerated manner and walked slightly ahead of the others. He wore baggy low-hung jeans and was shirt-less. His chest, arms and neck were so heavily and hideously tat-tooed with what at first or even second glance could be interpreted as meaningless gibberish that Don and Vince might have been jus-tifiably forgiven for not noticing that his head was shaved.

"Yo! What up bros? Look, man, ah wanna axe you sumptin," the large tattooed man asked Don and Vince.

Troutdale is a small town of about 14,000 people and after awhile the residents started to recognize the locals, but as these four got closer Don and Vince, who once again had the 3:00 p.m. to 9:00 p.m. shift, knew they had never seen them before. When they were about 20 feet away Don, who grew more concerned with each closer step they took, gave the command. "Stop. Turn around and leave now."

The four young men stopped, but they didn't turn around or leave. From about a block away, Alison who sat peering out Kelly's upstairs bedroom window could just barely see Adam as he aimed his rifle toward the south and placed his wide-open, deep blue right eye a few inches behind the eyepiece of his scope.

The tattooed man smiled, held out his open palms and as the other three remained a few yards behind answered Don. "Aw we wan is sum waddah and sumptin ta eat and we will go."

Vince said, "Go find another town to beg in. Get out now before there is any trouble."

Just then, one of the two waiting in the back lifted up his black sweatshirt and produced a pistol, pointing it at Vince. "You. Get us some food now. Bring it back in less den one minute oh yo friend will die."

Don froze, but Vince removed his sunglasses and placed them on his head.

Adam saw the four men when they arrived, but was now focusing through his scope only on the bald headed one. The pistol appeared. Adam began to slowly press on the trigger. About a second after the man holding the pistol said the word, 'die,' Adam, barely noticing that Vince had started to place his sunglasses on his head, nailed him in the right temple with a single .308 round.

The other hooded men immediately turned and fled running as fast as they could toward 257th. The dead man's baggy pants wearing comrades each grabbed the front of their oversized jeans with both hands and stumbled away as quickly as they could waddling away in their probably stolen expensive yet oddly unlaced athletic shoes. All three chose to abandon their late friend and to also abandon what was probably far more important to them: the pistol, which remained lying a foot from what remained of its former owner's head.

Don walked over and picked up the pistol. He paused to inspect it as he glanced at the three fleeing strangers. He then turned to Vince and asked, "Show me how this works. I should plan on carrying it from now on."

Bill, Joe and Jimmy heard the single loud explosion and Joe went to investigate. He slowly jogged to the street entrance, turned right and waved up at Adam, who waved back. He jogged south a few dozen yards and saw Don and Vince standing alongside the body.

Don explained what just happened. Joe turned to give Adam a big smile and a strong supportive thumbs-up. Joe then volunteered to drag the body away and dump it alongside 257th, where eventually someone might see it and carry it off for disposal.

Chapter Thirty-Four

While Joe was dragging the body down the middle of the street it was 10:00 Wednesday morning in Shanghai, but the Shanghai Stock Exchange would not be opening for trading as it did at 9:30 most weekday mornings. The panic that had started in the USA the day before, hit Asia like a 500-year tsunami and many major Asian cities were scenes of horror and smoky ruin as the sun crested over the Pacific Ocean Wednesday. Only the island nations of Japan, Singapore and New Zealand escaped the carnage. Many nations were hit hard, but China was hit the worst.

China had already been reeling from the loss of cheap oil imports after the Three Hour War and as July first neared, an estimated 110 million jobs had disappeared as factories closed one after another as the North American and European economies contracted. Severe gasoline and diesel shortages disrupted the shipment of goods. China, which by last December consumed 10.2 million barrels of oil each day, only produced 3.6 million. This meant that as the Three Hour War broke out China needed to somehow find 6.6 million barrels of liquid energy each and every day in order to survive as a modern nation. Over the past 15 years, the volatile and unstable Middle East had become their primary source and it could no longer supply them.

As July arrived they were still only able to import 3.5 million barrels of oil per day and at $240 per barrel it was likely all they could afford. Their Strategic Petroleum Reserve now contained 270 million barrels, which could theoretically provide 30 days of fuel, but was being prudently saved for emergency military uses and other than a 500,000 barrel withdrawal in late May, remained largely untapped. Long queues at filling stations became common as fuel shortages worsened. Various fuel rationing schemes and a five-month long ban on Sunday driving failed to quench the Chinese population's insatiable thirst for fuel and resources.

The highly urbanized nation of 1.3 billion people relied increasingly on trucks for moving the daily shipments of food and basics into their densely populated cities. The newly forming 100 million strong army of unemployed along with an additional 300 million rural poor was having great difficulty simply feeding itself and as July first rolled by they were growing very desperate and very hungry.

Over the past six months food shipments from overseas were getting increasingly unreliable causing prices to increase. Food shortages appeared. Black markets for essentials emerged. In response the Chinese government granted police sweeping powers to execute hoarders and black marketers in summary street trials, which by late June had become commonplace yet were largely unreported by the media.

Although China's rail system was arguably among the world's most advanced, factories still relied on diesel burning trucks to move the bulk of their manufactured goods to markets and to ports for overseas shipment. As the fuel crisis worsened, unsold goods stacked up in warehouses and production slowed everywhere. Unemployed and hungry workers had been protesting in ever-larger numbers since January, ending an amazing forty-five year long period of relative domestic peace in that historically strife-torn nation. Some would say the unfolding Chinese fuel crisis was inevitable due to the effects of peak oil, but the unbelievable suddenness with which their economy was unfolding shocked even the most hawkish among the recent many and increasingly vocal doomsday prognosticators.

As the carnage and horror in North America unfolded, the Chinese government chose not to allow their banks or stock markets to open Tuesday morning. Hong Kong, Tokyo, Singapore, Sydney and the rest of the Asian markets quickly followed suit. Factories and shops throughout China remained closed. Food markets in many cities were ordered shuttered. Crowds formed in the early hours and as the morning progressed, they grew larger and increasingly furious. Food prices, which had already doubled in the previous 12 months, worsened overnight. Riots broke out all across Asia as the growing numbers of unemployed joined with those who had in just one day lost their life savings. It was a violent release of anger the world had never before witnessed.

Urumqi, a city in Xinjiang with 1.4 million people, erupted as the day began. This remote city had felt the brunt of the food and fuel shortages occurring throughout China over the preceding six months. Ethnic Uyghurs and Han Chinese had been waging violent street battles against each other since April. The army was repeatedly called in to quell the ethnic violence but most agreed the army presence, which was openly sympathetic to the Han majority, only made things worse. The rapidly unfolding financial crisis released a floodgate of open warfare throughout the region. By late Tuesday morning hundreds were dead and fires could be seen throughout this western regional capital. As the crisis exploded Tuesday morning a state of martial law was proclaimed throughout Xinjiang. As the army prepared to once again move in, an unnamed high-ranking military officer was ominously quoted saying that this was going to be the last time the army would be called. The gloves were being removed and the well-organized Uyghurs prepared for a final yet futile defense of their ancestral homeland.

As a state of martial law was being announced in Xinjiang, violent unrest broke out in most other Chinese cities as well. By 11:30 a.m. local time, People's Liberation Army soldiers were patrolling the streets of Hong Kong, Tianjin, Wuhan and Shenzhen. In Guangzhou, the police initially set up barricades preventing the protesters and anyone else from reaching the Yuexiu district. In fact, most of Central Guangzhou was peaceful and well protected, but the Inner and Outer suburbs erupted. PLA units prepared to move out in full force as martial law was declared throughout China.

The rioting that broke out in Shanghai Tuesday was totally unexpected. This sophisticated modern city was considered the jewel of China and few were prepared for civil unrest, and especially unrest on the scale that occurred Tuesday morning. It started in the early morning as thousands of students and their supporters joined with tens of thousands of unemployed workers marching toward city hall located in the Huangpu district. The crowd grew, as hundreds of thousands of residents of this beautiful city could not access their bank accounts. They marched right into the city center.

By 10:00 a.m., rumors of a pending month long bank holiday panicked the city of 20 million and fearing their life savings had disappeared, the population rose up in a spectacular fury. Supermarkets and popular outdoor markets were quickly looted and much like what happened in the USA, banks were dealt the brunt of the fury.

By 11:00 a.m. an estimated four million people were in the streets of Shanghai demonstrating. As martial law was being declared nationwide, all Internet and cell phone communication from China suddenly stopped. The door to China, which had been cracked open by President Richard Nixon back in 1972, was once again slammed shut. The army's response to the rioting was never known.

Chapter Thirty-Five

Europe was nailed next. When the Monday morning crisis hit in the USA, it was already afternoon in London and European markets were preparing to close. Across the EU stock markets immediately caught wind of the wave of bank failures and closed an hour or two early, depending on the city. Banks closed at their usual hours, and as night fell across the continent things appeared normal, but that was just a brief calm before an unimaginable storm.

The deepening fuel crisis had hit central and western European countries hard. Of the 27 sovereign member nations of the European Union, not one was self-sufficient in oil. Even prior to the Three Hour War, the pricey $144 per barrel oil was beginning to slow down the member states' economies. By the time the war hit, the EU was consuming 13 million barrels of oil each day yet they only produced 1.6 million barrels per day. Eight million barrels per day of what they consumed was in the form of crude oil and other fuel imports such as gasoline and diesel, while the rest was made from coal and other fossil fuel liquids as well as ethanol produced from grain crops. After the war struck, imports of oil fell to four million barrels per day and it was impossible to make up the deficit. The EU, like Asia, began to power down. All other oil-producing nations in the world were pumping flat out and no matter how much technology and financial investment resources were applied to get oil production to increase, oil production continued its relentless decline.

In the EU, the market rate had been the chosen mechanism for rationing oil. Initially, demand was reduced through higher taxes. This form of rationing worked fine until the price of oil shot up to around $250 per barrel. There was no price high enough to significantly slow demand. In France, motorists queued up for hours to pay four euros a liter. In Sweden 4.5 euros seemed reasonable and gas lines several kilometers long formed across the entire EU early each morning. Throughout the UK, ration cards were distributed allowing each vehicle ten liters per month at market prices, which as June ended was two pounds per liter. The system allowed motorists to purchase ten additional liters for three pounds per liter over the posted price, but that was the limit.

Bicycle sales went through the roof as commuters throughout Europe switched to pedal power. Moving produce became difficult and as imports of fresh fruit and vegetables declined, local vegetable growing centers were started in vacant lots and in people's yards. Hundreds of parks throughout the EU were converted to orchards, but it would take several years before they bore fruit and it simply was not going to be enough to feed over 300 million people. As the movement of goods grew costlier and unemployment increased, hunger spread. Immigrant communities throughout the EU were hardest hit and by spring unemployment among immigrants exceeded 50% in Germany. In the Muslim section of Paris unemployment was estimated to be running at 80%.

Their situation only worsened after a string of gruesome daycare center bombings, which occurred on the 30th of April. Two hundred and seventeen children were killed and over 200 injured in the coordinated suicide attacks. The victims were targeted well and were almost all ethnic Caucasians. An Islamic extremist group claimed responsibility and the thirteen attackers were all found to be immigrant Muslims from Saudi Arabia and Pakistan.

Anti-immigrant sentiment exploded throughout the EU. By May 3rd, race riots were underway in dozens of cities and towns. Throughout Germany many ethnic non-Germans were forced to abandon everything they owned and flee for their lives. News reports showed long lines of non-Germans walking and biking along major highways. As the economic situation worsened, right wing political parties throughout the EU grew in influence and openly called for the immediate deportation of all immigrants starting with those receiving public assistance. As summer began, even the Social Democrats were supporting calls for an immigration moratorium. Anti-immigrant sentiment had not been this extreme since the 1930s, and as Tuesday morning arrived it made a terrifying turn for the worse.

News reports from North America and Asia created a sense of tension and impending doom throughout the EU that had not been felt for many decades. Banks remained closed and a four-day bank holiday was announced throughout the EU. It was unusually warm in Western Europe. Large crowds formed in most cities and ominously, they formed along racial lines. The stage was set for a monumental disaster.

Cash machines no longer worked and by 9:30 a.m. supermarkets in Paris, Stockholm, and in dozens of other major European cities were being looted. Televised news reports clearly showed the overwhelming majority of the looters were non-European, which fanned the flames of racial strife even more.

In Amsterdam, where public assistance payments had recently been severely slashed due to the crisis, several hundred thousand angry Muslim immigrants gathered for a noon protest demanding more food assistance. By 11:00 a.m. more aggressive elements among them were smashing store windows, turning over cars, attacking police and shops. Soon, businesses throughout the city were being ransacked. The police response was swift. Images broadcast on television and Internet news sites showed helmeted police officers wading into the crowd swinging batons and spraying the protesters with gas. The crowd fought back violently and before the Internet and television services went silent shortly after noon, shots were being fired from both sides.

It was a story repeated throughout Europe. In Moscow, which had not experienced long gas lines, food was getting more expensive and long queues were forming at markets and to older Russians it seemed reminiscent of the Soviet era. By late March, gangs of Russian men had started patrolling the food queues in most major cities throughout Russia. Non-Russians were pulled from the lines and threatened. Many were beaten. A few were killed. In Saint Petersburg, 26 African immigrants were removed from several food lines on the warm morning of May 15th, and stabbed to death by a large mob of skinheads. Few Russians complained and police failed to identify the attackers, all of whom remained at large.

Fear spread among immigrants and hundreds of thousands throughout the EU made plans to return to their native homelands. By the first of June, there was a two-week wait to find a seat on a flight to any Asian city, but returning flights often arrived with a hundred or more empty seats. Flights from most major European cities to Turkey, Pakistan, India, Iraq, and to an assortment of Middle Eastern and African capitals departed full and arrived back in Europe nearly empty. A mass exodus of non-indigenous Europeans was well underway.

Chapter Thirty-Six

As soon as Joe arrived back at the entrance to the Strawberry Park neighborhood, a Troutdale police cruiser pulled up. Officer Costello looked out his car window and tipped his sunglasses lower, "How are things going?"

Don replied, "Depends on who you're askin'. I'm fine. We're all fine here, but food and medicine are running low for some. For many, in fact. As far as I know everyone's still safe tho' and doing as well as can be expected."

"Just to let you know, the Safeway is now being looted and there's nothing we can do about it. In fact, there's not a whole lot we can do about anything. So whatever food you have at home will be it for quite some time," Officer Costello nervously replied.

'Plus," he continued, "all the police cars will be out of fuel soon, and after tonight police patrols will be on bicycle or on foot, if at all. I mostly stopped by just to let you all know residents could soon be on their own for protection: the 911 emergency response system is no longer functioning." This meant that by tomorrow, everyone in town would be officially on their own for all emergency services.

As he prepared to do a U-turn and drive away, Costello gestured with his thumb toward the body he had just passed and further suggested, "Please … and I'll use the word 'please', use restraint defending your neighborhood."

Then he slowly slid his sunglasses down over his nose once again and stared briefly at each of the three men. As a few quick gunshots cracked in the distance, he paused a moment, then smiled, "At some point civil order will return and those engaged in excessive vigilante actions could be prosecuted."

The police car drove off. Joe then said goodbye to Don and Vince and after waving up at the nearby roof at Adam, he returned to help watch the footpath with the others.

Meanwhile, Kelly and her mom were busy in the Lee house preparing dinner for everyone. Deborah had planned to bring dinner out to Jimmy and their two new friends. However, after having a few more neighbors drop by asking to borrow this and that missing dinner ingredient, it might appear rude for them to eat in front of those who might be doing without. So she decided to leave their dinners in the refrigerator. The men could have dinner when their shift was over.

When the after-dinner chores were done, Kelly and her mom decided to relax a while. Deborah took a nap on the couch, and Kelly, rather than watch the TV, which was showing fewer and fewer stations as the day went on, powered up her laptop and went straight to Google for the latest news. Each time she turned on her computer she was somehow a bit surprised she could still get Internet access. Although it was unusually slow, she managed to once again get an Internet connection.

She was hoping for some encouraging news but none was to be found. Starting with the local news, she read that gasoline and diesel supplies remained exhausted throughout Oregon and that with the refineries no longer receiving crude deliveries, there would be no gasoline indefinitely. Nearly all supermarkets throughout Multnomah County and the rest of Oregon had been looted. With the nation's trucking industry halted it would be a long time before food deliveries arrived anywhere.

The governor of Oregon briefly announced that a state of emergency was in effect, but since 4,000 Oregon National Guard soldiers had just been deployed to Iraq and Saudi Arabia, local guard forces would be thinly distributed. Twelve of the 36 National Guard armories throughout the state had been closed due to budgetary reasons. This included the armory in Gresham. Few people were surprised when the National Guard presence remained unseen throughout East County.

The charismatic and upbeat mayor of Troutdale, Jim Wright, who had just been overwhelmingly re-elected to his second term, was quoted during an online interview published on the official city website, "Let me get straight to the point. Everyone needs to remain calm, but we also need to immediately organize neighborhood community patrols. Police are no longer able to perform duties as they did before the crisis. The National Guard is busy elsewhere. Stores are empty and no food deliveries are expected. People living near the Sandy River should plant vegetable gardens immediately. I am asking church leaders to allow citizens to plant food crops on church property once water supplies stabilize. All city parks are now available for vegetable gardening, but water access could soon be a problem. City water should remain on for at least another week, but after that the well pump generators would be out of fuel. Steps are now being taken to keep water flowing longer, but for now, I strongly urge everyone to restrict water use to drinking and washing. Prepare to use the Sandy River for water, but due to assorted contaminants, avoid getting drinking water from the Columbia River. God bless each and every one of you." That was the Mayor's final official communication with his constituency and he was never heard from or seen again.

What he didn't say was that he'd been riding around the city on his bicycle all afternoon asking everyone to remain calm, but with refrigerators getting ever closer to empty, an uneasy mood was already developing. Although the city police had performed heroically in the initial hours of the crisis, it was apparent that the citizens would very soon be on their own. Cell phones were out. Police and fire vehicles were nearly out of fuel. Local hospitals were overwhelmed, running low on many drugs and supplies. Some were being robbed and looted of pharmaceuticals. Soon they would be completely unable to cope. By the next morning, police and fire response would be non-existent. As Kelly read this, she saw her mom, who had not rested properly for two days, sleeping peacefully next to her on the couch and decided not to wake her.

Chapter Thirty-Seven

After reading the depressing local news, Kelly soon found that getting up to date news from around the world was next to impossible. She was able to get a handful of stories. Most were second-hand and few were very positive.

The Internet connections out of China had been cut. There was absolutely no news coming out and it was the same with Vietnam, South Korea, Australia, the Philippines and a number of other Asian nations. Japan was one of several exceptions and it appeared to be weathering this disaster better than many countries. In Singapore a strange and uneasy calm prevailed, as public and private motor vehicle traffic came to a complete halt as their remaining fuel supplies were saved for the armed forces and the police. The tiny island nation continued to receive water supplies from Malaysia, but food supplies would soon pose a serious concern. The now-worldwide bank holiday extended to Singapore and, like the international banking system across the globe, theirs too remained closed. Army units had fanned out across the strict tiny island nation and authorities let it be known that looters would be shot on sight. Police and soldiers loaded up with ammunition just in case. They had been fortunate so far in not experiencing the rioting and looting that had struck other major Asian cities. Energy saving restrictions had been implemented such as a ban on the use of air conditioning while the use of hot water was prohibited. A food rationing system was about to be put into effect, but additional detailed information was not available.

News from country after country in Europe told similar tales of bank closures, fuel shortages, race riots, lootings, and entire neighborhoods ablaze. Governments throughout Europe had been severely weakened and destabilized by the rapidly worsening sovereign debt crisis. Faced with the shocking spread of the financial crisis, they were completely unprepared and found themselves powerless to intercede.

In Moscow, long lines of immigrants and non-Russians were reported packing into cars and trucks moving south along highways M4, M5, and M6 starting on the 29th of June. Many were pushing bicycles and crude carts loaded with personal effects while others simply walked with the clothes on their backs. Tens of thousands of Azeri, Tatar, Armenian, African and other non-Russian ethnics could be seen moving south from St. Petersburg along the M10 highway starting hours after six members of the famous St. Petersburg Mosque were arrested. They were suspected of planning and financing the June 24th suicide bombing of a large suburban day care center that killed 77 Russian children and injured dozens more. It was the latest in a string of Muslim attacks on day care centers, which had struck numerous European cities over the past few months. The Russians were famous for being an unusually friendly and patient people but their patience and tolerance had reached its limit and they lashed out ferociously.

On the evening of June 28th, an estimated 400,000 angry and vengeful Russians besieged the mosque, ransacking and utterly destroying the historic century-old house of worship. They demanded the deportation of all Muslims and non-Russians and began attacking people suspected of being followers of Islam. Several thousand people were killed in the overnight attacks.

Non-Russians, who had over the previous several months been occasionally attacked while waiting their turn in lengthy food queues, were now being attacked on sight while on buses, sidewalks and even in their homes. When they made it home, many found their apartments ransacked and more than a few had been set on fire. This time instead of simply being attacked, they were told to leave the city. Police stood idly by, completely powerless to stop the unfolding brutality and an exodus the scale of which had not been seen in Europe since the days of Stalin began to unfold.

In Paris, rioting flashed throughout many parts of the city resulting in destruction far exceeding that of the riots of 2005. Entire sections of the city had completely run out of fuel and food. People were getting increasingly desperate. As the temperature outside reached 42 degrees Celsius, rioting broke out in the 13th and 18th arrondissements, destroying nearly every market and shop in those predominately Muslim districts of the city. Supermarkets, shops and warehouses had been completely cleaned out and ransacked. Many were set ablaze during overnight rioting. By morning entire neighborhoods remained on fire and police and fire units refused to go near them.

News from elsewhere throughout Europe as well as from South America and Africa was pretty much the same. India managed fairly well for now, but with most trucks and other vehicles slowly grinding to a halt, unrest was inevitable in that densely populated and poverty stricken nation. Within two days India went totally dark, and there was no more news. In many rural villages throughout Asia and Africa no one would know for many years what had really happened as the crisis unfolded. For many small, isolated villages, life would continue pretty much the same as it had for centuries and as if nothing had happened. For others, unbelievable suffering would strike hard and fast.

Kelly thought about the personal tragedies. The individual hardship and the suffering that was to come were almost too much for her to bear. She grew more and more frightened, but at the same time she desperately wanted her mother to see her as strong and capable so she forced herself to be tough. As she read on it was hard to avoid trembling at the terrifying news. It was becoming increasingly apparent that a disaster of unprecedented proportion was unfolding across the entire globe. In the coming days millions of people -- maybe even tens or possibly even hundreds of millions of people or more – throughout Europe, Asia and the rest of the world could starve to death. The four horsemen had saddled up and were once again riding tall, eager to do their work.

In her small section of the world, Strawberry Park, she knew most people had on hand only enough food to last a few days. If food did not arrive within a week or sooner, her friends and neighbors would slowly starve to death. She also knew that before they starved, they would get desperate and do things they ordinarily would not think of doing. She gazed lovingly at her sleeping mother a moment, then ran upstairs to talk to her sister. She knew exactly what they had to do.

Chapter Thirty-Eight

Kelly sat by her sister and spoke quietly to avoid waking her mother, "Alison, please listen to what I have to say. I don't think we can stay in the house much longer. We're running out of food. A few families in our neighborhood have already left. More are planning to go. Many other houses are also running low on food. People are stopping by already asking for handouts. Soon they'll get really hungry and start taking from our garden. It's the only vegetable garden in the neighborhood. No one else has one. Once that starts it will only be a matter of time before their growing hunger turns their requests into pleas, and then their pleas will become desperate demands."

Kelly stopped and stared at Alison a few seconds, then continued, "After that, who knows what they'll do! Soon," she paused a second, "soon, we'll be forced to flee anyhow. Maybe it would be best to leave before people started going crazy with hunger."

Alison, looking a bit depressed replied, "We have enough food in the house to last a few more weeks and we can easily defend it. Plus, we really don't have anyplace to go. Larry and Maggi have their farm in Sweet Home, but it's too far away. We'll never make it with the shooting and robbing going on. Anyhow, we wouldn't last a month out in the woods somewhere. Where would we go? We'll eventually end up raiding houses for food like the rest of 'em."

Kelly was not convinced at all. "More and more strangers from Portland are wandering into our town begging for food. All day long they try to get in from the footpath. They're all asking for food. If we left fairly soon," Kelly explained, "we wouldn't have to fight to guard the rest of the family food stash, which," she reminded Alison, "is dwindling much faster than we expected."

"Plus," she pointed out to her sister, "the gas pressure is getting weaker and the electricity could go out any time, according to Steve down the street. He works for PGE and he says he's surprised the 'juice', as he calls it, is still on. At any time cooking food will be impossible. And after that, we'll be forced to leave anyhow. Why not plan for it and set ourselves up someplace where we might be able to hunt or plant some food? If we do it real soon maybe, just maybe, we'll have a shot at making it through this disaster."

Alison, suspecting their mother had awakened, put her finger to her lips. "See if mom's still sleeping. I don't want her to hear us talking like this."

Kelly tiptoed to the upstairs railing, peeked over, and saw her mom soundly sleeping. She looked so peaceful. Kelly returned to her room and saw Alison looking out the window while cradling her dad's old, but still perfectly functioning Chinese MAK-90 rifle. Kelly sat on the edge of her bed, gesturing toward the rifle and alluding to the other weapons. "We'll probably have to use these pretty soon."

Alison said nothing and kept looking out the window. She noticed Adam, who once again appeared to be getting ready to shoot. After a few seconds she saw him gently lay his rifle back down on the dark sheet covering the warm tar roofing shingles.

Kelly then told Alison more about the incident on MLK. "I had had no choice shooting that man on MLK. If I hadn't he would have shot Joe and then shot me and Bill next."

"I know that, Kelly. I'm really proud of you. So are mom and dad."

"All my training and practice with Chris worked. I didn't hesitate even a split second before pulling the trigger," Kelly went on, "I'm not very comfortable about it, but would do it again if I had to in order to protect us, but the thought of killing our neighbors to save a few days food gives me the creeps."

Kelly digressed off topic a moment. "Dad has already lost his parents, and all four of his brothers. Plus, if this crisis isn't resolved – and it looks like it won't - mom may never again get to fly to China and see her family. In other words, we are all mom and dad have left. We have a responsibility, no, we have a duty to stay healthy and alive to help them if this gets any worse, and I think it's going to get a whole lot worse very soon."

"Alison, I don't want to kill anyone again. If we stay here much longer we'll have to respond with deadly force just to guard a few weeks or even a few days' worth of food. It all just seems so pointless and unnecessary. Starvation is gonna settle in right here in Strawberry Park no matter what we do. I don't want anything to do with killing our neighbors."

Alison nodded in agreement. "Do you really think we could make it to Sweet Home, where dad's friends live?"

Kelly thought a few seconds. "Maybe we can make it there later, but for now the only way to get that far is by killing a path through the crazy hungry people out roaming the streets."

There was still a glimmer of hope, and Kelly told Alison what she read on the city website. "The mayor says the problems are all getting addressed."

Alison spoke up, "I heard him. He rode through Strawberry Park earlier today on his bicycle accompanied by Councilman Black. I talked to him while you were watching the window. He said the water should stay on at least a week, maybe longer, but we should plan on the gas and electricity shutting down any time.

His opinion, well, he said he's sharing this with as many people as he can, is that this situation, as he called it, would soon be resolved and things would get back to normal fairly soon. He has full faith that state and federal authorities have a clear handle on things, at least that's what he said, but his eyes spoke of fear. So did Councilman Black's."

No one could blame the popular mayor for touring the town trying to spread a face of calm, but few believed a word of this and the constant gunfire and relentless smoke in the air testified in support.

Kelly told Alison about her plan. "Okay. I've been thinking hard about this all day. I'm going to ask Joe if we can all stay in Corbett on his family farm, at least for a few weeks or until things calm down."

She explained further, "The money we have might not be good much longer, but maybe we could work on his farm or offer some ammunition or maybe even pay him in some of dad's gold or silver if he would let us stay."

"That's the best idea I've heard all day, Kelly. But what if he says no? What then? Are you going to ask soon?" Alison said.

"We'll always do our best, sister, but as soon as they all get back from the footpath I'm going to ask Joe."

"You mean, Joe-Joe?"

"Sister, we're not like that … not that I'd mind, if you know what I mean."

"Kelly, Joe seems like a really neat guy. Definitely good looking … hot, even. But what if he has a bad temper, or drinks, or chases other women. You better get to know him better first."

"Don't worry. He's never laid a hand on me or said anything stupid. Anyhow, this is our best chance, but I don't want him to think I'm asking because I like him … which I kinda do."

They shared a good laugh at Kelly's surprising remark. Kelly sat with her sister awhile talking about high school, college and the good times they had growing up in Strawberry Park.

Chapter Thirty-Nine

At nine, as it started getting dark, Jimmy, Joe and Bill came back to the house. While Kelly was at the upstairs window, Alison fixed everyone a cold glass of tea. All but Kelly sat at the dining room table near the front window.

Alison stared briefly at each of the three men's faces imagining what they would look like if they could not shave or shower any longer and she started giggling. She smiled and said, "You're all going to start looking a whole lot different in a few weeks. No more showering, no hot water, no shaving … maybe even lose a little weight, which, and she pointed at Joe's tummy, might not be all bad."

Joe and the other men laughed.

She had their attention. Everyone was in good spirits. "Mom and I have been watching I-84 from the upstairs window and although a few cars are moving, there are no trucks heading into or out of the city. There've been no trains either. No National Guard trucks are seen yet either, which is very bad news."

"No trains? That means no train horns. Finally, we have peace," said Jimmy.

She moved to sit down at the dining table and exhaled deeply. "More people are dropping by to borrow from us. Jackie dropped by earlier and asked to borrow toilet paper. At some point we'll have to say no. Either way, what we have in the house isn't going to last us ten days and without any way to boil water, well," and she softly giggled, "maybe we should think about taking a little vacation – like maybe to Sandy or Corbett!"

Only her dad caught the little joke, which was directed at their planned August vacation to South America. He understood exactly what she was trying to say and he too started laughing as did Joe, but as quick to grin as he was, Joe would laugh at just about anything but this time had no clue what they were all laughing about. He was just happy to see everyone laughing.

Jimmy had already mentioned the possibility of leaving town to Deborah, but he did not want Kelly to miss the important discussion that was obviously coming so he called to her, "Kelly! Could you please come downstairs a minute?"

Kelly came downstairs right away and stood near the table still holding the rifle. "What's up, dad?"

Jimmy looked at her. "Could you please set that rifle down a minute sweetie?"

She leaned it against the hallway wall. "Sure dad."

"I've been talking to Joe and Bill a bit while we were outside. I told them that in the few hours we'd been guarding the footpath, we've turned away several dozen people and many had to be told more than once to leave. Adam had to shoot one at the street entrance tonight. Guy deserved it, but many of those walking by now are families begging for food. Soon the wandering masses will grow, they'll get frantic and begin to take extreme measures. Gangs are going to form. Maybe even large ones, like small army-sized ones. Things around here could soon get very, very dangerous," said Jimmy.

Joe interrupted Jimmy. Joe had seen it before during his deployments and he knew from personal experience what unspeakable horrors desperate people were capable of inflicting on others.

"It is going to get very ugly in a few days. I can feel it coming. I have a question for you, Mr. and Mrs. Lee. And, of course for your daughters, too."

Joe rarely spoke so formally, so even though Bill knew what Joe was going to say, he started wondering what else he might have on his mind. Over the years Joe had dragged Bill into so many messes it was impossible to count them all. "I am wondering if you, the entire Lee family, would join me on my family farm in Corbett until things settle down."

Joe had earlier that evening borrowed Kelly's laptop for a few minutes while she was working in the backyard garden. He emailed his parents. It was the last email he would ever send. In it he didn't need to tell them about Kelly. He spoke often about the cute barista at Starbucks who called him Joe-Joe. At 31 and still single, his parents had been starting to wonder about him, and they were now happy to hear him mention her name, which he was starting to do more often.

It took Joe 20 minutes, but he struggled through finding the words and hitting the tiny keys and wrote, "Hey mom and dad, I'm coming home in a few hours and should be there around two in the morning. I already told you about the Lees. They're not an ordinary family. This family is hard working, friendly and best of all they're, well, basically they're a well-trained and well-educated small army! They won't be a burden to us at all but an important asset. Until things settle down they could help in the berry fields, expand our vegetable garden and teach us a few things. They garden like crazy! You should see what they do. Kelly's mom wrote a few no-meat cookbooks. We could use her because there won't be any meat for a long time. Her sister is smarter than anyone on earth. That's what Kelly says. You should meet her. She's only 24 and already has a Ph.D. in physics! Most important, mom and dad, they can help defend our farm."

A reply came quick, but they did not know about it until they sat at the table.

"You have an email from your parents, Joe," Kelly, who had just popped open her laptop again happily announced.

"What's it say?" asked Bill.

"Yeah," replied Kelly who had set the computer down in front of Joe, "What's it say?"

"Whoa. Cool. You can all come! Here, read this."

In it they let Joe know they trusted his judgment and approved, telling Joe they could use the help. "Bring 'em on up, boy! We're starting to seal off the town, but I'll explain the Lees to everyone up here so the sentries will let 'em in." Joe's dad concluded, "Joe-Joe, we can use the help!"

"Joe-Joe?" Bill laughed. "How come everyone's calling you Joe-Joe lately?"

"Shut up, Bill," he glared.

Bill smiled and did as he was told.

Joe spoke more, regaining his rarely used, but very effective and persuasive serious voice, "We talked about it a bit outside, while on patrol at the footpath. It might be best if everyone started packing right now. We must leave in a few hours."

Chapter Forty

Packing was going to be a lot harder then they thought. During the past 25 years of marriage, the Lees had collected a houseful of possessions, and most of what they owned would be left behind. Jimmy hoped he could return in a few weeks to check on the house, but what would remain after the starving had rampaged through? Would the desperate bother stealing anything or simply go for food? Would they even have the strength to go through all their precious book and memento boxes? Would they sleep in the beds? The questions were endless, but deciding what to take now was tough because they could only take what would fit in Joe's Hummer and in the family Toyota.

Starting right away, the first thing they did was gently lay Jimmy's gun safe down in the back of the Hummer – with Jimmy's other rifles and handguns still in it. It must have weighed 600 pounds, but with Joe lifting on one side and Bill and Jimmy on the other they were able to carry it to the truck and slide it right in. With the somewhat lighter top end resting slightly up on the folded-down back seats it was a perfect fit. Jimmy had 4,000 rounds of Chinese 7.62x39 ammunition. He bought it back in the early '90s for ten cents per round. They were recently selling for over a dollar each. He also had a few hundred rounds of ammunition for each other caliber and it was all stored in surplus ammo cans and they, along with extra magazines and other various spare gun parts, holsters, and related weapons gear went in next.

Then the remainder of the household food they took was packed neatly into six large plastic bins and set within the perimeter rails of the full-sized roof rack. They also packed vitamins, all the spices and several dozen assorted bottles of alcohol between which they stuffed as many t-shirts and as much underwear as they could fit. The essential pots and pans went into two bins. The kitchen knives, flatware and assorted utensils were tossed into the same bins.

Next, Deborah set out one large plastic bin each for basic clothing. Moving quickly, all their cargo pants, jeans, stockings, underwear, a few shirts and the toughest boots they had went in bins. Their warmest winter-wear as well as assorted belts, hats and gloves went in a few more. They had to leave most of their clothing behind, including all their suits and dress clothing. An assortment of blankets and other bedding went tied on top of the bins. Four tiny sleeping bags were stuffed above the safe.

The Lees were avid readers and although they had primarily used e-readers for the past few years, they still had a collection of many hundreds of books, but they could only take a few. Deborah grabbed her copy of "Edible Plants of the Northwest," and her copies of the home organic gardening guides she had published several years back, while Jimmy took his four-volume set, "How Things Work" and a few of the family's Buddhist texts. Alison and Kelly packed a few of their university science textbooks as well as a few cherished childhood books.

After loading the four bicycles way up on the top of all the bins and blankets, Jimmy placed the bicycle tire pump, spare bike tires and tubes, flat repair kit, and a few towels and garage rags as well as his two small toolboxes into the trunk of the Toyota. None of the Lee family took any medication, so thankfully that was not a concern. Jimmy also had a small amount of emergency cash and packed it into the same ammo can as his modest collection of silver and gold coins, which he placed in the overloaded car trunk with the other things.

Kelly packed her cherished laptop, but they left the family desktop as well as nearly all of their books and furniture. Everyone stuck their cell phones in their pockets and packed the chargers. Alison grabbed both of their hard-earned black belts. With the exception of a small box containing soap, shampoo, razor, toothbrushes, dental floss, an emergency medical kit and a few other odds and ends, nearly all the bathroom supplies had to be left behind. "Just one towel, each! Each of you go grab a good thick one!" Deborah reminded all of them.

She then issued a last minute reminder, "Don't forget to pack the toilet paper. Pack all of it!"

Deborah and Jimmy hurriedly went through the family file cabinet packing into a single small cardboard box a few essential documents, birth certificates, diplomas, checkbooks, passports, licenses, pink slips for the scooter and car, as well as the house title and a few assorted business records, plus two reams of copy paper along with as many pens and pencils as they could find. Most of their family documents and records would remain filed away in boxes and left behind.

Chapter Forty-One

By 12:30 a.m. they had finished packing. After some deliberation they voted to lock the house doors rather than leave them unlocked as Jimmy suggested. It was three to one. If someone broke in, repairing the damage would be fairly easy.

"Why leave the doors or windows unlocked? Force them to make some noise when they break in." Alison insisted, "That way maybe someone might hear it and stop them. We might get lucky."

Jimmy thought to himself. "Wow, that girl is always so full of common sense. I should just do what she says all the time."

They all took one final walk around the house picking up their shovels and other garden tools, the long water hose, which could be filled and laid outside to make hot water even on cool days, and four bags of chicken manure.

Deborah froze for a moment, and then she ran back into the garage and grabbed a shoebox that was filled with tiny envelopes containing a wide assortment of non-hybrid vegetable seeds. She thought this might be the most important box of all.

Jimmy then went back inside. He quickly packed a few more select Buddhist books including the family sutra collection as well as a few Buddha statues and iconic wall hangings into a box.

Kelly, with her handgun holstered under her pink hooded sweatshirt and a spare magazine in each of the front pockets of her loose-fitting faded blue jeans, rolled her scooter from its place in the garage and into the driveway and started it up. She unplugged the trickle charger and stuck it in her front hoodie pouch. It still had nearly a full tank because she had just filled it Monday morning during the daily 5:00 a.m. to 6:00 a.m. motorcycle-only hour. Alison, who had successfully completed Chris McClanahan's combat firearms course four years earlier, hopped on the back wearing her favorite tan Danner Marine Temperate Military boots, tan cargo pants, and a black hooded sweatshirt. She carried the AK attached to a sling on her back. Like Kelly, each of the two oversized front pockets of her cargo pants contained two 30-round magazines filled with exactly 27 rounds of 7.62x39 surplus Chinese full metal jacket ammunition which was manufactured decades earlier but still worked like new.

Jimmy and Deborah piled into their overloaded Toyota while Joe and Bill hopped into the Hummer and they all headed away from the family home. They stopped at the street entrance to give last minute goodbyes to the two men standing watch, Chad and Adam.

"Three other families have left in the past few hours. We're heading out too. The place is evacuating. We're leaving for my sister's house in Mosier at five this morning," Adam said.

"Our family's going too. It's getting too dangerous here," said Chad. "We're almost packed already."

"Best of luck to all of you, and to your families. Well see you all soon," Jimmy replied.

But Jimmy was sad. He knew he would never see any of his friends and neighbors again. An incredible and unexpected new chapter in his unusually interesting life was about to begin and as he thought about it he grew increasingly apprehensive. Worrying about the health and safety of everyone who lived in Strawberry

Park would accomplish nothing and help no one, so they focused on the task at hand and moved on. It was a dark, nearly moonless night: three days away from a new moon. Before they had made it six blocks the entire city of Troutdale, which until that moment had remained lit up by countless streetlights, and probably the entire county, maybe the entire state of Oregon, maybe even the entire country, suddenly went absolutely pitch black.

"Whoa!" Joe said.

"Yup. I've been expecting that to happen," replied Bill.

The street lights they just saw go out would never again shine.

THE BERRY FARM

Chapter Forty-Two

With Joe leading the way and the scooter following behind the Toyota, the three vehicles slowly chased after their piercing headlights, moving deeper into the total darkness and out of Troutdale toward the historic century-old Stark Street Bridge. The bridge would take them across the Sandy River and then up the hill into the Corbett farmland. They drove across the bridge and turned right on the Columbia River Highway. Before they got another 50 feet, they ran into a roadblock and stopped.

Fearing a sudden migration of hungry and desperate masses, the good old boys and girls of Corbett had banded together Tuesday morning, strategically placing a few very well-armed men and women on each of three main roads into town. One group was positioned along the Crown Point Highway just up the hill from the Vista House, one was stationed a few hundred yards east of the Troutdale Bridge, a stone's throw from the river, and the third was this one, positioned just across the Stark Street Bridge. There were a few other small country roads leading in and out, but the three they road-blocked would catch most of the traffic for now. For the cars or other people they missed, there were occasional bicycle patrols riding back and forth through Corbett from Larch Mountain Road to the schools. No one was wasting gas driving unless they wanted their tires cut open.

Joe and Bill were quite impressed, but not all that surprised, that their old buddies had arranged this roadblock so quickly. Joe stopped his easily recognizable black behemoth gas-guzzler which he had, against nearly everyone's advice, purchased for $5,000 last November, in the middle of the road and quickly killed his engine. The Toyota and the scooter stopped close behind, with engines silent. They were greeted through Bill's side window by the sentries: the twin Mershon brothers, Johnny and Don who had been guarding this stretch of road since noon Tuesday when the road into Corbett was closed.

"Hey, Joe. Hey, Bill," Don said. "We have patrols running around all over Corbett, but they're all spread out, just getting started. We could use some help."

"Those the Lees?" Don asked.

"Yup," replied Bill.

"Yeah, we've been expecting them," Don said. "Your dad rode his bike down here about nine-thirty and told us they would be with you. He told us to let them in and no one else. Him and the Chief are running the show for now so for now we just do what they say."

"Count us in," Bill said. "Let's get the Lees settled in. We can join up in the morning and help patrol somewhere."

The Mershons were eager to tell them the latest Corbett news, and were just as eager to find out what was going on outside their small hillside community. They traded stories for a few minutes.

While Joe and Bill talked with the Mershon brothers, Kelly patiently waited in the middle of the darkened road with her sister, while her dad shut off the Toyota and waited in front of Kelly's scooter for the boys to finish so they could all pass through. "We're stopped at a security checkpoint, Kelly. Isn't this stupid? Look. Sentries."

"Yup." Kelly replied. "Quite odd. Hope they let us in."

"I think we could take those two skinny guys out," Alison replied half-jokingly.

"Easily. I mean, look at them," said Kelly. "But probably not the guys in the trees above the road.

"What guys?"

"Listen carefully. I can't see anyone. Hey! Look! Now you can see one in Joe's headlights. Three, no four trees up from the road. He has a rifle. He's partly hidden by a tree. He should hide better. Maybe find a bigger tree, a big rock, maybe."

"He is hiding, he's just really fat. He's bigger around than the tree."

They both laughed a minute at their tasteless fat jokes while they continued waiting.

"We have strict orders from the Corbett Citizens Committee, which was just formed Tuesday morning, to turn around anyone who didn't live in Corbett or Springdale," Don, who did most of the talking, said. "Your dad told us to expect you guys so we're going to allow the Lee family to enter, however, no one else will be allowed in. That includes migrant farm workers too. Ya can't use them on farms no more. They can't come in. We've been turning them away all day and all night long: dozens and dozens of them. Maybe more. They're bringing their friends and families too."

Many migrant farm workers had labored at local farms for years. Not anymore. All visitors and employees were being turned away or ordered out.

Bill and Joe very briefly explained to the Mershon brothers who the Lees were telling them the new family would be staying and working on the Happy Berry Farm until things settled down and that they would definitely be sharing guard duty.

"Yup. We heard all about them. Pleased to meet all of you," Johnny smiled at the short caravan lined up behind the Hummer.

He continued, "Regular guard and patrol schedules are being prepared now, but until then we'll remain on sentry duty here without relief. Messengers on bikes are delivering us supplies as needed. We're all set here. There are five men assigned to guard this bridge, but two are sleeping at the state park a few hundred feet up the road next to their bicycles, while the last one, Pat O'Malley is wide awake up in the trees over there, pointing east, looking down at us through a rifle scope, just in case. Wave at Pat, guys! He can hit a fly at 500 yards, but he works best when he's alone."

"I know. He can handle hitting a fly almost as easily as he can fly off the handle." Bill said.

Everyone laughed at Pat's well-known reputation as the best shot in town, a heck of a nice guy generally, but also more than a bit of a hothead, which everyone jokingly blamed on Irish whiskey and his Irish heritage.

"We had a real rush of vehicles we had to turn away Tuesday, as people scrambled to leave Portland and Gresham. We advised them to try to make it to I-84 and then east to Hood River or maybe head south toward the Willamette Valley farming areas. But none were allowed into Corbett after noon. Not one," Johnny said.

Don spoke up excitedly, "Two truckloads of rednecks from Gresham took offense and tried to rush past us this evening. They pointed rifles at us. See that truck in the river? That's one of 'em, the first one. Pat nailed 'em good. One shot. As usual. Nailed the driver. Smack! You should have heard it. His truck went right into the river. He's still inside, I think. The others guys in his truck swam to shore. The other truckload took off over the bridge back to Troutdale. Those who made it in earlier, or who made it to friend's houses, or were camping anywhere in Corbett, or along Larch Mountain, almost all of them were ordered out at gunpoint. This town is scared to death, I tell ya."

"Things will calm down in a while," Joe replied. "See you guys soon. Be careful."

As Joe pulled away from the checkpoint he looked at Bill. "Security will need to be bolstered with additional armed men right away. In a few days, a week, who knows ... we'll be under attack. In fact, I see a small war coming at us, yeah, a small war. It's coming for sure. It could start at any time."

"Yup," Bill said, as he waved at Pat, "any time now. I feel it too. If we're lucky it'll be a small war, not a big war."

In Multnomah County there were probably somewhere around 500,000 firearms in private hands. As hunger set in deeper, thousands of them could be used in a final desperate hunt for food meaning for many of them a deer-hunting trip across the Sandy River. By now word was spreading that armed men were turning away anyone crossing the Sandy. All it would take is a coordinated attack by maybe a few dozen well-armed men to take out both Sandy River checkpoints. Two or three sentries would not be enough. A better and more powerful defense strategy would be needed by early tomorrow or Corbett would be overrun in a matter of days. But after three hours' sleep in the past two days, a few hours' rest was on top of everyone's agenda.

The caravan wound up the Columbia River Highway in the protective total darkness. It snaked its way along the narrow, tree shaded backcountry roads to the 100-yard long gravel driveway leading to the home on the Happy Berry Farm. As they pulled up to the Hancock family house, headlights flashed a quick view. Jimmy said to Deborah, "Wow, check out how big and well maintained this farm is. I wonder how many people are living here right now?"

"Joe said three," replied Deborah. "Him, his mom, and his dad. That's it. Just three. Well, seven now, counting us."

It was nearly 2:00 a.m. when they turned off their engines and gathered near Joe's Hummer. It was totally dark outside so Joe left his headlights on directed at the house's deep front deck. Within a few breaths of the unusually calm 70-degree summer air, Joe's mother and father appeared at the door, quickly running down the four wide porch steps to greet their son and his group of friends.

Introductions were briefly made, and noticing how exhausted everyone was, Joe's mother, Mary Kay, quickly raised her lit candle, and stepping carefully led Jimmy and Deborah through the front door and upstairs to their interim housing; a well appointed, spacious bedroom furnished in solid beautiful wood antiques that looked like they had cost a small fortune. "This room once was Joe's great-grandfather's. He slept here until he died many years ago. It's been vacant since. He built this house back in the '20s."

"Thank you," Deborah said.

"Yes, thank you so much," Jimmy added.

Jimmy remained quiet after that. He had never experienced such a gift and did not know quite how to deal with it.

Deborah said, "Your hospitality is ... I just don't have words for it. We'll talk more tomorrow. Okay? Right now everyone's dead tired, no doubt."

"Welcome home, Mr. and Mrs. Lee. This will be your room for as long as you like. Again, make yourselves at home."

Alison and Kelly were shown to another upstairs bedroom in the spacious old five-bedroom farmhouse, and in the warm air they flopped down on top of their twin beds and were asleep within minutes.

Their tired parents parked themselves flat out on the raised antique king-size bed. In a blink they too fell asleep shoeless but otherwise fully dressed, knowing that the next morning would start a day they would always remember: the first day in their new hometown.

Chapter Forty-Three

At 7:00 a.m., after a solid five-hour rest, Jimmy woke up and nudged Deborah awake. There was no need to get dressed since they slept in what they wore the day before. They started the day off by spending a few minutes getting to know the Hancocks, and hopefully start things off with them on a positive note. The first thing they would do is donate all their food to the family kitchen, but the two unopened 500 count jars of multi-vitamins would remain hidden in their winter clothes bin. It might come in handy if for any one of a thousand reasons they had a falling out with the Hancocks or who-knows-what might happen. Plus, if the disaster continued, as they feared it might, by winter and spring food could get scarce and they planned on getting all four of them through this calamity alive one way or another.

When they opened the door to the bedroom, the wonderful and familiar aroma of freshly brewed coffee coming from downstairs got them smiling.

"Deborah, you smell that?" Jimmy asked.

"Yeah, nice."

They walked downstairs and found the oversized functional farmhouse kitchen. Deborah and Jimmy walked over to Mary Kay and she gave Mary Kay a happy greeting, "Good morning, Mary Kay! What can we do to help?"

"There's going to be plenty to do this morning. Maybe you could start by mixing and pouring the pancakes," Mary Kay cheerfully replied. "There'll be plenty to do around here after that. You'll see."

Jimmy piped in, "Excuse me, ma'am. Which way is it to the bathroom?"

"Go straight down that hall, make a right at the end and it's the only door on your left."

After making a few wrong turns in the large farmhouse, Jimmy found the bathroom. While using it he wondered if the water was running out, like it was in Troutdale. Should he flush or even waste water washing up afterward? He wondered a moment. He compromised. He flushed, but did not waste what could be the last of the water by washing until he found out about the water supply.

When he got back to the kitchen, Joseph was talking to Bill, who was leaning up against the counter sipping his black coffee. Bill, who stayed rather than walk the mile home in pitch darkness, was still groggy having slept on the living room couch.

"Hi Bill. Good morning, Joseph. I'm Jimmy Lee. I barely saw you last night in the dark. Thanks for everything. We really appreciate your hospitality and generosity. We won't let you down," Jimmy said as he introduced himself once again to Joe's dad, Joseph.

"I heard all about you and your fine family from Joe and again just now from Bill. Quite an impressive crew you have here, Mr. Lee. Quite impressive," replied Joseph. "This is July and we always have a ton of work to do around here, but this year, well, you know anything could happen. We'll all have to be on our toes."

Jimmy asked him the question that was on his mind, "Yup. Hey, Joseph, what's the situation with the water supply."

Joseph smiled and replied, "We're in luck there, Jimmy. Water ain't on our list of problems. Corbett water is gravity fed from a spring way up on Larch Mountain. It'll flow freely with little maintenance for years. They built it that way on purpose. The pipelines'll need periodic inspection, maybe some minor work now and then, but that'll be it for the time being. Yup, we're good with water."

Bill then spoke up, "Jimmy. We do have one major issue we gotta address immediately. I just heard from Scott Harger, our neighbor to the south. He dropped by earlier and said several groups of people crossed the Sandy before daybreak today. A town meeting is set to start in about 45 minutes in front of the Country Market to plan a response and we should attend. We have to chase 'em out. More are coming, too. They're looking for food, and they'll hunt down all the black tail deer if we let them. These people all have to be chased out. It could get messy. You ready? We should leave in a few minutes. The meeting starts at eight. It's a twenty minute walk."

"Yup," replied Jimmy. "I'll let the girls know. They'll wanna come, too. Where's Joe?"

"Sleeping," Mary Kay said. "He should get up. He needs to be there to support his dad. It could get rough. Yesterday a few idiots gave the Chief a bad time, but we need him to lead us through this disaster. Joseph shut them up, but ya never know what could happen. The Chief needs everyone's help and support."

Chapter Forty-Four

Chief Jack Dutton, 63, was in charge of the small, unincorporated town's volunteer fire department. He operated the only real estate office in town and was well respected by all. Although Corbett was unincorporated and had no elected officials, the school board was elected every four years and Dutton had served on the board since 1984. He was 6' 2", a solid 195 pounds and an enthusiastic supporter of the town's only school and especially its impressive athletic department. Like most people in Corbett, he was in excellent physical shape for his age, regularly biking to the top of Larch Mountain with friends: a tough 30-mile round trip for a person of any age. He did not need to stand on a box as he spoke. When he talked, his voice rang loud and people listened. He was considered one of the few unofficial town leaders along with Reverend Scott Golphenee and Joseph Hancock.

Standing next to the Chief was Scott Golphenee, the well-respected pastor of Mt. Hood Christian Church, the largest church in Corbett. The Chief would need his support and he would also need the support of Joseph Hancock, who was just now walking up to the gathered crowd with his son, Joe, and three members of the Lee family, Jimmy, Alison and Kelly.

When he called the hastily arranged meeting to order at 8:02 a.m., it was already 66 degrees outside. The east wind was barely moving. The weather was perfect. It was no doubt going to be a very nice day. Without the national weather service or a host of other weather experts guessing how hot or cool or wet it would be, predicting the weather from now on would be a guessing game. But it was now July 3rd, and everyone knew it would be sunny and warm for the next few months.

There were about 450 men and women gathered in front of the Country Market. Not counting a few high school sports events or the Easter Sunday sunrise service at Mt. Hood Christian Church, it was possibly the largest gathering ever held in Corbett. One man drove his SUV, but everyone else arrived either on foot or by bicycle. Most had lived in or near Corbett all their lives and knew every hill, stream and tree for miles around.

More trickled in as the Chief, as everyone called him, told the gathered crowd in his usual formal manner, "Good morning everyone. You all know Reverend Golphenee and most of you know me. I'll not sugarcoat this. We have a life and death emergency on our hands. Law and order has broken down throughout the state, and probably throughout the country too. The whole government seems to have collapsed so it looks like we're on our own. I believe our town will soon be under attack. Groups of people including hunters were seen walking through our fields east of the Sandy River this morning. I just got the good news that they were all peacefully turned back. But more, many more, will be trying to get in during the hours and days to come. The Mershons tell me dozens were turned away at the Stark Street Bridge overnight. O'Malley had to shoot one. Lots of farm workers are trying to get in, too. With all the fresh food in Multnomah County spoiling in the heat they'll get hungrier and more desperate all the time. We can't let 'em in. They'll strip our town bare. They'll hunt down every last deer and probably eat our livestock and pets, too if we let them. Then we'll all starve. We can't let that happen."

He raised his voice as he continued speaking to the crowd, "The rules of law we have always lived with are now suspended, at least for a while. We must focus with single-mindedness on saving our homes and farms, the town itself, and our very lives. With nearly a million people living nearby and all of 'em facing starvation, the few we see heading our way now will soon grow in number until they're swarming like locusts, stripping away everything we have unless we stop 'em now. If we allow 'em in to strip our farms and deplete the forest wildlife …" Reverend Golphenee nodded in agreement as the Chief paused a moment, noticing he had everyone's complete attention, "… they will only satisfy their hunger for a few days, maybe a week or two at most. Then if we allow 'em to do this they'll then all starve shortly afterward anyhow. But if we protect what is ours we can get through this time of horror and offer our children a decent shot at a safe future."

With so much to do, he kept it short. "In conclusion, I must warn you in clear terms to not waste ammunition. What we have right now is most likely all we will ever have. At least until help comes, which I suspect will be never. I'm talking about maybe forever. As the number of invaders grows in the coming days, defending our homes and farms individually will bring certain failure. Therefore we must organize and defend ourselves as one."

Everyone loudly applauded, offering the Chief total support as he spoke once more, "There will be no more gas burning. No lawn mowing. Like I said yesterday morning: No. Driving. At. All. Use bikes or walk. We talked about this yesterday and I thought we were clear. Everyone agreed on this. Now we're serious. If I see anyone driving a truck, car, or motorcycle or in any way wasting gas in this time of crisis, I'll personally rip 'em apart. We need the last of it for scooters and small dirt bikes, and they're used only for emergency messenger use."

He then briefly lightened up the crowd a bit, "I don't mean rip the person apart, heh ... but I'll do way worse than that. I will sic Big Joe Hancock on anyone found wasting gas."

"Whoa," Joe whispered to his dad.

To the amusement of the crowd, Joseph raised both his massive arms high into the air with fists clenched and yelled, "And my boy Joe's a lot tougher than he looks, but don't hurt or tease him because then everyone'll find out what a big crybaby he really is."

Turning serious, the Chief continued, "If anyone feels they'll have trouble pulling a trigger in self defense on an attacker there will be no hard feelings whatsoever from me or hopefully anyone else ... but they'll be expected to serve in other ways such as cooks, medics and messengers instead. If anyone has a problem this way, let Reverend Golphenee know right now. He'll give you something else to do. There's plenty of work. We all gotta pull together. All of us must do our part."

A few started clapping. Then more. Then the entire crowd erupted in loud cheering and applause.

After the crowd died down, the Chief spoke again, "The Fourth of July celebrations are postponed. We can have a party after things settle down. But for now we must remain vigilant about guarding the town perimeter. We simply can't allow anyone in. Send 'em back or maybe kick 'em south walking toward Sandy. There're plenty of farms that way. Okay, one more time. Do. Not. Waste. Anything. Especially gas. Those days are over. From now on we walk or ride bike."

Jimmy, Joseph and his son Joe then overheard Jeffery Rogers, an obese wealthy middle-aged landowner he vaguely knew, complain to someone standing near him, "Why were the Lees allowed in? One of my best friends was turned away at the Stark Street Bridge yesterday." He grew louder. "He was willing to buy a piece of land on the spot! He had a half-million dollars in cash with him in his Jaguar. It isn't fair. This is a bunch of total garbage."

A few nodded in meek agreement with the massive, intimidating businessman.

Joseph, with the single exception of his son Joe, was probably the toughest man in Corbett. He walked over to the fat businessman and stood less than a foot away from him, staring into his eyes for a very uncomfortable moment making the Chief, Reverend Golphenee, and everyone else pause and turn.

"How many children do you have, fat boy?" Knowing the answer was six.

The obese man nervously mumbled out, "Six."

Joseph pointed at Joe and barked loud in the man's face, "I have only one child – Joe. Everyone here knows Joe except you! You don't know him because you're never around. Riding through town in that hundred thousand dollar Range Rover of yours you don't know anyone. You might have been rich yesterday fatso, but soon you'll be starving. Why? Because you have no idea how to work. You never have. Look at your fingernails all clean and manicured. Your money and gold mean nothing any more!"

He then gestured toward Jimmy and said, "His daughter, Kelly Lee, saved Joe's life two days ago and therefore without the Lee family, Joe would be dead."

Joseph was known to have lost his temper more than a few times in his youth, but it had been many years since someone set him off. Joseph was not someone to mess with and his temper was rising fast. A few people stepped away. In his prime he regularly bench pressed 550 lbs. He once benched 545 while drunk with a lit cigarette sticking out of his mouth. He was generally sweet as a bowl of strawberries, but when someone hit a nerve, watch out.

With his huge 22 ½ inch biceps mightily powering his hand forward, he forcefully buried his sizeable right index finger deep into the fat mans massive belly, "My Joe is worth more than all six of your fat lazy kids combined. Listen to me, boy. If I ever hear of you saying another word against the Lee family I will personally barbeque you. You hear me, boy?" He then shouted it a second time. "YOU HEAR ME?"

Joseph, struggling to refrain from punching the still-silent obese man in the face, which probably would have killed him, stood staring at him a few seconds and started twisting the man's left ear, "I asked you a question fatso. You hear me?"

"Yes. Yeah, I hear ya. I hear ya." He stammered trying to not reveal to those around him the intense pain racing fast and deep through his skull.

Joseph then pointed at the shiny newer Range Rover parked next to the Country Market. "What's that doing here? Is that yours?"

The man meekly nodded.

"Did you drive that piece of crap here? Everyone knows we can't waste gas anymore. What the hell's the matter with you?"

Without waiting for an answer, Joseph walked over to the man's costly SUV, withdrew his 12" Cold Steel knife from its leather belt holster and punctured its two rear tires. Then the two front were stabbed. He then turned to face the Chief. "That, sir," he paused, "that is no longer an SUV parked in front of the gas pump. It's our new filling station. We're gonna use it for siphoning fuel into small motorcycles and scooters."

He then stared hard at the obese man once more, "You got a problem with that fatso? Lose some weight you useless flabby bastard. In fact," he turned to face the crowd and spoke in a loud, firm voice, "if any of you waste gas, sleep on patrol, or use more than your share of food you should be banished or shot. This is a fight for our very survival! There are a million starving people across the Sandy desperate to have what we got. A war could break out any hour."

"And about the Lee family," he continued, "the Lee family does not come here to beg. The Lee family has brought with them an assortment of seeds, weapons, skills, gardening knowledge and training far greater than what most of us in Corbett have. Look at Kelly!" He pointed at Kelly, who shyly looked down at the ground in front of her and kicked a small stone. "You may have read about her in the papers or saw her on TV. Everyone heard about what she did. She's the girl who stabbed that knife-wielding maniac in Eugene last summer. She stabbed him with his own knife. Right through his damn adam's apple. She's a national hero for God's sake! And then there's Alison. She's standing right next to Kelly. She's a nuclear physicist. Heck, I can barely pronounce it. How many of you are physicists? None? I thought so. She's probably the smartest person in Oregon. Their dad, Jimmy here, he's donated 3,000 rounds of AK ammunition to our militia stockpile. How many of you have donated even 500 rounds? 100 rounds? I thought so. Maybe a few of you kicked in a few hundred. And his wife, Deborah? She's unbelievable! The whole family is vegetarian. We're all going to be mostly vegetarian for a while so get used to it. My boy tells me she wrote two vegetarian cookbooks and a rack of guidebooks on organic gardening. She can teach us how to prepare meals without meat. She'll show us how to garden without fertilizer if it comes to that. We'll ALL learn from her. She's been up since dawn and she's already out teaching Mary Kay how to plant beans and make a proper compost. Y'all know we need a dentist, a doctor, a permy culture expert, however you pronounce that, and a few others I can't remember right now. Well, the Lees also bring a fantastic gardening and cooking expert: Deborah. Her knowledge is just as important for all of us as having a doctor."

After Joseph calmed down, the Chief skillfully took charge. "Okay, okay. We all hear you. Moving right along," he paused and smiled.

Reverend Golphenee quickly cut in, "First, excuse me there a second Chief, just a second. First, let's all welcome the Lee family!" he shouted.

Loud cheering broke out among the crowd as Mr. Rogers slowly turned and headed home. More than a few walked over to shake hands with Alison, Kelly and their father and welcome them to Corbett.

The Reverend continued, "One more thing. We discussed this yesterday, but there are so many more people gathered here today I should ask it again before we move along: Does anyone here have a problem with the path we're taking. The path of protecting our hill from invasion and depredation?"

The response was dead silence from all. Reverend Golphenee and the Chief together scanned the crowd for about fifteen seconds.

"Okay, then it's unanimous. Now back to business," the Chief shouted.

He pointed at Mary Lou Rainier, who sat at a small table near him smiling brightly though suffering with the intense pain of a horrific toothache, which would wait because there was not a single dentist in town, "Volunteers for our town militia are needed right now. Sign up with Mary Lou here. She's preparing the roster."

Almost everyone knew Mary Lou. She was the gregarious and friendly secretary at the high school across the street. She was as beautiful and optimistic as a bright summer sunrise and had worked there for 15 years without aging one bit. Her husband, Ed, 44, was considered the luckiest guy in town. He was handsome and healthy as a horse at 5'11" and 175 pounds without a single grey one yet to sprout among his thick brown head of hair. Not only was he married to Mary Lou, but he was also the sole maintenance supervisor with the Corbett Water District, making him the guy with the nicest wife and the steadiest job in town. Plus, he knew how to keep the water flowing.

There was a very good reason the Chief asked her to create the militia volunteer roster: she was like a sister, mother, or friend to all, but more importantly for the critical mission at hand, she was a person no one could say no to.

As people lined up and signed up, Mary Lou asked each volunteer a few simple questions. And they were questions she never could have imagined ever asking. "Do you have any serious health problems? Are you a current or former police officer or do you have any military combat experience? What weapons do you have? How much ammunition can you donate?" The questions were repeated as each volunteer stepped up to her table.

"Next!"

The next in line immediately obeyed, stepping forward.

Jimmy and his two daughters were near the front of the line. Knowing writing paper could someday run out, Jimmy noticed that Mary Lou wrote very small, neatly noting the replies on the carefully written form she had made by hand the previous night.

"Next!"

And the next volunteer stepped quickly up to her table.

Mary Lou and her husband knew just about everyone in town and they were very well liked. Her husband was widely rumored to be able to fix anything. He was currently making solar cookers, which were going to be needed if the power remained out.

In the distance a few rifle shots could be heard as Mary Lou and the Chief began to break the volunteers into groups of four to six and direct them out on various patrol assignments. The instructions they received from the Chief were simple and few, "Everyone gets turned away. No exceptions except doctors, dentists, and organic farm experts, among a few others on the short do-admit list. If the patrols encounter anyone wasting fuel or ammunition they would be told to stop and report the incident to me later. There can be no exceptions. If they refuse to stop, send a runner at once for help. If anyone gives you trouble let either Reverend Golphenee or me deal with 'em. We'll explain to them why they must stop being wasteful."

Before the crowd left, the Chief spoke once more. "Only ten percent of the people in town came to this meeting: fewer were at the meeting yesterday, so word is spreading. Some still may not have heard about our new militia yet, but everyone has to do their part. During this time of crisis everyone living in Corbett is a member of the Corbett militia and there can be no exceptions. Everyone either fights or supports the fighters. Nothing is more important right now. Nothing! All outsiders must be ordered to leave, with the few exceptions listed with Mary Lou. If anyone refuses to leave they must be forced out using as little ammunition as possible. Seize their weapons and ammunition if they refuse or resist in any way."

The Chief continued, "In addition there will be no exceptions for old buddies or relatives seeking entry: all must be turned away. Farm workers and all other employees have been ordered out. Employees trying to enter must be turned away no matter how long they've worked for a family. We may not even have enough food for the five thousand people living here."

As tough as it was, anyone allowed in would just represent another mouth to feed. From now on just about everyone would become a farm worker so there was no more labor shortage.

A few exceptions, of course, included the disabled and elderly. They were people who could no longer farm or fight. They were allowed to serve the community by performing clerical duties such as loading magazines, counting and distributing seeds and anything else that came along. A few performed menial chores at Reverend Golphenee's Mt. Hood Christian Church, which was located a few hundred yards west of the store. Until the situation stabilized, Corbett was closed.

Chapter Forty-Five

At 8:30 a.m. the four-man unit assigned to guard the road up the hill from the Vista House was increased to ten. They were moved down the hill a half-mile to the Vista House parking area allowing better protection and a greatly improved view of the highway leading up from the Columbia River. This group had an excellent scenic view of the Columbia River and could see traffic on I-84 as well as on Highway 14, across the river in Washington. They could report if any trains were seen rumbling along either side of the river as well. Plus they had a clear view of the northern sky and could see if any planes were flying, although none had been seen for 24 hours. They would be expected to remain on sentry duty there 24 hours a day, sleeping in shifts in the large parking lot. They were assigned one bicycle messenger to bring them supplies and report back to town with any news or sightings.

The Mershon twins, who had earlier reported seeing hunters cross the river, and the three men who stayed with them were allowed a few hours rest as the first of the fresh, well-rested new men began arriving at 8:40 a.m. They would help guard the Stark Street Bridge and the nearby shoreline.

By 8:50, the few men stationed near the Troutdale Bridge were reinforced with 24 more men all armed with rifles or handguns.

They rode down the hill on bikes packing additional ammunition on their backs. One former army medic was among them. He carried what few medical supplies he could. They expected to see action at any time. Four sharpshooters hid in nearby trees mindful of the orders to allow no one to pass, but also to not waste ammunition with warning shots or misses.

At 8:55, a gathering of about two dozen pick-up trucks and several dozen armed men appeared to be setting up camp alongside Stark Street, just across the bridge. Country music blared from truck speakers as the men and women in the growing crowd inspected their rifles and gear. They gathered near the entrance to the once very pricy, but now very demolished River Restaurant. Worse, more vehicles were arriving every minute. They were even starting to park in the restaurant parking lot and were lining up alongside the road.

Josh Daugherty, a skinny high school junior, was immediately sent pedaling back up the hill as fast as he could to report this ominous development.

It took Josh 25 minutes to pedal up the long hill and reach the Country Market. The Chief, who was now acting as the de facto general of this newly-formed militia, was busy addressing a few of the gathered older military veterans regarding the surprise surplus of firearms and the shocking shortage of ammunition. He suspected many people were hiding their ammunition at home, and he really could not blame them. If a serious influx of humanity suddenly crossed one or more of the Sandy River bridges, they could be overrun. It would be impossible to stop a wave of hundreds of vehicles or thousands of starving people if they rushed in all at once. The Chief was very concerned and nervous but he did not let it show.

On the other hand, he was quite pleased to discover that one of the local hermits, Charlie, had just told the Chief about a box of dynamite and some plastic explosives he had illegally stored in his garage. A week ago he could have been arrested and jailed in Inverness, the huge county jail in northeast Portland. Newspapers would have shouted out headlines calling him a terrorist, an insane man, a psycho and even worse: he probably would have never seen freedom again. Instead, starting today, he was going to be the town hero.

They were just then talking about how it could be put to use when Josh rode up to them with the bad news. "They're here! Dozens of pick-up trucks! Maybe a hundred or more rednecks! More are coming! They're all getting ready to cross the Sandy River right now. They got guns! Rifles! Hurry!" The first feared hungry crowd had finally appeared. They were at the Stark Street Bridge and their numbers were growing fast.

Two of the Vietnam veterans, well into their 60's, knew their way around explosives and volunteered to try to take out the Stark Street and Troutdale Bridges.

"I think I can take it out," Charlie, the younger of the two told the Chief. Charlie was rumored in some circles to be the person responsible for the occasional explosions that echoed across Corbett every few years. As a result of one minor error in judgment twenty years ago he was nearly deaf in both ears.

"Go for it," replied the Chief. "Take 'em both down. Do it now."

"What?"

"He said, WE CAN TAKE OUT THE BRIDGES NOW," his friend Tim shouted.

Charlie smiled.

Many locals in Corbett had joked for years that if chaos swept over the urban areas west of them both century-old Sandy River bridges would have to be destroyed in order to keep a swarm of terror from reaching them. These two old men did more than simply joke about it: they prepared for it. They knew that the bridges must one day be blown. They had studied the bridges for years and knew exactly what to do, where to place the explosives. Today they were no longer considered to be among the handful of town loonies. Soon, their names would be chiseled into a stone memorial recognizing the town's heroes.

Chapter Forty-Six

The older one, Tim, had a 2007 BMW F-650 running on dirt tires. Together they rode straight to Charlie's house to load up. After slipping into his Kevlar vest, Charlie filled the bike's hard plastic saddlebags with dynamite and everything he would need to set it off. He hopped on the back behind Tim and they took off down the hill to the river.

When they got about 200 yards east of the Stark Street Bridge, Tim killed his engine. He quietly coasted the rest of the way. Long lines of trucks and cars now stretched up the Stark Street hill along both sides of the road past what remained of the fine dining restaurant that had been ransacked and looted of meat and liquor early that morning. Charlie hopped off the motorcycle as soon as it stopped. He reached into the side bag, pulling out exactly what he needed. So far, none of the people gathered had stepped foot on the bridge itself, but unless they could take out the bridge fast, it would only be a matter of time before they tried and the bridge became covered with blood.

Tim pointed at Charlie, then gave the universal 'hush' sign with his finger to the armed men on their side of the bridge and he restarted his motorcycle. He paused briefly telling one guard that the bridge would be blown up in a few minutes. Then he rode north as quietly as possible toward the Troutdale Bridge. Meanwhile, about ten yards upstream from the Stark Street Bridge, Charlie slipped into the thick undergrowth carrying a canvas bag filled with his share of the explosives.

Three minutes and 20 seconds later, after waving and smiling at a few of his buddies gathered at the base of Woodard Road, Tim arrived at a point 100 yards upriver from the Troutdale Bridge and shut off his engine coasting as far as he could. He parked his motorcycle behind the rain-weathered Lewis and Clark historic marker sign and dug into the other saddlebag. He quickly grabbed his explosives and told the handful of guards to stay back from the bridge a few minutes. Tim then jogged to a point just south of the east end of the bridge where he disappeared into the thick underbrush. He was nearly invisible to the growing crowd of people gathering in nearby Otto Park as he crept in his old faded green BDU's to a point near the bridge footings where he stopped, quickly set the charge, then climbed back up to the road. He calmly walked back to his motorcycle, started it, waved goodbye to his buddies, and slowly rode east to get Charlie.

At exactly 9:42 a.m., just as planned, two large explosions rocked the lower Sandy River valley. The east ends of the two historic Sandy River bridges were ripped apart and collapsed, reducing them to twisted wreckage resting on the river bottom. They would remain where they fell until generations later when the steel finally oxidized and the wooden roadway broke off from its mounts and washed out to sea.

Tim, who had ridden his motorcycle along every road east of the Sandy, knew his town was not safe yet because trucks could still cross the Sandy River. All they had to do was drive across the I-84 Bridge, and after taking the first exit, backtrack to the Columbia River Highway. However, a railroad bridge crossed the Sandy River about two hundred yards south of the I-84 bridge. If it collapsed, blocking the Columbia River Highway just north of Lewis and

Clark State Park, vehicles accessing Corbett from Troutdale would be forced to head several miles down I-84 then climb up the NE Corbett Hill Road or take the Crown Point Highway exit where they could be easily stopped. Tim suspected few would try that.

He took off back to Corbett, stopping briefly near the Stark Street Bridge to pick up Charlie, who had by then, as planned, started walking back up the hill to Corbett. Both rode without helmets. Tim could hear Charlie perfectly. As he rode, Tim spoke over his shoulder to his nearly deaf buddy Charlie, "We have another job. We gotta take out the railroad bridge somehow. We gotta set another charge, a much larger one this time: large enough to take out the railroad bridge and we gotta do it right now."

"Huh?" Charlie replied.

But they had to do it quick. Right now, anyone could drive right in. "After we hit the railroad bridge, we gotta see what can be done about blocking NE Corbett Hill Road." Tim yelled.

"Huh?"

All Tim had on his mind was blocking that access road. With dozens of fallen trees and maybe a few intentionally set rockslides no vehicles could pass. He stopped a moment while passing the Country Market and shared his idea with the Chief. The Chief concurred and immediately ordered several crews with chain saws and heavy equipment to go down the hill. By 10:55 a.m. the rough backcountry men of Corbett had blocked nearly every road leading into town. Only one more needed to be closed.

Preparing the explosives was fairly easy for Tim. Two 25-pound charges, which is what he initially estimated would be needed, would hardly deplete his once-secret explosives cache. For many years he told no one about it fearing people would think he was crazy, and sharing this with anyone might get him arrested. Nevertheless, they were now glad he had the explosives and he was glad he no longer had to keep quiet about them, but he would still keep them hidden.

He had the charges prepared and packed on his motorcycle in less than ten minutes. "Let's roll, pops."

He quickly sped back down to the bridge taking Charlie with him in case he had trouble.

"What?" Charlie shouted.

When they reached the large parking lot just south of the Troutdale Bridge, they paused briefly explaining to the men stationed what they were going to try to do. They asked for some men to provide protection and cover for a few minutes and a crew of six responded, riding their bicycles to Lewis and Clark Park where they stopped and watched Tim and Charlie get to work.

Tim and Charlie arrived at the railroad bridge a minute later and paused a few moments to study its design to determine precisely where to place the explosives. Instead of dynamite Charlie brought C-4, which was much better suited for a heavy bridge of this kind. The east support tower was too solid to fall west and block the narrow access tunnel. Taking it down would be impossible. Tim had plenty of experience blasting buildings and tunnels, but very little with this type of structure. He climbed onto the tracks themselves and studied the bridge a few minutes. He then placed each charge 75 feet apart just under the rails. If it went well, twisted steel rails and debris should collapse across the roadway and into the river. At 10:23 a.m., after placing the charges, they quickly moved back 100 yards and waited another minute for the explosion. It was perfect. Clearing the heavy rails and debris that fell across the narrow stretch of road would take powerful equipment working several hours. It was doubtful that would ever happen.

Tim and Charlie rode back up to the Country Market, which was by now looking more and more like a guerrilla army command post. They shared the good news of the successful explosions. Raised fists and more than a few loud cheers and whistles rang out as the two hermits smiled, basking in the glory of their good work.

"What do you want us to blow up next, Chief?" Tim cheerfully asked.

"Oh, we'll think of something, Tim, don't you worry. Ain't that right, Charlie?"

"Huh?"

Chapter Forty-Seven

The Country Market was still closed, but the small dirt parking area was beginning to look more and more like a military command post. Serious-looking men and women wearing jeans and boots as well as others dressed in tan and green BDU's and the newer military issued ACU's chatted and milled around small tables covered with maps protected from the never-ending east wind by carefully placed rocks. Numerous rifles and a few ammunition boxes were lined up along the shaded north side dirt parking lot behind the tired old structure and folding chairs were scattered about. A few old men silently stuffed bullets one by one into long rifle magazines. The only sound was that of men and women softly speaking and the wind's occasional howl. The town's tall, grey haired leader was standing next to a small picnic table with his arms folded across his chest. He was deep in thought staring silently at a wind-shook map.

He knew blocking the access roads was only part of the victory. With the early Mt. Hood runoff nearly over, the Sandy River was still too deep to wade across; however, it could always be crossed by boat. In a few weeks, the river level would drop. Then it could easily be waded across in many places. People would continuously patrol the woods near the shoreline and prevent anyone from crossing. Small groups of men and women were now out patrolling doing just that.

But it was now July third, and the man everyone called the Chief knew they had to start planning long-term. He was well aware that if the masses of hungry and desperate people from Portland and Gresham were allowed in they would strip their farms and town bare in a matter of days. Worse yet, what if they organized themselves and attacked en masse? There was no way to predict what could happen, but one thing was certain: allowing them in would serve no purpose whatsoever. While some were tearing their little town apart in cruel ways the imagination could not visualize, others would quickly hunt down and eat all the wildlife on their side of Larch Mountain and beyond. After that, what would the invading masses of starving people do? The Chief did not even think of it. No matter how cold and heartless it was, they had to be stopped. There was no sign of the government coming to the rescue to straighten things out. There was no other way: they would protect themselves.

How can they possibly plan for this? The townspeople must act based on the assumption that the people living in Corbett could successfully keep thousands of hungry city dwellers out. This was going to be the current focus and it placed an immense burden on the Chief and the other town leaders.

It was time to forget about farming as a business and instead start planting food crops for their own use. Some locals became quite wealthy selling to wholesalers while others with smaller farms barely got by. However, farming solely for the town's use would be a huge change for all. They had grown comfortable after many decades of selling their vegetable and fruit crops to urban stores and the occasional summer tourist who self-picked and that practice was about to end forever.

Many growers had become used to the practice of hiring migrant farm workers. This had accelerated during the '80s and by now few local high school kids and local part-timers participated in the annual harvest. This had changed overnight. It was clear that from now on locals would be doing the farm work, as they had always done up until a generation or two earlier, so relying on outside labor would no longer be done. Some migrants had worked on the same farms for years, but the stark and harsh reality was that they were no longer needed. They would pose an unacceptable level of resource burden and were being told to leave or turned away if they were encountered by a patrol.

The Corbett lifeboat was full. Normally around 5,000 people lived in and around Corbett, but with many stuck in far-flung places during summer vacation it may have dropped to 4,500 or less. Most of them were in far-away cities and would never return. Even still, with 4.500 people living on the hill it may have overshot its sustainable population limit, meaning in time, the population might decline even further and it would be a harsh process.

More than a few living on the Corbett bluff were dependant on medications that would soon run out. Several dozen retired farmers required oxygen canisters to assist them with breathing. Two of the school kids needed weekly transfusions. Dozens were prescribed a bewildering array of assorted psychiatric medications and when they ran out, things would get more than a little crazy. Several hundred had severe physical disabilities and could not perform hard work. Hundreds were alcoholics or illegal drug abusers and would soon experience withdrawal symptoms. Hundreds more would soon be forced to quit smoking. About 40 of the residents were under 18 months of age and would require periodic medical attention. Corbett had exactly one doctor and he was an 82 year-old neurology specialist who once worked at the now-ransacked hospital formerly known as Mt Hood Medical Center. He was about as useful to them now as an MRI technician. Country medicine would someday make a comeback, but not right away. What Corbett needed now was someone to serve as a general practitioner or many of the people in need of medical care would die.

Those needing a dentist would be out of luck. Corbett had exactly two veterinarians and precisely zero dentists. Mary Lou might have to skip the novocaine and have someone yank her painful tooth out the old fashioned way: a string tied to a doorknob or by a pair of muscular hands twisting a pair of pliers. But she was not alone. Everyone eventually needed a dentist.

Summer was just getting underway and there was plenty of time remaining to plant new crops. They had to switch gears and change focus to growing the vegetables and grains that could hopefully feed the hillside population through the coming winter and into spring, if it came to that. Those not actively involved in patrolling would be invited and encouraged to perform hard labor on various farms in exchange for meals. A community meeting would be held to discuss which farms would grow what crops as soon as the threat of invasion had passed and the town perimeter had been made safe and secure. Until then, small home gardens were springing up everywhere and in weeks they would be producing a bumper crop of assorted vegetables and roots.

Chapter Forty-Eight

By 11 a.m., as soon as they found out the bridges had been destroyed, Kelly and Alison sprinted back to the berry farm. Jimmy, Bill, Joe and his dad returned shortly afterward to prepare for patrol duty. Shortly after they arrived, the men were surprised to discover that Alison and Kelly had already changed into loose-fitting dark cargo pants and long-sleeved denim shirts. They were ready and eager to go out on patrol. In fact, while the men were getting ready, they tried, but were unable to lift their family safe out of Joe's Hummer. The men walked over to the truck and saw that the safe had moved about a foot. They lifted it the rest of the way out of Joe's Hummer and set it in the driveway. Joseph tipped the safe back an inch and slid the scoop of his dolly under one end.

"Here Joe. Roll it in the barn," said Joseph as he pointed at the dolly.

"Sure dad," replied Joe.

Joe tipped the red hand-truck toward him at a 45-degree angle and wheeled it backward through the gravel and into the barn while everyone stared in amazement.

"Just set it down next to the bench press, boy," yelled his dad.

"Why's he using the dolly? The safe is only about 600 pounds. Why doesn't he just pick it up and carry it?" laughed Bill.

"Look at him. He's pulling that dolly like it's empty," said Jimmy.

"Daddy, maybe you should help him," said Alison.

"Looks like he's got it under control, Alison."

"It's okay. I've got it. I can control the weight better alone."

Alison and Kelly each carried Chinese-made MAK-90 rifles equipped with leather slings and with a dozen spare magazines shared between them. They looked like a pair of Sandinista guerrilla fighters standing alongside their mother and Mary Kay. The young women were ready for just about anything. Joseph, concerned that so few of the people in Corbett knew the Lee family, expressed a valid concern that it would be dangerous for the Lees to go out on patrol unescorted especially looking like they were dressed for war. He suggested to Jimmy that they make it a six-member patrol and that Deborah and Mary Kay would be safe staying behind working on the farm until the first patrol ended. Both women heartily agreed, reminding the others that there was a ton of work to do around the farm.

Jimmy went into the barn and opened the safe. He reached inside for his late father's old AR-15 rifle, which he had loaded many months ago. He also grabbed ten 30-round magazines, which he had already filled with 28 rounds each. With no idea what they might encounter, he gathered all the magazines and placed a freshly filled one-liter water bottle into his canvas handbag. Jimmy owned one Kevlar vest, which he and Deborah insisted Alison and Kelly trade off wearing each day. He then handed her back the bulky medical kit Deborah had just brought out and left it with her rather than be burdened carrying the extra weight. He reached once more into the safe and pulled out a 9mm handgun and a few extra magazines and handed it all to her as well. "Here, sweetie, take this. You might need it."

"Thanks Jimmy," she replied. Deborah took the weapon and spare magazines. "How nice it will be when things finally settle down. I love you all. Please be careful."

After the six said their goodbyes, they walked off through the tidy rows of nearly ripened blueberry bushes toward the Sandy River. They disappeared over a hill.

"How are things in the city?" Deborah asked herself. She could see smoke rising here and there off in the distance, but they were too far away to hear the gunfire. "In fact," she wondered further, "how are things in cities across the country, even throughout the world?"

Chapter Forty-Nine

The situation in Portland had deteriorated faster than anyone expected. A 44-year-old Corbett homeowner who was trapped in downtown Portland arrived late-morning Wednesday on foot after a terrifying two-day, 25 mile meandering hike through northeast Portland and Gresham. He hadn't eaten or slept in two days and when he arrived he was famished and dehydrated but much better off than most of the people he saw.

"Crowds of people are stopping cars just about everywhere," he explained. "They're robbing anything of value from everyone. Bodies are lying around rotting in the streets. I could hear women screaming. Lots of them. There was nothing I could do. Nothing at all. Fires are burning everywhere, too. It looked like the entire east side of Portland and all of Gresham was on fire. Entire apartment blocks were on fire. The air was full of smoke and stunk of rotting meat. Pharmacies and supermarkets were looted and burned to the ground. No fire fighters could be seen anywhere. It was a total nightmare. I'm really hungry and I need to sleep."

After eating, he told those gathered at the General Store more of his story. "Walking during daytime was too dangerous. Early Tuesday morning I felt lucky to have reached the Multnomah County Sheriff's Department parking lot on 122nd and Glisan where me and several hundred others seeking safety had gathered. Just before sunset Tuesday evening, a deputy came out of the green sheriff building and spoke to the terrified crowd and told us to leave. She explained that we could no longer be protected since only three armed officers were still in the building, and by morning the building would be abandoned and then there would be none. Just after midnight the three deputies all snuck out and left in a cop car. Shortly after they left, I started hiking straight up Glisan with a group of three other men who were trying to reach Troutdale. It was completely dark. We had to run for our lives on four separate occasions to escape gangs of young men wanting to steal anything we had. They had flashlights and chased us. We ran away as fast as we could and we all got away each time. We had nothing to give them. They would have killed us. It was so dark we couldn't see a thing. We constantly bumped into signs and tripped over bodies. It was a nightmare."

When he calmed down a bit, he went on, "A mass hysteria has taken over the entire city. The weak, sick and elderly have no chance. So many bodies are littered about dragged or dumped along sidewalks and left to decay in the heat. I can't stop repeating that. It was horrible. After Monday, there was next to no civil authority to be seen anywhere. I saw no national guard, and only a few police officers on Monday … none on Tuesday … none today. Gunfire was constantly cracking away. It wasn't until I got halfway to the Country Market that the sounds of firearms had faded."

Thankfully, he reported no large organized groups heading east as many in Corbett feared might happen.

It was hard to imagine what the situation was like in larger cities such as Chicago, New York, Detroit, Miami or Los Angeles. The collapse was so deep and sudden and with the Internet out and no radio or television, it became more and more clear that no one would ever know.

Chapter Fifty

By 11:45 a.m., Jimmy Lee and his daughters started their patrol along with Bill, Joseph and his son, Joe. They walked within earshot of each other, but scattered about ten yards apart to avoid offering an easy target. They had absolutely no idea what they might expect, but were prepared for almost anything. Between the six of them they carried around 1,000 rounds of ammunition split evenly between .223 and 7.62x39 rounds plus several extra magazines each for their handguns. They didn't fire a single round.

It was going to be hot, and with no weather service all they could do was estimate how hot it might get, which is something that everyone would find tough getting used to. In the past, all they had to do was touch their cell phones and a complete weather report appeared on the screen. No more. To learn the weather, they would study the wind speed and direction and read the clouds like their ancestors did.

While they silently walked and carefully scanned the trees and river below, Jimmy, who was keenly aware of current events and trends, had several decades earlier earned a masters degree in history. He thought deeply about what could have possibly caused such a sudden collapse of their society.

He knew that every society throughout human history went through a process of birth, life and death. Much like all organisms, all societies also passed through these same three life stages, and there were no exceptions. But what fascinated Jimmy was the process of the collapse itself. Why now? Why so sudden? Thinking back in time, he knew the Roman Empire decayed over a period of many centuries and a major population decline was part of that process. On the other hand, the Mayan Empire declined very fast: declining over a period of a few months or years, but much of the population that survived the initial encounter with the Spaniards scattered or were absorbed by others.

Some societies fall apart for unknown reasons, such as the Anasazi Indians of the desert southwest. Other cultures, such as the Polynesians who settled Easter Island underwent a population overshoot. They consumed and destroyed their environment by removing their energy base, which in their case were the trees. Shortly afterward they experienced a very rapid and violent die-off, the final stages of which was witnessed and recorded by European seafarers.

Jimmy knew that modern society existed almost solely due to the ingenious exploitation of fossil fuels. This resource exploitation transformed society in ways past cultures could not have possibly imagined. Nutrient depletion of farmlands and water scarcity were no longer impediments to growth as irrigation took on earth-shaping proportions and fossil fertilizers brought renewed life to long-dead farmlands. Centuries prior to the widespread use of fossil fuels, the world's population had been roughly stable at one-half billion, finally doubling with the western expansion eventually reaching one billion by the start of the 19th century.

As fossil fuels began powering farm equipment and transportation, crops could be far more easily grown and the population exploded, reaching two billion by 1927 and then three billion by 1960. The worldwide green revolution exploded during this time. It exploited fossil fuel based fertilizers allowing huge per-acre production increases in basic grains, which could now easily be grown in nutrient depleted soil. This allowed the population to surge even more, reaching six billion by 1999 and then seven billion by 2011.

With the appearance of oil powered cargo vessels, food could be inexpensively shipped anywhere. Industrialized nations could easily and cheaply ship farm equipment and trucks anywhere on earth in a matter of weeks. Without oil none of this would be possible, but cheap energy allowed farm production and population growth to explode upwards.

Across the industrialized world, people were suddenly able to easily transport themselves great distances on land using automobiles powered by cheap oil. Distant densely populated suburbs sprang up far from urban centers, and 50-mile commutes eventually became commonplace. Wars raged across several continents as nation after nation fought, struggling to maintain a steady supply of precious oil. None of this was cheap, however. Millions of lives were lost. Ancient cultural traditions disappeared. The new oil-based financial order required an ever-expanding economy, as any economist will easily explain, and if it started to sputter for any reason and failed to expand, a major financial crisis was inevitable.

As the new decade got underway, the United States as well as a number of European countries required massive financial bailouts of one kind or another. Fearing a domino effect, central banks of the more powerful nations came to their rescue as nation after nation could no longer service their national debt obligations. A sovereign debt crisis was well underway, but an assortment of clever and increasingly complicated interventions had thus far kept the outright collapse of any one nation at bay. But what would happen when the largest nation defaulted?

The thought of that occurring was too terrifying for most to contemplate. Contemplating the outright collapse of civilization sent shivers up the spines of everyone in positions of leadership throughout the top levels of government and finance. In fact, a subgroup of a German military think tank called "Center for German Army Transformation, Group for Future Studies," produced a document called, "Implications of Resource Scarcity on National Security," and highlights from the report were published by the German publication Der Spiegel early in the decade. It warned of the outright collapse of German society if energy became scarce or too costly.

However, more than a few knew this is exactly what would inevitably occur as oil production plummeted, and after peaking, it became clear that the decline would occur sooner rather than later. The doomsday scenario was more and more becoming a topic of top-level discussion among military and political leaders all over the industrialized world. For the last year or two, it was no longer limited to whispered discourse among those considered to be on the fringe.

The feared financial disaster loomed ever closer. The U.S. economy started to sputter long before the year began. The reasons were many, but deficit spending played the leading role. By 2010, 40% of the federal budget consisted of borrowed money. Last year the figure had reached a staggering 75%. The federal deficit had meanwhile reached $14.3 trillion as 2010 came to a close, and was now, as war costs escalated and tax revenue decreased, over $21 trillion. Meeting the payments on this mountain of debt required low inflation and an expanding economy, neither of which were present as summer approached. Increasing the debt limit could not go on forever, and the new congress finally put a complete stop to it. A period of extreme austerity and belt-tightening was about to begin. Getting the nation's financial house in order was the only way to forestall disaster, so the nation's business and political leaders believed.

Chapter Fifty-One

As worldwide oil production began its slow descent following the peak oil production year of 2005, economic expansion and growth in oil importing nations became impossible. Higher energy prices and increased military expenditures caused further economic weakening and, as many in the financial community had long predicted, interest rates and inflation continued to rise.

If any one of the countless and highly interconnected and incomprehensively complex links in the world's economy suddenly weakened the entire financial infrastructure could completely disintegrate in a hurry. The Israeli New Year's Day attacks and the resultant oil price surge followed by Monday's sudden bank closures may have been the last straws resulting in the complete shut down of the world's economy. The world's financial system appeared to have completely died. Bringing it back to life would prove to be impossible.

As a Buddhist Jimmy knew and firmly believed the core premise that all things are impermanent. This meant everything in existence including sub-atomic particles, grains of sand, stones, planets and the entire universe itself went through a process of birth, life and death. This process included humans and their constructs as well, meaning all nations are inherently unstable and impermanent, but facing the reality of the end of the US government and all of modern civilization was mind-boggling. These thoughts and more raced through Jimmy's mind as he quietly walked thorough the fields and woods along the east side of the Sandy River. He knew that the cause of the historically recent surge in the world's population was the sudden exploitation of cheap and plentiful energy used in transportation, industry, and, most importantly, in agriculture through the fossil-based fertilization of nutrient-depleted farmlands worldwide.

Jimmy knew that the primary destabilizing factor was that this single finite resource was the sole foundation of modern industrial human civilization. Since peaking, oil production had declined each year and worse yet, the decline appeared to be accelerating. The decline had been partially offset by converting food crops into liquid fuel but the sad side effect of that desperate measure was much higher food prices and civil unrest much like that which swept through many Muslim nations during 2011. The New Year's Day attack and the Iranian retaliation were the sucker punches that left the world's economy staggering and only one punch away from toppling over. All it would take would be one single uppercut and it would fall.

That uppercut occurred two days ago. When the newly elected Congress voted to allow the market to solve the deepening financial crisis this disastrous outcome was definitely not what they expected. Based on what little they knew and from reports people had gathered talking to stragglers, the fight appeared over. The nation's economy had collapsed and it was not going to be easy to re-start. Did that mean a historically unprecedented population crash would soon be underway? He desperately wanted information. He wanted to find out what was happening across the USA and throughout the world, but with no Internet and no electricity the only way the people of Corbett would get any news from outside would be on an amateur radio powered by wind or solar generated electricity.

Chapter Fifty-Two

At 3:30 p.m., Jimmy stopped dead in his tracks and called out to the other men in his patrol, "Hey! Any of you know anyone with a ham radio."

Bill replied, "Yup. Pete Roth. He has one."

Jimmy should have known. Pete and his wife, Linda lived along Larch Mountain in a house built partially against a hillside. He and Jimmy were motorcycle buddies back a few years ago and rode their motorcycles through the hills of East County many times. Pete was probably the smartest person in town. He was an amateur inventor who lived on a three-acre piece of land on the west slope of Larch Mountain, about six miles directly east from where they were now patrolling. His equipment and gizmo-littered garage, where he spent most of his time, was about the same size as his 2,500 square foot house. The two were pals who had rode motorcycles together now and then, but he had no idea Pete was among the estimated one million amateur radio buffs worldwide because the subject never came up. Desperate to find out what was happening on the outside, he made up his mind to bike out to Pete's house as soon as possible.

The Hancock and Lee family patrol assignment was going to last until midnight and after a 12-hour rest another 12-hour shift would start again at noon Thursday. This schedule would repeat until further notice by the Chief. He would inform Mary Lou of any changes, who in turn would dispatch messengers on foot or on bike. To conserve fuel, scooters and small motorcycles would only be used in emergency situations, and the ban on the use of personal cars and trucks remained firmly in effect. After finishing their patrol they would sleep light tonight. Everyone knew the universal wake-up signal was a weapon firing. If that were to occur, immediate response by all off-duty militia members was mandatory, allowing those on patrol elsewhere to maintain their assigned positions.

The Wednesday patrol went quietly throughout Corbett. The Lees and the two Hancocks were able to chase away a half-dozen hunters and a few desperate lost souls, sternly ordering them to cross the Sandy River or get shot. None refused. Thankfully none were shot. Other patrols reported similarly. Shouting out the harsh penalty for refusal was tough on all of them, but they knew the unspeakable terror that would occur if Corbett got overrun and that outcome was unthinkable. This was the time to focus on sharing compassion toward those living on the Corbett lifeboat. After things settled down: maybe in a month or two, it might be safe to cross the river and offer aid to survivors, but for now, all of their attention was going to be focused on establishing a safe perimeter and getting a late crop planted. Everything was subordinated to these two goals.

Chapter Fifty-Three

At 8:00 a.m. on the Fourth of July, after a very quick eye-opening yet refreshing cold shower, Jimmy and Alison said goodbye to those awake and hopped on their bicycles, following Bill to his nearby tiny house. They were eager to get to Pete's place to see if he had picked up any news from outside on his ham radio, but Kelly and the Hancocks were still sleeping, so the three told Mary Kay where they were going and headed out early. Deborah didn't know how to ride a bicycle yet, so she stayed behind and got busy picking blueberries. She would soon learn how to ride a bike. Besides walking, it was now the only way to get around town.

Alison and Jimmy were impressed by how efficient Bill's small and tidy house was. He proudly showed it to them. "It only has a few hundred square feet of living space, but with that six-foot deep wraparound deck and with the sleeping area located in the loft, it really seems much bigger. It stays nice and warm for next to nothing, too. I keep my hybrid bike chained and locked to those eyebolts, as you can see. They're securely attached to the right side deck. I don't know why I go through all the trouble of locking my bike. Must be something I picked up in Oakland. Out here, I never even bother to lock my front door. Funny. I lock up the silly bike but leave the door unlocked."

After unlocking it, the three rode off into the sun-filled quiet morning air and pedaled three miles up Larch Mountain Road to the Roth's house.

At 8:25 they arrived at the beginning of Pete's long gravel driveway and walked their bikes up to his closed gate, which was about 50 feet from his house. Bill called out, "Yo Pete! Linda!"

They waited until one of them walked out to greet them. They felt it might be considered impolite to walk right up to someone's door armed and unannounced this early in the morning so they waited by the gate. Surprising either of them might be bad for one's health.

Pete's house was built in a modern style featuring a full 360 degree perimeter balcony with the lower floor constructed partially underground, constructed soundly with concrete blocks against a gently sloping hillside. The solid concrete foundation held back ten feet of earth on the north side and was ground level on the sunny south. The air temperature in the lower floor, where he and his wife slept during the summer, never rose above 68 degrees even if it was over 100 outside.

Pete and Linda were avid gardeners. They had nearly an acre dedicated to growing food for their own use and to share with friends. To accommodate their edible hobby, Pete built a cleverly constructed watertight underground food storage room, carving it right into the foundation. Its strong wooden shelves could hold hundreds of jars of assorted canned vegetables, jams and the wide variety of homegrown fruits he and his wife prepared each late summer. By October each year stacks of plastic bins contained potatoes, onions, and assorted vegetables kept fresh for months in the sub-50 degree cellar.

At one time, many decades in the past, it was common for the people of this area to grow as much food as possible for their own use and store it all in this manner. Unfortunately, the home-gardening craft had slowly faded over time and recently fewer than

5% of the people in Corbett grew any significant amount of their own personal food. Local farmers generally relied on one highly fertilized and pesticide-saturated crop, which they sold to wholesale produce distributors. However, those days were over. The farmers would start growing organically and diversify their crops strictly for local consumption whether they wanted to or not.

After a few minutes, Pete and Linda walked out on their deck.

"Hi!" Pete called out, "What brings you all the way up here this fine morning?"

Bill replied, "We heard Linda was fixing everyone breakfast. We didn't want to miss out!"

After hugs were shared all around Bill quickly got to the point, which was his no-nonsense personal style and part of his charm, "Have you heard any news from outside on your ham radio?"

"Yup," Pete said. "C'mon in and first have some tea. We'll tell you all about it."

Pete and Linda invited the group in for a cup of their home-grown tea made from blackberry leaves and mint, both of which grew wild on their property and offered an unusually refreshing and tasty hot or cold drink. All visitors to their home were served their special tea whether they liked it or not, however most enjoyed it very much. They refused to discuss business until they were started on their third cup, a friendly tradition he picked up while assigned to serve in Afghanistan 10 years earlier.

As they stood out on the south-facing section of deck, they saw a few black tail deer wander by. Pete casually commented, "If the city folks are allowed in all the deer will be gone in a few days."

Linda laughed at that, and replied, "If the deer were all gone we wouldn't need six-foot cyclone fences around each of our fruit trees anymore."

Alison, who had spent all of her adult life buried in academia, had been wondering why the Roth's fruit trees were each surrounded by tall metal fences. "So that's what those fences are for."

To avoid appearing too 'city' she said no more, and simply laughed along with the others.

After a few minutes, Pete was on his third cup. "We're hungry for information from outside too. I spent an hour on my old hammie after we finished patrolling our section of eastern Corbett late last night. We made three contacts. One was from a rural part of southwest Georgia, another from just outside Yellowstone National Park in southwest Montana and another who was a guy living in eastern Oregon. All three lived in secluded areas. They offered no additional details about the crisis and other than mentioning that the Internet and cell phones no longer worked and the electricity was out everywhere they offered little. They said they were too busy to talk on their radios more than a few minutes each day and had been unable to make contact with anyone yet, just us."

There was much work to be done and a purely social visit was unthinkable now. It was time to get back to the Hancock farm and help prepare the five-acre plot the family had designated for vegetables and root crops. "Thanks, Pete. Goodbye Linda. We really gotta get moving. We start patrolling at noon. Keep us informed if you hear anything at all. We're dying to get any news at all from outside," said Bill.

"I'll keep trying. Linda knows how to operate it now, so she'll try as well, but we can only use it a few minutes each day because it consumes too much power. We still might get lucky and hear something."

"Yup. I'm a regular hammie now," Linda happily quipped as the three waved and smiled back then carefully pedaled down the long gravel driveway.

Patrol duty was going to be the same 12-hour shifts each day until the town's perimeter was safe and secure. They had no idea how long that would take. Everyone knew the lack of information from outside most likely meant the news would be too horrible to contemplate. Vigilant patrolling was now even more important.

Chapter Fifty-Four

At 10:00 the three arrived back at the Hancock farm and headed straight to work in the garden. They were preparing it for the assortment of summer vegetables that were now germinating in tiny trays. Onions, radishes, carrots, potatoes, and a variety of leafy vegetables would be planted soon. It was hard work and they were glad to be doing it before the afternoon heat arrived.

Deborah and Mary Kay were both needed on the farm to prepare the five acres Mary Kay had designated for planting. It was no different from what Deborah had done for years, but a hundred-fold larger. They were assisted by a group of 11 high school students who had been assigned by JP Lenet, the high school PE teacher, who was in charge of assigning older high school students onto work crews. The group of older kids arrived early and had been hard at work on their farm since 7:00 a.m. They had to work in order to eat. And they worked very hard. For most it was their very first job. Their pay was going to be the same as it would be for adults: breakfast, lunch and dinner in exchange for hours of brutal fieldwork.

Some of the students were out of school for the short three-week summer break. Many were in poor physical condition yet everyone strongly believed the healthy exercise would do them some good, especially their parents. A few of them had to learn the hard way that in order to eat one had to work, and that this simple primeval law now applied to all.

One of the students, 17-year-old Sandy Winters, was quickly gaining a reputation for laziness and constant complaining. She had approached either Deborah or Mary Kay numerous times during the morning to complain about the other kids working on the farm. It was one thing after another. Her beautifully painted fingernails had never felt soil in her life and her body was covered in a three-inch layer of soft body fat, which for her 5'4" had her scaling in at an even 180 pounds. She was quite clear, repeatedly telling everyone that farm labor wasn't her kind of work.

Deborah and Mary Kay struggled constantly to motivate her to do her part and to stop her sustained whining and tattling, but with so much work to do they had much more important matters to focus on. Shortly before lunch, they both had enough of her constant disruptions. "Go see Mr. Lenet," Mary Kay told her, "and get going right now. Go. You are welcome back when you are prepared to work but until then stay away." For Sandy there would be no lunch today, but she would learn a valuable lesson.

She skulked away, angrily waving her one inch long orange fingernails, "I'm telling my father."

At 2:15 p.m., she was back on the farm wearing old oversized boots with her fingernails freshly trimmed to the quick. Her father had escorted her and sternly told Deborah and Mary Kay they could be as harsh with Sandy as they wished and to let him know immediately if she slacked off or gave them any more grief in any way.

Deborah and Mary Kay smiled to each other knowing Sandy would learn quickly. It was close to 80 degrees already and Mr. Lenet's office was almost two miles away. Sandy would soon learn to manage without toilet paper, soap, shampoo, dental floss and all the other personal hygiene luxuries everyone had grown accustomed to. She would soon learn to pick dirt out of her fingernails, floss her teeth with tough blades of dried grass or sturdy twigs and be happy with cold showers. Most difficult for her today would be transitioning out of the open-toed red plastic sandals and into the ragged boots she now wore. But the transition would be difficult for all of them and more than a few would not make it through the summer. Sadly, as the weeks passed by, the population of Corbett slowly started to decline as dozens of residents' life-saving prescription medicines ran out.

Chapter Fifty-Five

By late Thursday afternoon the various patrols along the west side of Corbett reported a moderate increase in the number of attempted incursions. Most expected a surge of river crossings over the first week or two followed by a gradual decline as the grim and dark harvest cut deeper into the fields of humanity. The people they did encounter swam or floated across the river on assorted debris, all fleeing the horrors of the city. Few were armed and all of them were filthy and desperately hungry. For safety reasons, patrols were warned to remain a safe distance away from any outsiders in case they were sick or carried hidden weapons. No one in Corbett had any unusual illnesses and they wanted to keep it that way.

They were mostly just regular people who had somehow managed to escape the cruel mobs. They stayed hidden in the city as long as possible clinging day after day to their hope that some kind of government rescue would occur. They eventually ran out of food and grew thirsty. Fearing help would never arrive, they finally fled across the river. It was the only direction to go. Terrified of the increasingly violent gangs and the prospect of starving to death, desperation made them move out. Nearly all had reached the river by walking fast through the city during the moonless nights because gangs controlled the streets during the daytime. For the first few days, once the sun set total darkness prevailed. In an odd twist, that now meant safety, yet few took advantage of it because they remained burdened by an ancient deep fear of the dark.

Very few crossing the river were women or girls and at first no one knew why. Days later when the organized attacks began, they would understand the reason. It was so sad and was simply never discussed again.

A few joyous families had reached what they thought was the safety of the river. It was heartbreaking to turn them away, but all were forced back across the river without further discussion. Many on patrol suggested to the increasingly dirty and tattered people that they forage on wild greens and blackberries while heading south toward the large farms surrounding Sandy, Eagle Creek or Estacada.

As soon as the last remnants of state authority stopped functioning, the violent criminal gangs rose to the very top levels of the new violent society and their rise to power happened literally overnight. The ones at the top quickly ate, drank, smoked, raped, killed and injected their way through the stinking and rotting carcass of Multnomah County. In Gresham and nearby northeast Portland well-organized predominately Mexican street gangs kicked in door after door in an indiscriminate rampage seeking food, drink, drugs and women. They often attacked in groups of twenty or more. Houses guarded by armed citizens had no chance as the brave occupants eventually ran out of ammunition. This was the source of the non-stop distant gunfire reported by the Corbett patrols. The festival of fear and terror ran during the daylight hours and began anew each morning at sunrise. The darkness offered only a short-lived sanctuary.

WAR

Chapter Fifty-Six

This Sunday morning started out differently than others. There would be no church services this morning. Instead of hymns what people listened to throughout East County was the sounds of gunfire as the stronger of the hundreds of newly formed criminal kingdoms saw their looted supplies dwindling. In this perverted and final competition for control over the city's rapidly decreasing resources, the weaker gangs were extinguished and the stronger ones were made more powerful.

By mid-day Wednesday, the Multnomah County Inverness County Jail, whose ever-growing all-male population had now reached sixteen hundred inmates, ran out of food. The jail had transferred all its female inmates downtown several months ago to make room for the recent upsurge in male detainees. By Wednesday they had gone five days without a single supply delivery and the situation was getting increasingly tense because by Tuesday, the jail was running low on guards.

Early Thursday morning the few remaining guards, acting in what they believed to be a noble and humanitarian Christian gesture, opened the jail doors depositing hundreds of desperate, hungry and in many cases very violent criminals onto the streets of northeast Portland. The guards felt they simply couldn't stand by and watch them starve to death in their cells, although one particularly heinous murderer was intentionally left locked up in his cell. He died in his dark sweltering room Friday after drinking all the water in his small toilet. His decayed remains were eagerly worked over by rodents. Insects encouraged to breed by the hot summer air eagerly consumed the rest of him. His skeleton rested on the floor of his cell and remained unseen for decades.

Most of the freed men scattered, but by 10:00 a.m. a hard-core group of over 500 starving souls aware of the perilous state of affairs throughout the city, held a mass meeting in the jail parking lot. They formed what they called the Inverness Army and declared war on the city's remains. Their goal was dominance and power, but after being cooped up in jail spending the last two days with nothing to eat, their immediate objectives were food, drink, drugs, guns and women. After a late-morning freedom-filled Fourth of July rampage along Halsey Street they turned right on 136th and tore apart the upscale Glendoveer neighborhood. It was cleaned out by noon.

This ad hoc gathering of mostly black and Hispanic gangsters emerged from their morning and afternoon festivities having met all five objectives. They were now armed, drunk, stoned, in possession of a handful of young women and they were now very well fed. Aware the food and booze they had gathered into their flotilla of shopping carts would last only a few more days, they chose to wage what would become the final war of conquest over the many three-day old weaker kingdoms suddenly reigning supreme over the many East County neighborhoods now being stripped bare and burned.

The small-time street gangs that had quickly taken over in East County consisted of splintered sets of the Tortilla Flats, 18th Street, Surenos, Nortenos, and the toughest gang of them all: them all: the Trece. The Trece had grown fast in the past two years fueled by drug profits and was allowed to grow powerful due to recently reduced law enforcement funding. The Trece dominated the drug sales action along the MAX line and along Stark Street. Dozens of murders and countless drive-by shootings had occurred in East County during the past year and most were credited to this one violent gang. As tough as they were, they were no match-up for the Inverness army of thugs. By Saturday the Inverness Army had either killed or recruited nearly all nearby competition with the exception of the Trece, which remained powerful south of Burnside.

By Monday, the Inverness Army exerted their unquestioned authority over 30 square miles of Northeast Portland. Deep into Gresham, their new conquests quickly fell one after another. The few black gangs, such as the Hoover Criminals 74, the Kerby Block, the Columbia Villa Crips and the Rollin 60s had been largely squeezed out of the mostly Mexican dominated Gresham and Troutdale area. The black gangs clung to power west of I-205, but the Inverness Army was not concerned about territory to the west and wisely left them alone. Their ever-expanding authority was now clearly identified by their black spray painted symbol: IA, for Inverness Army. They skipped few streets as they fanned out waging a brutal and relentless block-by-block bloody battle across what was left of the eastern part of the county.

Through ruthless conquest their territory expanded rapidly. By Tuesday, July 9th, they reigned supreme over a smoldering ruin stretching from I-205 to the west, the Columbia River to the north and all the way to 201st Street to the east. It seemed as though nothing could stop them.

Just as they were picking up steam, resource depletion interfered. They were once again running low on food. The southern border of this growing kingdom meandered between Division and Stark. This is where for many days to come the fiercest fighting over the remaining food, drugs, alcohol, women and gasoline would be waged.

The brutal skirmishes along Burnside weakened both the Inverness Army and the long-established street gangs most of whom originated in California. The IA had peaked at around 800 members before starting to decline as they suffered terrible losses and defections during violent fights and near-constant heated battles. Dozens of Mexican gangbangers, many of whom were in custody facing deportation defected, rejoining their sureno companeros who controlled much of the turf south of Burnside, but not the MAX line itself, which was considered strictly Trece turf. Dozens more freed black gangsters and drug dealers defected as well, hooking up for security with their Rollin 60s and Hoover crews west of I-205.

By July 10th, a truce was finally reached establishing the southern extent of their increasingly fragile one-week old empire to territory north of Burnside. The conquest of the remaining still-undemolished lands to the east would be granted to whomever moved in quicker, and the Inverness Army wasn't about to be left behind. The leaders of this army left about 200 men guarding key intersections along their newly negotiated southern border while the remainder joined with several hundred fresh new recruits and prepared for war. The incursion east started at first light.

Chapter Fifty-Seven

The attack on Troutdale began on July 11th, early Thursday morning. Just before daybreak a few men piled into stolen trucks filled with weapons, ammunition and supplies but most walked right up the middle of Glisan from 162nd where they had assembled and prepared the previous afternoon. Ninety minutes later they reached $242^{nd,}$ and they divided into two deadly groups as previously planned. They struck fast and furiously. Screaming was soon heard from within hundreds of once-happy homes. Fires from the unfolding rampage would soon ignite, burning all day, and long into the following night. The smoke and flames from their terror were visible for miles around. The Corbett patrols watched from the safety of their side of the river wondering what was happening far in the distance.

One group of about 175 marched into a once-beautiful suburban neighborhood called Cherry Lane. They warned the few remaining residents to get out immediately. Most remaining residents fled through the nearby golf course and scattered, never to be seen again. A few tried to defend their homes but within one hour the entire area was utterly defeated. Most homes were looted and then set ablaze. Shopping carts were filled with booty. Trucks were loaded up and moved out. The same story was repeated in neighborhood after neighborhood as the larger contingent of the criminal army smashed the western side of the small livable city apart. Resistance in a few areas was fierce, but most people fled or surrendered according to those who fled and were intercepted by the Corbett militia. Those fleeing across the river were directed south and ordered out. Those who remained behind surrendered to the IA and were shown no mercy.

The Inverness Army suffered considerable losses but by nightfall all of Troutdale west of 257th Avenue was completely ransacked and in flames. The attack left hundreds of bodies strewn along streets, blocking sidewalks, and decaying into dust in burned-out homes. Some were gruesomely displayed in once well-trimmed but now dried out and yellowed front yards.

The survivors among the conquering army had little to celebrate other than a fresh new supply of booze and stolen clothes. This epic battle had nearly depleted their remaining ammunition leaving them perilously low with less than 2,000 rounds. Scrounging through abandoned houses boosted that to 5,500 rounds but it was all in a confusing array of assorted calibers. However, it would take hours for the intoxicated former jail inmates and their heavily tattooed new eager recruits to assemble and properly distribute this ammunition among the now fashionably dressed soldiers. For now it was party time.

The soon-to-be hungry and exhausted survivors of the Inverness Army would wake up Friday not only suffering harsh hangovers, but also counting their losses. They suffered 42 dead and another 55 seriously wounded. They did gain a few dozen new recruits as they pillaged their way east from 242nd to 257^{tth} Avenue, however many defected to Gresham, joining with the Trece and more than a few fled south and disappeared.

When the criminal soldiers of the IA finally sobered up the next morning their newly self-promoted commanders knew they possessed only enough food to last a week. Their remaining soldiers were ordered to invade deeper east. By late Friday afternoon the bloodthirsty army had smashed and burned its way to Troutdale Road. However, a terrific fast-moving firestorm happily fed by the relentless hot winds threatened them from the rear, forcing them to move deeper east. The army rested until 9:00 a.m. Saturday morning before making a final push to the Sandy River. This final half-mile push from Troutdale Road to the river proved easy since nearly all residents who could had fled overnight, fearing the advance of the army and the flames.

Accurate news was impossible to get, but the people of Corbett found out through a few fleeing survivors that Troutdale was defeated and subdued by the IA in a three day long episode of violent pillaging. More than a few homeowners chose to fight rather than flee, but waging war alone against a highly motivated and hungry army of thugs proved futile and the city was now in their hands. A 48-hour non-stop perverted party featuring the most debased debauchery imaginable was well underway. The few remaining residents of Troutdale were the featured entertainment.

When the party died down, the final city before reaching Corbett had been stripped bare and burned by the wave of sadists. The damage they delivered was much like what they delivered to all the other places they had pillaged on their relentless and cruel march east. As the flames around them died down, they could see there was only one direction to go for more food: across the Sandy River. They knew Corbett would be watching, so they carefully planned a surprise attack.

The final battles to control the rapidly decaying carcass of the once-mighty American Way of Life were repeated throughout the nation. Similar battles were occurring, they later found out, throughout the world. As terrifying and brutal as things were in Multnomah County, the situation in most other larger cities was far, far worse. News from outside the Portland metro area would be many months in coming but for now, as far as news was concerned, the residents of Corbett knew only the ominous sounds of gunfire. It relentlessly banged out a steady symbolic call of death as if it was The Four Horsemen's version of the Morse code telling anyone listening that they were now coming.

Chapter Fifty-Eight

By Saturday morning, the twelfth day after the disaster struck, the militia patrolling the western boundary of Corbett heard less gunfire from across the river. They still saw the flames flickering on the horizon, but it was just more of what they had seen since the disaster first struck, and by now they thought little of it. If they had known what terrors lay waiting to attack them from across the river they would have beefed up patrols, but for the next few days, each shift was the same: scattered arrivals of desperate and starving people who continued to be intercepted, interviewed and turned away.

Fantastic tales of a crazed criminal army marching east out from Portland through Gresham were largely dismissed as the exaggerated rants of starving people frightened out of their minds or the incomprehensible babblings of the flat out deranged.

By the morning of Tuesday, July 16th, the patrols along the Corbett side of the Sandy River had become eerily monotonous. The same men and a few women patrolled the same hills and farms, and mostly during the same times. The shifts were exhausting 12-hour ordeals with no days off. Each day the roving patrols were expected to work a few hours on farms getting ready for summer planting or picking fruit. They were getting increasingly exhausted and a few risked permanent banishment or worse by sneaking catnaps during the mind-numbing boredom of the midnight to noon patrol shift. Rumors were rampant, but none were caught. The Corbett militia was getting more and more complacent.

The Inverness Army knew when the foot patrols were about to arrive by the river and where they went next. They watched where the bulk of the forces patrolled: down river from Dabney State Recreation Area, starting not far upriver from the remains of the Stark Street Bridge. They saw few patrolling in the east near Larch Mountain and only a few dozen at a time patrolled upriver east of Dabney.

They observed the militia closely, taking cautious note of its strength and size. A few cautiously swam across the Sandy River, crawled up the embankments, and returned with more valuable information about the citizen militia. By Tuesday morning none of the trespassers had been seen and their existence remained unknown to those in Corbett.

At noon Tuesday, Jimmy and his daughters along with Joseph, his son, and Bill started their 14th consecutive noon to midnight patrol covering a meandering two or three mile long stretch of hilly treed territory between the Sandy River and SE Gordon Creek Road just across the river from Oxbow Park. This was their area of responsibility. As usual they spread out keeping a ten-yard distance from one another as they silently walked through the woods and across fields along the east side riverbank. They varied their times somewhat but their path varied little, and by now it had become well worn and easy to walk in the brightening moonlit night.

Another group of six well-known local men patrolled to the west of them between the river and Hurlbert Road. They consisted of two Vietnam veterans in their early 60s: Pat O'Malley and Steve Nelson who daily patrolled with four strong and fit young men in their mid-20s: Chris Saunders, Corey Anderson, Joe Tweedy and Kyle Howard. All six were recreational target shooters and autumn hunters but the two older men were experts in long-distance rifle shooting and Pat, who led the group, was capable of etching into a paper target a red circle of paint out of a bright thumbtack at 200 yards. Chris and Kyle were fearless Afghanistan war veterans and each had experienced plenty of combat. Patrolling the east side of the river's 'S' turns: three, mile-long loopy turns in the river, were the responsibility of these two groups. At 12:30 p.m., as they were just starting their increasingly routine patrol near the very end of SE Stevens Road, Chris made a grizzly discovery.

Chapter Fifty-Nine

The Inverness Army had compiled considerable information about the Corbett militia during the past five days. Most of the information was gathered by secretly observing the movement of the patrols from across the river.

Considerably more information was picked up when three thugs silently crossed the river early one morning and invaded an isolated farmhouse along SE Stevens Road. They had been observing the Hoffman's farm for two days and knew the owner lived alone. The 58-year-old was a stubborn old man who refused to join the militia claiming he could defend his farm alone, as he had done for decades.

They entered his house through the open front door at 9:45 a.m. on the sunny Tuesday morning of July 16th and quickly tied him up in his kitchen. Brad Hoffman was 6'1" and weighed over 350 intimidating pounds, but at the frightening sight of the handgun placed under his fat chin by the smelliest of the smiling home invaders he offered no resistance. They stayed for nearly two hours before returning across the river and heading back to Troutdale. They drank Brad's hot coffee and ate well during their informative two-hour visit. They questioned Hoffman in a friendly manner for about a half an hour then they got serious and busy. A washcloth went in his mouth to silence the coming screams while they went to work torturing this lone farmer. They snipped and sawed away for over 90 minutes, occasionally pausing briefly to ask a few key questions. He tried in vain to scream ever louder with each cut of the saw and each click of the shears, but the cloth restricted his breathing and muffled his voice. Every few minutes they would remove the cloth and ask another question.

A red pool spread wide on his kitchen floor as he offered more and more useful information. Desperate for an end to his suffering, he gladly told everything he knew as his sizable body was slowly twisted and pruned apart piece by piece. He watched in horror while his various parts were unceremoniously paraded across his living room by an ever-grinning, green-eyed assistant who each time toed open his screen door and tossed the dripping portions out on his front porch.

Through this cruel and sadistic interrogation the Inverness Army discovered a wealth of information. They discovered older male teenagers were undergoing six hours a day of basic fitness and combat preparedness training on the high school soccer field under the guidance of their PE teacher, Mr. JP Lenet. He was a retired marine sergeant and veteran of Desert Storm. They found out that all roads into Corbett were impassible to vehicles due to fallen trees, rockslides or solid fixed defense positions. The farmer told them the Corbett militia expected an attack near the blown bridges at some point, but were in the dark about when or what form it would take. The men wielding the pistols and pruning shears also learned that the Corbett Country Market, which was still stocked with dry goods, was where the bulk of the common weapons and ammunition was stored and this would be their first target.

Most importantly, he confirmed their belief that the shift changes for patrols was at noon and midnight meaning from about 11:45 a.m. to 12:15 p.m. and from 11:45 p.m. to 12:15 a.m. the river was largely unpatrolled. They also now knew a curved section of the Sandy River near Oxbow Park was generally unguarded and that is exactly where they chose to make their incursion into Corbett early that afternoon.

Their plan was simple and, they thought, clever. They would initially sneak 40 well-armed men across the Sandy River in groups of ten in a diversionary action. This smaller group would cross the river on the I-84 Bridge just north of the collapsed Troutdale Bridge over a two minute period starting around noon. Their objective was to fake an invasion from the northwest. This group would then firmly establish themselves on the north side of the crumpled rail tracks south of the freeway near Lewis and Clark State Park firing upon anyone they see. The goal was to draw as many of the Corbett forces in that direction as possible thereby allowing a larger group of invaders crossing near Oxbow Park to safely enter and move into town.

The primary invasion force consisted of over 300 men. They planned to wade across the shallow and slow-moving Sandy from Oxbow Park at 12:15 p.m. during the end of the shift change period then quickly move north to SE Gordon Creek Road. They expected no opposition as they moved up the hill from the river. Next, the plan was to pierce directly into the heart of Corbett by way of SE Evans Road and they were all eager and excited to get going. The distance from the river crossing to the Country Market is about two and a half miles and they planned to arrive in the very heart of Corbett in about 45 minutes. Thus far, as they cut their way across East County, they had encountered little significant resistance, and they expected an easy time here as well. But they couldn't possibly anticipate meeting up with the Hancock and Lee patrol near Hurlbert Road and none of them could've imagined O'Malley's unbelievable accuracy.

Chapter Sixty

The fake attack began on July 16th at noon, right on schedule. A static patrol along the river near Lewis and Clark Park spotted about 40 men moving east crossing the I-84 Bridge. The group ran in small groups moving south to the railroad tracks next to Lewis and Clark Park, quickly setting up their positions and opening fire on anyone they saw. Generally a few men with rifles were stationed high up on Broughton's Bluff offering a bird's eye view to the northwest, but at noon there was no one positioned there. By 12:04 four Corbett militia members had been shot. Two of them were killed, including Scott Pritchard, a well-liked husky man who had served as an army reservist for many years and Mike Houston, a cantankerous retired Coos County deputy sheriff who rarely smiled or slept and had been on duty since 10:00 p.m. the previous evening. Both remained where they fell. The two wounded crawled to safety but would suffer in pain waiting nearly an hour until they could be evacuated.

A scooter messenger stationed in the park immediately rode up the hill into Corbett to announce that an attack was underway. It was seven miles, but with no traffic he made it in eleven minutes. He reached the Country Market at 12:18 "We're under attack!"

he excitedly yelled. "Dozens of men are attacking over the freeway bridge. They're coming from Troutdale! We need help now!"

Thirty-five men were sent as reinforcements including twelve recent high school graduates. They were quickly summoned and stuffed into three heavily overloaded and teetering pick-up trucks. At 12:33 they left lumbering toward the park to help repel what everyone believed to be the long-awaited major invasion. The fake attack was working perfectly. The main invasion force near Oxbow Park had already started moving across the river miles to the south eighteen minutes earlier.

The Chief and other community leaders decided early on that the Corbett militia didn't have enough volunteers to support the luxury of a second interior perimeter patrol. They had approximately thirty square miles to protect but only 600 capable men and women under arms, with another 500 at various levels of training under Mr. Lenet. That meant only 300 were on duty at any one time. In reserve, 150 reinforcements were assigned to remain stationed near the Country Market, allowing only 75 of them on duty at any time. Many of them were out training on the high school soccer field or helping Mr. Lenet. With 50 assigned to man fixed posts such as the Vista House and Lewis and Clark Park, this left only 200 at a time out on foot patrol. They were scattered far apart well beyond each other's voice range patrolling across the many hills and valleys making up this lush rural farmland. The number of militia members was growing daily as Mr. Lenet graduated more and more out of training and into armed defense assignments, but it was still considered insufficient to repel a major invasion.

Most of the people living on the bluff, as many locals called it, were too young, too old or too unfit to serve in the militia. Many had never fired a weapon and anyone Mary Lou categorized as unfit for combat was allowed to serve in a variety of other positions such as medic, remain working on farms, or continue training with Mr. Lenet until he thought they were ready to fight. A sense of urgency prevailed at the high school as the training moved forward at a frenzied pace while everyone sensed an unknown danger loomed ever nearer.

The Inverness Army couldn't have planned it better. They knew only 12 armed men and women patrolled the soft underbelly of Corbett on its southwest side. Through the trees they had seen the two overweight older men carrying the long, funny-looking rifles and laughed. They had no idea what those two heavy-set old men could do with their odd-looking Soviet Dragunov SVDS sniper rifles.

None of the defenders were near the river as the lines of invaders held their weapons and ammunition high and dry crossing the waist-deep water. By 12:40 p.m. the primary invasion force was marching up the hill on the east side of the Sandy River. They brought weapons, all their ammunition, a growing hunger and a sense of eager desperation, but no food. They were arrogant, optimistic and undisciplined: a fatal combination, which led them to become noisy and sloppy as they moved en masse up the hill.

Chapter Sixty-One

Chris and Kyle were always sharp and alert, listening to everything including the birds and the ever-present whistling winds. If something was amiss it was in the changed tones coming from the trees and fields. They rarely spoke a word and walked ten yards apart, but could communicate freely with the hand signals they had mastered in the high, dry desert mountains of Afghanistan.

At 12:20, as they approached the farm of Brad Hoffman, Chris stopped dead in his tracks staring in the direction of Hoffman's farmhouse. He wondered why would there be so many crows flocking to his front porch. He hand signaled to Kyle to move with him directly toward the front of the house, but to increase their separation at 20 yards apart. There was only one thing that could attract so many scavengers. Chris had seen it before. Kyle silently signaled to the other four to set up positions watching closely for anything and anyone.

Pat and Steve immediately fell deep into the tall grass and keenly searched in all directions peering deep into the bushes and trees through the scopes of their powerful rifles. Corey and Joe, who preferred to be called 'Tweedy', moved apart and disappeared into a nearby copse of trees and silently listened and waited while nervously gripping their rifles and sweating buckets in the humid 85-degree early afternoon heat.

The men on patrol had no electronic communication and when Chris approached closer he desperately wished he could contact the Lee and Hancock team patrolling a mile or two to the south. When he finally reached the edge of the front porch of the Hoffman house he started to fear for his patrol; in fact, he started to fear for everyone.

"Oh my God! Oh my God! Oh my God!" He repeatedly whispered over and over again to himself as his heart rate suddenly lurched to 160 beats per minute.

Hoffman, or, more accurately, what remained of him, was displayed in dozens of pieces still dripping between the 2x6 planks of his front porch slowly turning the dirt below a deep dark red. The crows fled momentarily, but would soon return to obediently perform nature's required clean-up work, leaving the scraps for the town mortician. Knowing Brad lived alone all Chris could do was slowly back away, regroup with his friends, and plan what to do next.

"Kyle, you're the fastest runner here. I think you should go now. Run to the General Store and get some help," Chris suggested, fearing this could be much worse than an attack on one farmhouse.

Corey had been running and training daily before the disaster and was actually the fastest runner in the group. He spoke up, "Hey guys, sorry Kyle, but I really think I can make it there faster."

Pat held up his left hand, "Corey, we need you with us. You're bigger and if we need someone with strength ..."

Corey looked at Kyle.

Kyle nodded approvingly.

"Fine. You do it then," Corey grudgingly agreed.

"See you guys in a few," Kyle replied. He started running fast up the hill, planning to meet up with them again as soon as he got back. Kyle was carrying more than 40 pounds of weapons and gear, but he had trained for years running with 60 pounds so he moved fast.

Chris quickly briefed the others once more on hand signals and pulled out a few small tan plastic cases. He passed them around. They all stopped a minute to paint their faces and hands slate green, mustard and black as they had done countless times before.

"Let's hook up with the Hancock and Lee group right now," ordered Pat. They spread out and started walking east without further discussion.

In fifteen minutes Kyle reached the intersection of Bell Road. He would have reached it a few minutes sooner but he was carrying a holstered handgun plus his AR-15. Eight fully loaded 30-round rifle magazines added considerably to his load. He planned to jog the final two miles into the center of Corbett, but immediately after reaching Bell Road the rumble of truck engines moved down the hill toward him and he stood in the middle of the road waiting to greet it.

It was a sound made by internal combustion engines and other than an occasional scooter buzzing by he hadn't heard that sweet sound in weeks. He found it strange and waited in the middle of the street for the trucks to reach him. The three trucks rounded the curve overloaded with armed and excited men speeding toward Lewis and Clark Park where an attack was underway.

"Stop! Stop!" Kyle excitedly stood in the road jumping up and down and waved for them to stop, but they ignored his appeal and blasted right by waving at him as they roared through the historic Springdale district.

Three scooters followed close behind each carrying a passenger.

"Stop! Stop, Dammit!" Kyle tried once again.

All three scooters carrying two people each slowed down, then stopped to find out why Kyle was still jumping up and down in the middle of Bell Road frantically waving his arms.

"We had an attack! Hoffman's been killed. He was torn apart by someone! I think there might be a big attack about to start. We could use some help."

"They're attacking the Lewis and Clark Park right now!" Jesus, one of the three operators told Kyle. "Dozens of them, all at once. Like a half-hour ago."

"This could be the big one." Kyle said.

"Jesus and I'll ride back up and tell the Chief," said Chelsie Morris, his passenger, who spoke for the small scooter group. "You guys all ride back down to the park."

The two scooters immediately buzzed down the hill.

"Okay, I'm heading back to my patrol," said Kyle. "They'll need my help pretty soon, I'm afraid."

"See ya," replied Chelsie, "I'll tell the Chief what you found. Please be careful."

He immediately started running back to SE Stevens Road to meet up with his patrol. He ran faster this time and at 12:45 he reached the Hoffman farm. He saw hundreds of crows hungrily flocking about, but no sign of his patrol. Then the softly echoed explosions of gunfire came from about a mile to the east. It was unmistakable. He instantly sprinted through the fields and woods in that direction, running faster than he ever had before.

Chapter Sixty-Two

The three hundred desperate armed men crossing the Sandy River had Mother Nature on their side. The spring thaw started earlier than normal and the river level had dropped considerably. None of the men crossing got wet above their belts and all their firearms remained dry. It took a little longer than planned for everyone to wade across but by 12:35 they all made it. They gathered along the east bank to check their gear and drain water from their shoes. Within a few minutes they were marching north in an undisciplined yet very dangerous 100-yard long disorganized mass. Their shoes, socks and pants were still soaking wet and they were growing hungrier, but their spirits were high as they trudged along SE Gordon Creek Road joking about having lunch at the very center of town by 1:30 p.m.

"Almost lunch time!" One of them shouted. "Comida, cervesa and senoritas! Oh yeah! What else is there, amigos?"

"These country cracka's all have some fine sauce stashed. Ah be so thirsty ah cain't wait!" said another.

"Den it soon be cracka' hoe's fo all da bro's!" Another chimed in with a crazy grin as he started dancing obscenely in the middle of the street inches away from another man, both eagerly bumping and grinding away on each other.

A chorus of laughter followed by a scattering of crude remarks rang out in response as the colorful mob happily marched up the road.

The others in Kyle's patrol didn't expect him to return for quite awhile. Therefore they moved east fast, hoping to join forces with the Lee and Hancock patrol they knew were located somewhere across the river from Oxbow Park. It was an easy fast walk and by 12:45, as they approached SE Rickert Road from the west, shots were heard coming from a short distance down the hill.

The Lee and Hancock patrol had just started out. As usual they headed down SE Evans Road, planning to move into the woods and begin another routine near the river.

"Where're all the birds?" Alison commented to no one in particular, "usually I hear them squawking and singing when we start our patrol. I always look forward to it. I wonder where they all are?"

"Yeah, it seems mighty quiet today," her dad replied. "Maybe they found something to eat. If there's a dead animal nearby, they'll find it. But who knows?"

At 12:40 they found out. When they rounded the corner past SE Rickert Road they heard laughter and the chaotic yet oddly rhythmic drumbeat of feet clomping up the road from the river. Then there was more loud laughter. Much nearer.

"Joe, stay with me behind the guardrail. You four go hide up there! Get ready to fire as soon as you hear my first shot!" Bill quietly hissed as he pointed his left index finger up into the forested area north.

They fanned out and hid themselves among the fallen trees and underbrush that grew thick along the upper side of the road. Joe and Bill hid on the west side of the road near the guardrail and the others climbed up the embankment into the woods to the east.

It was now 12:44.

"It's almost show time," Joe whispered to Bill.

Bill nodded, "It's a small battalion!" he whispered to Joe.

Alison bravely whispered to Kelly, "I'll move deeper down the road and hit the ones in the rear. They'll think there are more of us that way."

She moved away from the road then headed down the hill and through the woods, frightened like never before. She had fired thousands of rounds while training with Chris McClanahan and knew how to shoot in a combat situation, but this was nothing like what she expected. It was absolutely terrifying. After quietly moving through the woods for several minutes, she hid trembling behind a thick recently fallen tree. She had a perfect view of the road and waited to fire.

No one asked this mob to turn back. The only requests to get out would be in the form of fast-moving lead. The four of them had spread out quietly, waiting fifteen to twenty yards deep in the underbrush until the first of the invasion force was about to pass. Ammunition was scarce. Each shot had to count. They carefully divided up the targets as well as they silently could. All six started aiming. They didn't wait long.

Bill fired first as planned. The other five instantly fired next. Alison hid alone, bravely shooting at those near the back of the force. All six carefully sniped away from each side of the road firing down the hill at their stunned targets, all taken by complete surprise. Within the first five seconds at least twenty-five men were lying dead or dying in the road. As each second passed more fell. Many more were injured. Blood flowed down the hot pavement in bright burgundy rivulets. These men would be shown no mercy. The invasion force was stunned and decimated. They spun into a wild panic leaving the dead and wounded in the road where they dropped. A few fled up the steep hill and into the trees on their right. All of them became easy targets and within minutes were shot dead by Jimmy, Kelly and Joseph. Others hopped the guardrail to their left scrambling in fear deep into the trees tripping and falling noisily as they moved down the bank and away from the road.

As they scrambled for cover, they poured hundreds of rounds of ammunition into the air and up the road in the general direction of the six defenders, but none hit anyone. Dozens more marching in the rear of the mass of men bolted from the pack in fear, running as fast as they could down the hill toward the safety of the Sandy River. Alison had a perfect view of them as they ran down the road passing between the trees. She picked off many who joined their buddies sprawled out dead on the hot road. A few got away and were never seen again, but by now SE Gordon Creek Road was littered with dozens of dead bodies. When Alison had no more clear targets, she went back up the hill through the trees joining Kelly, her dad and Joseph. Bill and Joe hopped back over the white guardrail aiming down toward the several hundred remaining men who had hopped over the rail. The four saw Bill and Joe looking over the white wooden railing and crossed the road to join them. They had no idea the O'Malley patrol was only a few hundred yards away as they hopped over the rail and moved closer to the attackers.

Moments after the gunfire started it suddenly stopped and the forest grew quiet once again. Pat O'Malley's patrol was patrolling through the trees along the river and heard the shots. They moved fast toward the sounds of gunfire, running straight upriver through the woods between SE Gordon Creek Road and the Sandy.

Pat shouted, "let's go! Move! Move!"

Within moments they saw the movement of men in the distance between the trees. They were about 75 yards away and heading straight at his patrol. Steve smiled at Pat and winked, pointing at two large boulders 10 yards down the hill, "Let's set up there and wait 'til they move closer." They knew every inch of this area.

"No. Let's pick them off right now," Pat replied, knowing what he could do with his rifle.

"30 seconds," compromised Steve, "you first."

Pat nodded in agreement.

They dropped behind the familiar large boulders and prepared to fire. Tweedy, Corey and Chris knew instinctively what to do. Without a word, they fanned out to take positions ten yards apart to the left of the two expert marksmen, completely hidden yet closer to the road. Saunders took a few steps toward the road and almost stepped on Kelly, who had partially covered herself with pine branches. She smiled at Chris and placed her left index finger to her lips. She then pointed 10 yards toward the road signaling to Chris where her dad and Joseph were hidden. She then raised three fingers and pointed where Bill, Alison and Joe were hidden. Those three were completely unaware reinforcements had arrived. All eleven of them were now together. They quietly and patiently waited.

They remained silent and motionless a few more moments until the few hundred frightened men in the trees moved close. They were within 50 yards. Then 40. 30. Still getting closer. The eleven of them desperately wanted to nail them all at once. With such a small defending force, the best they hoped for was to damage them so badly in the first few seconds that they would be forced to retreat. In ten seconds they got their one and only chance.

As agreed earlier, O'Malley would be the first among their group to fire. Pat was proned out peering into the trees from ground level from the left side of the large boulder. Steve was a few feet away doing the same on the other side of the same boulder. The noisy mass of men was fast approaching through the woods several dozen yards away from the road. They noisily crunched away on fallen branches and dried vines. He carefully set his crosshairs on the left eye of a man near the front who had suddenly stopped to stare to his right, in the direction of the road about 20 yards away. Pat took a breath and held it in. Two seconds later he pulled the trigger.

Chapter Sixty-Three

The two truckloads of men finally reached the remains of the Troutdale Bridge at 12:44 p.m. and stopped to disgorge its human cargo. The men piled out. "They came in from over there," a man shouted excitedly, pointing downstream, "we need you guys to set up position along the riverbank. Get going now!"

There was no gunfire coming from the north near the tracks. The defenders headed carefully north along the river. They brought additional ammunition and distributed it to those running low. Runners quickly moved out to re-supply the other well-positioned men hidden deep in the forest.

By 12:45 p.m. the diversionary attackers finally stopped shooting.

"They've stopped firing," one of the men quietly said, "they haven't shot a round in several minutes."

"I wonder what they're planning?" replied another.

"Stay alert!" said a third. "Expect anything."

The defenders were all beginning to wonder why such a small group had attacked and wondered further if they had stopped firing because they ran low on ammunition.

At exactly 12:49 p.m., less than an hour after they attacked, they got their answer: the attackers suddenly turned and fled fast, running back to the I-84 bridge. The men and women of the Corbett militia fired dozens of rounds at the fleeing force. At least four were struck by shots fired by distant sharpshooters who by now had positioned themselves high above the park on Broughton's Bluff. The dead remained on the I-84 Bridge where they fell. When it was over the militia believed it had survived its first major attack, but with two dead and more injured they were in no mood to celebrate.

A few minutes later, four brave volunteers ran out to the tracks where the 40 men had been firing and found they had left behind six more bodies, but no weapons or ammunition. The survivors wondered what this assault was all about. Something about this attack wasn't quite right.

"Why move in such a large force only to stop at the tracks?" one young man asked, "they couldn't have moved past the tracks. No way. They must have known they could not get past the tracks with such a small force. Something about this doesn't feel right."

The bodies of the two killed and five of the seven wounded were placed in the back of the trucks and driven back to the town's small fire station, which was serving as an emergency field hospital. Two of the injured had their wounds bandaged and were allowed to remain on duty. One of the two scooters remained behind in case other news developed, but the other one headed back toward the Country Market behind the trucks. No one was aware of the fierce war being waged five miles away. No one had a clue that anything was amiss elsewhere until the third scooter pulled up with the terrifying news about Brad Hoffman.

Chapter Sixty-Four

O'Malley's opening shot hit home, nailing the man precisely where he aimed, but Pat didn't stop there. He already had the next four shots planned out in his mind before the first shot was fired. Within seven heartbeats each had found its mark. Five men were dead within seconds. His accuracy was well known throughout the Gorge, but this performance was absolutely unbelievable, yet there would be only one witness: Pat – and he would never discuss it. He still had 95 rounds remaining, but wanted to go home with some of them so he needed each bullet to count.

Nelson did likewise, just as the invaders returned fire. A split-second after Pat fired, Steve let loose a carefully planned set of three trigger pulls each of which pierced an enemy's chest. He changed position, leaning over the boulder to carefully fire off a fourth, and just before he squeezed his trigger, he suddenly fell without a sound. He was shot in the middle of his forehead and died instantly.

"Oh no!" Pat rushed to his side, "ah, Steve ... no, no, no ..."

Meanwhile, Chris and the others had opened fire, hitting targets with well over half the rounds they fired. Over 100 of the attackers were killed or seriously wounded within five minutes. Dozens more had fled back toward the river. This sudden surprise counter-attack forced the surviving invaders to waste precious ammunition by firing hundreds of rounds wildly into the trees above.

Chris was struck in the left arm by one of them. A bullet tore through his bicep leaving his arm bleeding badly and hanging useless. Alison saw him get hit and went straight to his aid.

"Lie down on your back and don't move," she told him, "I'm going to fix you right up. Stay still, Chris. This will only hurt for a while. Seriously! I said, stay still!"

She cut off the remains of his sleeve with her black automatic Benchmade knife and roughly wrapped the wound with it. She expertly tied his injured arm to the side of his chest with his rifle sling and placed his handgun in his right hand.

"Here. Hold this. I'm now going to dig through your front pockets, so don't you dare move."

She then transferred his three spare handgun magazines from his left front cargo pocket to his right front cargo pocket.

"Chris, this won't be any fun for awhile, I'm sorry. But you can enjoy the pain later and after this is over there will be plenty," she smiled, "but right now you must keep fighting."

She slung her AK over her back, picked up his rifle and scanned the trees for targets. Then she helped Chris to his feet with her free hand.

"Alison, your shirt is torn. It looks like someone ripped out a piece of it."

"I didn't notice that. I fell running down the hill a minute ago. Must have torn it then. I thought I ran into a branch. It felt like someone punched me in the chest, but I got right back up and kept running. It still hurts."

"I don't think you hurt yourself falling. I think you've been shot!"

"SHOT?"

"Yup. You took a hit. Your dad's bulletproof vest stopped the bullet and saved your life. Girl, you're gonna have a nice big bruise to show off."

"Damn it. My shirt's torn. Ruined. I'll look at the bruise later, but I don't think you'll be on the list of people I show it to, no offense Chris. Now let's get moving." She then tugged on his right arm and led him toward the battle.

Kyle ran fast toward the long familiar sounds of battle as it intensified. He ran even faster when he heard it grow louder, as a good soldier always will. He could see his family home to his left and he feared for his mother and younger sister. Hearing the sounds of gunfire coming from near the river, yet unsure exactly where the friendly forces were, he took a chance and ran straight down SE Gordon Creek Road intending to bypass the battle and harass the rear of the invading force. That was his plan, but battle plans rarely work and his would be no exception. As he approached the 90-degree bend in the road the shooting stopped.

He kept running anyhow careful to make as little sound as possible. As he rounded the sharp turn in the road near the river at a full sprint, he ran straight into a scene of surreal carnage. Dozens of bodies were strewn across the road and each provided a dark red stain on the asphalt. There were dozens but he had no time to count. As he quietly walked among them he noticed quite a few still alive and within reach of their weapons. A few were barely breathing with their eyes closed. Several were in distorted positions writhing in pain. Two were on their backs watching him approach with desperate pleading eyes. He did not want to get shot as he walked through them and had to maintain absolute silence, so as he passed through he paused a few seconds at each, silently dispatching them with his combat knife.

After he passed the dead he peered over the guardrail and saw two men in the distance running alongside the river. At he looked closer he could tell they weren't the good guys. Kyle crossed to the center of the road and ran straight to the bottom of the hill. He found a hiding place between two large logs between the river and the road. He aimed his rifle downstream from his position and waited for them to pass. He crouched down quickly, finding absolute silence allowing him to be fully aware of everything around him. A few shots rang out from far away. Unfamiliar voices yelled in the distance. Then the shots intensified anew and moved closer. Terrified shouting began and it grew nearer.

Chapter Sixty-Five

The Inverness Army was shattered. Fewer than 100 men remained in arms and they had no idea how to defeat the defensive positions deeply entrenched along the river downstream from them. They believed dozens of armed men must be hidden among the large boulders and fallen trees. The attackers had no idea it consisted of only eleven highly disciplined and well-trained townspeople.

The invading mob was unruly and leaderless following instructions from nothing other than their incessant primal craving for food, alcohol, women and drugs. They knew food would only be found in the outlying rural areas because the city had been stripped bare, but they were now trapped by a deadly hidden foe. The bodies of their former cellmates were strewn along the highway and throughout the woods and they were scared out of their minds. It had been so easy rampaging across the city but now they were stunned. They didn't know what to do.

From among them, a lone frightened voice cried out the only sane move, "I cain't see 'em but dey goan kill us, dey goan kill us awl … I'm crossin' back 'cross dat rivva and I ain't never comin' back!"

The response was unanimous. Several shouted, "Let's get outta here!" The rest quickly voted with their feet.

As soon as the first few fled everyone started running at once. It was a mass unorganized retreat: every man for himself. Corey and Tweedy saw this and chased after them, running as fast as they could while leaping over logs and scraping themselves as they passed through blackberry vines in their hot pursuit. They paused together about every 50 feet to fire a few times, careful to make each shot count.

Pat got up and moved out, too. He went through the trees and blackberry bushes straight to the riverbank and then, burning with blind rage ran right at the fleeing invaders. He stopped every 20 yards to fire a few shots, each round dropping one man. O'Malley was on fire and just could not miss.

Bill, Kelly and her dad had been huddling together and saw the general retreat. They moved fast, running through the trees and firing, much the same as Corey and Tweedy were doing. Joe and his dad scrambled through the forest firing at any stragglers. Chris, heeding Alison's advice, moved out alongside her trying hard to keep up, while his pain burned brighter and he grew ever weaker. He jogged alongside her firing occasionally at those fleeing while pausing often to place the barrel of his handgun near another wounded man's temple, putting another seriously wounded yet still deadly dangerous enemy out of his pain. He reloaded his handgun several times. Grimacing in pain, he tightly held his handgun between his knees while quickly and nimbly ejecting each spent magazine onto the ground then expertly snapping another home with his good right hand.

It was a complete rout. The fastest among those fleeing reached what they hoped was the safety of the shallow river crossing point as Kyle patiently waited for his moment. The shore was only 25 yards from his position. When the first four started wading across he sighted in on them with his AR-15, gently resting it on a large log. "I see you, but you don't see me. Surprise!" He whispered as he opened fire. All four fell and floated off toward the Pacific Ocean.

Kyle waited for another group to reach the shore and went to work picking them off one by one by one. Bodies began to pile up along the shore. Others shot while crossing floated downriver. More arrived. More were shot. Kyle changed magazines once again and waited for yet more to approach.

After several minutes of non-stop shooting a silence fell along the river. Then a minute later he heard a twig snap somewhere behind yet close. He turned while keeping his rifle aimed.

Joe and Bill appeared out of the forest behind him.

"Hey! Am I glad to see you two! Get over here with me. We're safe behind these big logs and we have a perfect view of the riverbank."

They gladly joined Kyle. Now three defenders hid behind the large logs. A few more remnants of the Inverness Army appeared and not a single one of them reached the river.

The other patrol members soon arrived chasing after a few stragglers. Fifteen final attackers found places to hide and waited. But they were anxious and impatient. In time, one here and another there bravely tried to exit the forest and wade across the river. All were gunned down. Corey, Big Joe and Tweedy went about a mile up river searching for those who fled in that direction. They found five. Within minutes, four were hunted down and shot. Corey, charging out ahead nailed three of them. One of them surprised Corey, leaping at him from behind a thick second-growth tree and locked onto him with his fully tattooed right arm wrapped tightly around his throat. Corey, barely able to breathe, managed to unholster his Cold Steel American Lawman knife and repeatedly stab his attacker in his right thigh until he loosened his chokehold. Corey seized his moment and dropped low, then twisting his body, sprung right back up piercing him with a deep blade thrust to his neck.

The dead attackers were all stripped of weapons, ammunition and anything of value and then bodily tossed into the river. One had a large plastic bag partially filled with several ounces of a white powder and another large bag completely filled with a foul smelling brown powder. They saved it in case Denise Song Bird or the medics could determine what it was and possibly use it as an emergency painkiller.

After about an hour, the eleven remaining defenders spread out cautiously, moving step-by-step, clearing the forest of anyone still alive. Dozens and dozens of dead littered the forest floor. A few were found severely wounded, quietly whimpering in their pain. None of them were spared. Two were found to be playing dead. Soon they were no longer playing.

The militia started at the river and slowly moved up SE Gordon Creek Road, crossing back and forth into the nearby forest, gathering as many weapons and as much ammunition as they could carry. They had to make repeated trips.

Pat paused and kneeled awhile next to his old buddy, Steve.

"Where should we put all these guns?" Kelly said.

"Why not stuff them into these blackberry bushes for now. We can come back later and pick 'em up with a truck," replied her dad.

"Good idea!" Joseph said, "No one will touch 'em but we better hide 'em just to be safe."

It would require several truckloads to carry the newly found weapons and ammunition to town, but for now they had to put them somewhere and they didn't want to leave them lying out in the open. The immediate threat had passed, but one never knows for sure. They finished gathering up the weapons and paused a moment.

"We must first count the dead," Jimmy told the others.

"Whoa," replied Joe sadly. "There must be hundreds."

"Let's do it right now and get it over with." Kyle suggested.

And so they did: 52 were killed along the riverbank across from Oxbow Park. Five were killed upriver. Sixty-two were found lying dead in the road; 126 were counted in the forest west of the road. O'Malley was down to his last ten rounds of ammunition, meaning

90 men were hit by him, or at least that's what Tweedy would tell people for many years to come. The grand total was 249.

Dozens of attackers fled across the river when the shooting started. A few more may have snuck across later or fled into the hills. Patrols would be searching for weeks hoping to find them, but none were ever found. This meant the invasion force was 300 strong, maybe more: a battalion.

When the count was complete, Jimmy and his daughters stood by the road and softly chanted. Each Tuesday afternoon for the next seven weeks they'd pause briefly near the site of the battle and chant once again for those killed in battle.

Chapter Sixty-Six

When the count was over, O'Malley, with tears in his eyes reminded everyone, "There are still ten more hours of patrol remaining. We should get reinforcements in case any survivors are still wandering around. They all need to be hunted down. Plus, we need to get a truck down here and take Steve home." Then he fell once again to his knees and started crying alongside his fatally wounded buddy.

Without radio communication this wish wouldn't happen. No one else knew about the surprise invasion. They were on their own. It was hard to believe that thousands of bullets had just been fired yet no one outside this small group knew because the steep hillside where the battle occurred deflected the sounds into the Troutdale hills west of the river.

It was also hard to believe that only Steve had been killed and only Chris wounded. But these 12 brave souls were prepared to die defending their town. They were also intimately familiar with this land. Other than the Lee family all of them had hiked these hills and valleys for decades, heading down the hill to fish or just spending time outside walking. They knew every rock and tree and they had the high ground. Even the Lees had hiked along the river in the past, and for the past few weeks had done so for 12 hours each day. For nearly all of the invaders, it was their first time crossing the Sandy River.

The members of the two Corbett patrols were very well trained and intimately familiar with the weapons they carried. Most of the invaders carried notoriously inaccurate handguns looted from homes. Many who fell dead were unarmed. The rifles they carried were in a wide, even bewildering assortment of calibers. With the exception of Pat, all 12 militia members carried rifles that shot either .223 or 7.62x39 ammunition and they were all, once again, experts.

Now that the threat had passed, someone had to make the run back to town so Steve and Chris could get evacuated. Everyone looked at Kyle.

Kyle pointed at Corey, "It's your turn, bro."

Corey nodded once and without a word turned and with his pack on his back and his rifle in his hands he started jogging up Gordon Creek Road.

Chris, amazingly, didn't go into shock and was no longer bleeding. He was tough. His arm was badly torn up and he would need medical attention very soon.

Always the deadpan comic, Chris dryly commented through his pain, "I really hope the good looking veterinarian is on duty."

Everyone knew what he meant and a few softly laughed. One veterinarian was a 77-year-old man. He'd been drunk for the past fifty-five years and only worked on cows. People would often joke that he only worked on dead cows.

The other was a young, strikingly pretty 5'9", 25-year-old Native American. Her name was Denise Song Bird and with her long black hair waving side to side she looked gorgeous from a mile away. She was known to be single and a recent college graduate. It was no secret that Chris, half Indian himself, had been trying to meet her since she moved into town last February to set up her animal care practice. He'd been getting nowhere until now and still hadn't had a chance to meet her. The sweet thought of finally meeting her began to ease his pain and if he knew how well received he would be by her he would've smiled even more.

A truck would arrive within the hour. Alison volunteered to remain with Steve and Chris until it arrived. To distance the group from the scene of bloody carnage, Corey and Tweedy carefully carried Steve up the road a few hundred yards as far as SE Evans. They gently placed him on the soft ground alongside the road.

"We really need to get back out there and patrol." Tweedy said. "It's just me and Kyle. Maybe one or two of you could join us. We could patrol along the river … then everyone check back here in an hour. Does that sound good?"

"Yup." Replied Joseph. "Sounds good. How about Joe and Kelly. Maybe you two could patrol with them for a while. Would that be okay?"

"Sure!" Joe eagerly agreed. "So everyone – all of us, will meet back here in an hour. Right?"

"That's the plan." Joseph said. "Let's roll."

Kelly and the others nodded and headed out once again.

The O'Malley patrol went back out without Pat, but they avoided their well-used trails, returning in less than an hour.

Bill, Joseph and Jimmy walked back to the river; saw nothing unusual, and returned in an hour to once again meet up with the others.

Corey returned about an hour later with Rueben Moreland, who was driving his older pickup truck. Rueben, who had lost his lower left leg in a horrible motorcycle accident along Highway 14 in Washington several years earlier, had volunteered to help collect the dead and injured. Prior to the disaster, he worked as an apprentice mortician in Gresham. Since few knew what to do with their dead, he was now serving as the unofficial town undertaker. He and Pat carefully placed Steve in the back and covered him with one of the white sheets Rueben brought along.

"Pat, you wanna ride with Steve, or do you wanna head out on patrol with us?" Corey cautiously asked.

"I'll finish my patrol. Steve wouldn't want me to leave you guys."

"I'll watch over him," Chris said.

And with that, Chris and Rueben hopped into the cab and the truck pulled away in a cloud of dust.

The Hancock group was seen walking down the road as the truck disappeared over the top of the hill. A minute later, Pat, Kyle, Tweedy and Corey walked back into the nearby forest. It was 3:15 p.m. They had all resumed their normal patrols once again.

The O'Malley patrol headed east fast, back into their usual area. By 3:30 they were nearly a mile away.

Chapter Sixty-Seven

After the fighting was over their human sides became apparent. It was odd the way some of them responded.

There are no words to accurately describe the sheer terror of a gun battle, but not a one of them felt the full deep impact of this strange fear until long after the final bullet had been fired.

"I can't believe this," Kelly commented to her dad, yet the others could hear her, "but I'm so tired. I need a nap. Just ten minutes, please. Just ten minutes." It was a phrase she repeated over and over again to everyone's amusement.

Joe and his dad laughed.

Even Bill, who rarely laughed, joined in.

The brave defenders of Corbett knew they never wanted to fight again, but there would be no resting yet.

Several others said they were sleepy too, but none napped. A few in O'Malley's group were suddenly so hungry they tore through blackberry bushes feasting like it was Thanksgiving Day.

To Tweedy's amusement, Kyle and Corey had to be asked several times by Pat to get away from the blackberries and keep walking.

Tweedy suddenly found everything funny. He saw a bird dive at the ground and started laughing hysterically. He saw Corey, the only black member of the patrol, walking, "Dude, anyone ever tell you, you walk funny? You walk like a gorilla."

"And Pat, each time you take a step, your arms jiggle. Damn, that's hilarious! Kyle look! Watch. It's like Jell-O. See what I mean?"

"Don't light Pat up, Tweedy. Bad idea. Not today." Kyle advised him. Pat, generally nice and kind as they come, was known to explode unexpectedly, flashing into wild anger for no apparent reason. If it happened today he would have a good reason. "Seriously, Tweedy. Find someone else to screw with."

"Corey, you're still walking like an ape." He fell to the ground giggling wildly like a young schoolgirl.

"Kyle, did you see what that bird just did again?" More laughter.

Everyone and everything made him laugh. The guys were starting to worry. Something might be seriously wrong with Tweedy. "Maybe we should tie him up. Leave him with Mr. Hoffman." Pat said.

"I bet he'd laugh at that too. Sick bastard." Corey joked. "Hey, you guys want me to just shoot him?"

"I'll do it," Kyle quipped.

"No, guys, I'll do it," Tweedy said and started laughing once again.

And with that, Pat walked over and took his rifle away. Then he took his handgun and stuck it in the back of his belt. "Hey, Joe, I'll carry those awhile if you don't mind. Just walk with us. Laugh quietly if you like. Enjoy the scenery. Smile at the flowers if it makes you happy. But if you get too loud I'm going to shoot you."

By late afternoon, the once rock-solid Tweedy was in very sorry shape: mumbling as he walked, praying softly to himself. Crying occasionally. It appeared as though he had truly lost his mind. As the sun started to approach the horizon he turned quiet and sullen. He continued to walk with his buddies but he refused to speak with anyone. Corey, his best buddy, tried for hours to console him, but was unsuccessful.

By mid evening, just as it was getting dark, he suddenly snapped completely back to normal. "Sorry guys. I really don't know what happened back there. But I'm fine now. Really."

Pat continued carrying his guns but Tweedy took the next two days off during which time he slept almost continuously.

A few, Big Joe in particular, became so sad and depressed Kelly and Joe's father struggled to comfort him yet his crying continued. They all knew killing is wrong, yet they felt no true inner sadness shooting these terrible men. They knew the people of their town would have been treated much the same as Hoffman was by these men if they were allowed in, yet the carnage nevertheless deeply saddened Joe.

What Big Joe and the others didn't know at the time was that the Inverness Army had been capturing, raping, torturing and killing hundreds, maybe thousands, of people in the sickest and most sadistic ways possible for the past two weeks while they mowed and cut their way east. Defeating this army of madmen meant saving the people of Corbett unspeakable pain and suffering far beyond anyone's imagination. As brutal as the afternoon killing was, letting them enter would have been unimaginably worse.

Another thing they did not know was that another attack was coming. The 35 men who fled back into Troutdale across the I-84 Bridge planned to cross the Sandy River near Oxbow Park that afternoon. They were hoping to rejoin their friends who they now believed were enjoying the fruits of another mighty conquest. They had been eagerly and excitedly marching south toward the park since 12:45 p.m.

They walked up Troutdale Road to Division and made their way to SE Oxbow Road, picking up a few old buddies and a handful of new recruits along the way. At 3:45, without pausing, they started wading across the Sandy River, 45 strong. When the first ones crossed the river they climbed over a few large flood-swept logs and saw the bodies strewn everywhere: fifty-two of them rotting away in the hot sun. Bodies were strewn everywhere. People they recognized. Fellow inmates. Their old homies. All of them dead, lying in contorted positions. No weapons to be seen among any of them. The men paused and stared.

Chapter Sixty-Eight

On a hunch, Jimmy suggested they focus their afternoon patrolling along the river near Oxbow Park, where the attack had just occurred. He suggested a static or stationary patrol where the view of the river was best. This meant concealing themselves not far from where the last battle was waged. It was possible that what they encountered earlier was the first wave of another, possibly larger invasion force and if so they had to be ready. The others in the Lee and Hancock group agreed. Plus, they all welcomed the rest, especially Kelly.

By 3:40 they were still just the six of them. Reinforcements had yet to arrive because security patrols were getting beefed up everywhere. Scooters and small motorcycles were buzzing back and forth across Corbett burning up the last drops of Mr. Roger's Range Rover's gas. Mr. Rogers had other things on his mind. He was holed up in his spacious edge-of-the-bluff mansion fully engrossed with eating away at what remained in his once well-stocked pantry. When he was through he would focus on drinking his way through his wine collection, which was how he spent his final days.

The eager and excited scooter riders, mostly high school kids, busily buzzed across town. They sped this way and that in the hot mid-July afternoon happily checking up on everyone everywhere, but other than that one brief post-battle visit the Lee and Hancock patrol was once again entirely on their own.

They sat alongside the logs watching across the river for any sign of movement when Alison suddenly whispered, "Get down. Everyone. I mean right now! Joe-Joe! Snap out of it. Look!"

Another wave of armed men had emerged from the trees and started noisily wading across the Sandy River. This time it was a still formidable, yet much smaller group. They counted about 45 men. Most were armed. All were very dangerous and deadly.

Bill whispered stern commands to everyone, "Pick targets from left to right. Do not shoot until I do. Kelly, you're on the right, you start with the men on the right and work toward the center. Joseph, you start from the left and do the same.

Joseph's teary-eyed son strangely snapped right out of his deep post-battle depression. He instantly returned to normal as soon as he saw the danger. It was strange, even surreal. It was like someone flipped a switch on Joe. He instantly changed right back into his natural mental fight zone. It was nice to have Big Joe back again.

"I'll start with the third from the left," he said as he lined up his sights.

"I'll get those nearer the right," Kelly replied.

Everyone picked targets. Bill had the small leading group. They were approximately 75 yards away. Bill set his sights on the first person, but in his mind planned his next three or four shots. As soon as the first group crossed they saw the bodies of those who had died earlier and paused in shock just long enough for Bill to fire four quick shots. He hit the first three, but missed on his fourth shot. As soon as he fired, so did the others and a fusillade of ammunition rained out of the hillside delivering death to the smaller invasion force. Six rounds at a time, volley after volley, lead rained down on the invaders.

It was over within two minutes. Seven more bodies rested on the shore. Others were struck repeatedly in mid-stream. When it went quiet once again, nearly forty bodies had floated away.

"Whoa," Joe said, as he pointed. The bodies slowly floated downstream.

"Yeah. Whoa," Kelly replied, turning toward him, waiting to see if the crying would start again. Thankfully, it did not.

A scooter rode by minutes afterward. The teenage rider pulled up to them and stopped. She was over a mile away when the firing ended, and was completely unaware that a battle had just occurred.

She smiled at Joseph, "Hi! You guys need anything?"

Joseph smiled back at her a few seconds, "Thanks," he calmly said to her, "but nope. This patrol has everything it needs."

PEACE

Chapter Sixty-Nine

The bodies were summarily and without ceremony stripped of ammunition, leather, boots, belts and anything else that might be of value. Then they were dragged down the hill and tossed into the river. It took hours in the hot sun, but it was an ugly chore that had to be done immediately. Several wheelbarrows were used the following morning to complete the gruesome task. Numerous plastic baggies and neatly folded paper packets filled with assorted white and brown powders were saved and later turned in to Ms. Song Bird in case she might find them useful as painkillers for the injured or seriously ill.

The threat wasn't over yet. Nor would it be for many months as the ever-vigilant people of Corbett continued the 24-hour a day patrols constantly watching for anything amiss. More and more graduated from Mr. Lenet's training sessions and by August, as the number of trained militia members grew, occasional days off were scheduled. By September, patrol duty was reduced to eight-hour shifts, allowing people more time to prepare for winter.

There were no more attacks after July 16th. Several stray souls wandered by now and then in the weeks and months to come and they showed up in worse shape as time passed. All of them were asked what they did for a living in the old times, but none had experience in the critical occupations they so desperately needed. All were turned away, some by force. One refused and paid the ultimate penalty, but most were knocking on death's door when they arrived.

On the morning after the battles, Kelly and Joe walked together to the high school and sat on the soccer field. They talked about the attack and the killings, but they also talked about their future and the future of Corbett.

"Joe-Joe, at some point my mom and dad will need to have a place of their own. I know your family is just fine with us staying on the berry farm, but two families can't live in the same house forever."

"I know. I've thought about that too, but your family really gets along so well with mine. I hope you guys can stay with us forever!"

"Yeah, that would be nice, but that's not the way things work for some reason. I know some of the families who were out of town when the disaster hit will never make it back. Some of them were on vacation outside the country. Some went to Asia or Hawaii and others went to Europe. They'll probably never make it back. There're probably hundreds altogether who disappeared. Lots of houses have nobody living in them. We walk by them on patrol all the time. There are lots of vacant houses around and more will be coming vacant all the time. I know of a few houses that were homes for people who were on vacation in Europe, including that mansion overlooking the Columbia River. If someone doesn't move into that big house by next summer maybe my mom and dad should. Someone should stay in it. It's like a castle. I know the Chief wants us to give everyone who was away a year before people move into their homes and farms, but at some point people should stake a claim or something, at least so their property can be put to some use."

"Yeah, there's a lot of good property available, but it's kinda strange claiming a house someone else owns. Yup, it's a drag. I hope they all do okay wherever they are, but no one's going to be paying house payments or rent anymore," Joe said.

"Maybe we could ask the Chief, you know, he was always into real estate and might have some ideas," Kelly replied.

"Okay, I'm not going to suggest anything Kelly, but I think it might be better if your mom and dad talked it over with my mom and dad first. As far as you and Alison go, well, as far as I'm concerned all of you can stay as long as you want. We really like having all of you around on the farm and my mom and dad aren't so young anymore and can always use the help. I hope you all can stay forever. I really do."

Kelly and Joe stopped talking and stared at each other a moment. Finally Kelly said, "Hey, Joe-Joe, we better get going. People are going to start gossiping about us pretty soon if we're not careful."

"You're right Kelly. You know, you need to talk to Denise Song Bird about helping her with her veterinary work. I hear she's really busy and could use some help."

"I was thinking about that too, but it's only right if I keep doing patrols for awhile, at least until things settle down. But I do want to talk to her and, well, why don't we walk over there right now? Her place is only a five minute walk from here and we could be back to your mom and dad's in a half-hour."

"Okay, let's go. But people are going to see us walk in together and they'll start to talk about us as if we're, you know …"

"Let them," said Kelly as she smiled at Joe, "I don't mind one little bit. Now if we went together to visit with Reverend Golphenee, well, now that just might get people talkin'!"

"Yeah, that would be really funny."

"Whoa!" Kelly said, and they both laughed.

By the time they finished laughing they were half way to Denise's place. Denise spoke with Kelly awhile about her degree and her aspirations and invited her to work a few days a week starting right away, and as much as she wanted once things stabilized. As long as the Chief and everyone else was agreeable to one less person out walking patrol she could start tomorrow.

Kelly and Joe immediately went to see the Chief.

Kelly approached him in front of the store and asked him, "Chief, I have a question. Denise is really busy right now helping the wounded from yesterday and all that. Well, I just talked to her and she could use some help. Would it be okay if I helped her out, maybe just a few days a week? I'll still do patrols the other days and part-time after helping Denise, but she's the only real veterinarian in town and, well, she isn't doing much vet work lately. Mostly doctor work, if you know what I mean."

"Listen, Kelly. After the way you fought during the attack, well, as far as I'm concerned you can do whatever the heck you want. The twelve of you are heroes and Wally at the brickyard is talking about building a memorial stone to honor all of you. Start tomorrow if you like. Start right now! Listen, no one will complain if you decide to pick flowers for the rest of your life!"

All three of them laughed at the Chief's remark.

"Kelly, we'll all need another veterinarian pretty soon and I understand that's what you're going to college for, is that right?"

"Yes it is. Thanks, Chief. I'll go tell Denise right away. But I have patrol starting soon with Joe and everyone and we need to get home. Thanks!"

While Joe and Kelly started to walk back to Denise's place, Joe stopped a moment and smiled at Kelly. "See what I mean, Kelly? You always call the berry farm home now. I've heard you say that a lot lately. I think that's really nice. I like it when you call the berry farm home."

"I like saying it too. I really do, Joe."

"Whoa."

"We can skip the talk about my parents getting their own place, at least for awhile."

Chapter Seventy

The town of Corbett badly needed a dentist and Mary Lou and more than a few others suffered terribly in pain. Very early on the morning of July 20th a tall, handsome and fit-looking white-haired man about 50 years old and an exhausted-looking yet still very pretty slender woman in her mid-40s with short brown hair slowly walked up Bell Road, each carrying a large, black detachable motorcycle side-bag. Both were wearing new blue jeans, thick leather boots and heavy black leather jackets.

Gretchen Simkovic, a beautiful, tall woman with long, dark-brown hair was up early walking along the shoulder of East Bell Road. Her husband, Tom, was away on business when the disaster hit or he might have been walking with her. He had flown into Hawaii on the evening of June 30th, but he might as well have been on the moon. His final text message to her sent the next day read, "I love you G! Even if I have to sail, I'll make it home. Tell Michael and Elizabeth I love m n will c em soon!"

She was slender and solid like a beautiful bronze statue and with a two-gallon wicker basket in hand she moved gracefully along the roadside busily picking wild greens when she saw the disheveled couple cautiously approach.

She hated guns, but, aware of the deadly danger she pulled a handgun out from the bottom of her partially filled basket, and for the first time in her life she pointed a gun directly at another person, "Stop right where you are. Drop any weapons you have. Do it now!"

"I have a pistol. I'll set it on the road," the man shouted as he removed his weapon from its belt holster and carefully placed it on the pavement.

"Now both of you walk far away from it and sit in the middle of the road. Do it now. Start walking. I'll tell you when to stop.

They did as ordered.

"Now! Just sit where you are until others get here. Don't move! If you move I will shoot you both," she ordered.

They remained sitting in the road and quietly waited.

Gretchen didn't move closer. With her gun hanging at her side, she stood about 100 feet away staring at them for about ten seconds, trying to learn what she could by just looking. "Help!!!" She repeatedly screamed into the distance yelling as loud as she could into the silent and calm morning air. "Help! We have visitors!"

Without competition from the sounds of airplanes, cars, trucks, motorcycles, lawnmowers, farm equipment and all the other fuel-powered machines once constantly heard, it was hard to believe how far sound travelled in the now completely quiet air. Within a few minutes several people came running. More soon appeared on bikes. No one had seen these two before. As required, the strangers were instructed to stop and sit on the ground as soon as they were discovered. Then the instructions were to wait until help arrived. After the fierce afternoon battle, all trespassers were considered a threat and questioned about the conditions outside. All reported the same: hunger, destruction and death.

Within 15 minutes, a small crowd had gathered looking at the strangers from a distance. No one came close to them. If anyone looked sick only Denise Song Bird was allowed to get close. If they displayed a weapon after being ordered to sit they were to be shot, although none ever flashed a weapon after being ordered to disarm. It was just too dangerous to risk so the rules were strict. All visitors were presumed to be armed and extremely dangerous. Many were.

After a half-dozen others finally arrived, Gretchen moved a little closer and asked them, "Where are you two from?"

"Gresham," the man replied.

"Are either of you sick?"

"No. We're both just fine."

"Why are you here?"

"We've run out of water and food. We're hungry. Gresham is destroyed. Nothing's left. It's too dangerous to stay there."

"What's in the bags?"

The woman replied, "My husband is a dentist. I'm his dental hygienist. We brought some of his equipment just in case."

"A dentist? What are your names?" Gretchen smiled.

"I'm Karen. This is Stan, my husband. Stan Bohnstedt. Please listen. Across the river nothing's left. Almost everything is completely burned. Rotting bodies are everywhere. The smell is horrifying. It's a nightmare. We can't go back. We'll die there. Please, please help us."

With the ever-present east wind, the people of Corbett were thankfully spared the horrifying stench so many described.

"We made it to the Stark Street Bridge by motorcycle. We couldn't cross so we abandoned the motorcycle and just waded across the river," Stan said, "then we walked up this road."

Karen then smiled and proudly held up a large black leather bag, "These are some of his dentistry tools. It's his emergency carry kit. It's not the same as his office chair, but he can do a lot with what's in this bag."

Word spread fast. By noon the following day, Mary Lou was feeling much better and her painful molar was saved. By late afternoon a long list of patients had signed up at the new office of Corbett Dentistry, founded by Dr. Stanley Bohnstedt, DMD, and his assistant, Karen. It was located for now in a high school classroom, where they also slept, but in October they would get their own place when a suitable nearby home became available. He was busy right from the start and coordinated with Denise Song Bird helping her with many of the countless medical issues she and Kelly had been facing. His fee schedule was going to be different since money was now worthless. People now traded food or ammunition in exchange for his highly skilled dental work, but for those short on food he still couldn't resist accepting silver or gold and over time he began to amass quite a respectable hoard.

Epilogue

The never-ending planning and work required for everyone to prepare for the post-crash life was hard to imagine. Yet, as the weeks passed by, a new normal began settling in and it offered a sense of security and comfort to all knowing they were moving toward a common objective: survival. Most people noticed an improvement in their health. Fewer and fewer showed signs of being overweight and with no one in cars, people stopped and chatted a few minutes as they walked or biked past each other. The town became more and more friendly each day.

Long workdays were the new norm. People toiled hard from sunrise to sunset in exchange for three meals and a safe place to sleep. Children over ten were put to work picking blueberries, which had ripened nicely as the crisis unfolded. They were quickly dried on racks that were laid out on the hot paths of black road asphalt allowing them to be preserved for winter. Blackberries, which grew wild and plentiful, were smashed and made into wine and juice to provide nutrition over the winter and spring months. Cherries and all kinds of fruits were canned, dried and stored underground and in basements all over town.

Livestock was carefully counted and the numbers were frighteningly low. Horse, cattle, llama, and sheep breeding became a high priority. Grass-fed chickens were raised and bred in greater numbers. Groups soon felt safe enough to fish for salmon in the Sandy River, but they did so under armed guard. From the Vista House parking lot, people could still be seen now and then walking along I-84, so for safety and to avoid exposure to disease from the contaminated water fishing in the Columbia River would have to wait. The deer population had to grow, so a moratorium on deer hunting was put into effect until fall. For the next few years, meat would be a luxury.

Breads and grains would soon be gone. Wheat became a distant memory as the last of the flour was baked into the final loaves of bread. Next spring large fields of corn would be planted in hopes of providing some form of grain for people and for animal feed. Acres of barley would be planted and with no fear of getting arrested, a few small backyard marijuana fields started to grow. Tobacco plants soon appeared in greenhouses and when harvested would be worth far more than silver.

A ban on discharging ammunition remained in effect until the immediate threat of invasion was over. This prohibition eventually became permanent, but was relaxed for hunters who also needed to fire a few rounds to properly sight in their scoped rifles. Everyone agreed with this town rule because no one wanted to stop the next attack with stones and arrows. Most ammunition would be reserved for the militia, which meant for hunting, bow making would stage a comeback. Several bow-making hobbyists held classes in the high school teaching all they knew about bow design and construction. In the fall many were very successful bagging deer with their bows.

The adjustment was tough and it hit everyone, but some suffered more than others. The overweight, out of shape like Mr. Rogers had to get fit quickly. He chose not to and instead drank his way through his well-stocked wine cellar and died on Pearl Harbor Day. His 15,000 square foot mansion was appropriated as the new town center. Others saw it as an opportunity and by winter few would recognize them, but not Mr. Rogers. His millions of dollars and rolling acres of neatly mowed grass and trimmed shrubbery were valueless in the new economy. His $500,000 car collection was now worth less than a jar of homemade jam. His safely guarded gold and silver couldn't be traded for a cord of wood. He refused to adapt, sadly clinging to his wild fantasy that things would soon return the way they were.

The sick and injured could no longer get modern medical care and the townspeople did the best they could to comfort them. The elderly worked at home repairing clothes or preparing meals. All that mattered in the new economy was hard work from sunrise to sunset. Little else mattered. Those who were too weak to work wouldn't survive long. Those taking prescription drugs soon found their precious life-giving medicines and supplies forever depleted. They'd never get another refill. Nature would deal very harshly with them.

Denise Song Bird, the veterinarian, was also a student of Native American herbs, remedies and practices. She had an extensive library containing a wealth of valuable information on non-traditional disease prevention and healing. Kelly Lee, who had been interested in veterinary science since she was a child, became a student of hers and eagerly dug into her collection, devouring book after book. In August they opened a clinic operated out of a Corbett Elementary School classroom serving the people as well as their animals. More than a few times they had to dip into the brown powder found in the seized baggies to reduce the pain of the seriously sick and injured. Many patients were transported to and from the clinic on the back of Chelsie Morris's 110 mpg Aprilia scooter. Joe Hancock and Chris Saunders, whose arm had mostly healed by September, often dropped by the clinic offering to help in any way they could. The two men also chopped firewood for Denise and helped prepare her home for winter.

Wood was plentiful and the sound of chopping was heard all summer throughout Corbett, where the winters are cold, wet and very windy. Thousands of cords of wood were needed to properly heat the homes and freshly cut firewood was laid out along hot roads to dry faster.

Jimmy demonstrated how to easily make warm water showers by laying a garden hose full of water in the sun for awhile. After a few weeks of cold showers, everyone was thankful to learn this simple water heating technique, which worked even on cold, yet sunny days.

Everyone needed to learn organic farming techniques, which were practiced by only one Corbett area farm: Dancing Roots. Bryan and Shari, the owners of this highly productive organic farm on Woodard Road, had in years past sold their produce to various restaurants and to individual families, most of whom had waited years on their waiting list before they could enjoy its produce. They had practiced organic farming in Corbett for years and were considered among the best organic farmers in Oregon. Thankfully, they kept their farm and with the help of their close circle of neighbors it once again thrived. They immediately started teaching organic farming methods to the residents of Corbett. As popular as their farm was, this year there would be no paying customers for Dancing Roots. The land was situated perfectly. It faced south on a gentle slope and everything they produced was offered free to anyone who worked their land. They produced plenty to sustain themselves and offered a wonderful example others soon began emulating.

A few residents along the east bank of the Sandy River did exactly that, but as one after another ran out of food, most relocated onto farms where they toiled in the fields. A few who lived along or near the Sandy tried full-time fishing. They intended to trade the fish they caught for fruit, vegetables and other necessities, however it was still July and the main focus was on defense and farming. Some were slow to answer the call to help serve these basic community needs and for them, peer pressure was applied. A few men dropped by their homes and quite convincingly urged them to stop spending so much time fishing and sign up for patrol duty or farm labor. All complied, but some needed more persuading than others.

Deborah, Bryan and Shari held organic gardening classes daily starting on July 18th. The classes were held for three weeks from 5:00 p.m. to 6:30 p.m. in the high school cafeteria. With paper scarce there would be no handouts and few written notes, but important points were boldly noted on a large chalkboard and attendees were urged to repeat and memorize everything they learned.

The three instructors emphasized that variety and diversity was the key to a balanced diet. They drummed it into everyone they saw and the results were impressive. Lawns could no longer be mowed. They were now frowned upon and many were ripped out. Gardens were planted everywhere. Carrots, tomatoes, radishes, squash and potatoes were grown in every available space.

Fields of cabbage, which had been harvested for decades throughout Corbett, were planted once again. A Korean family living along the Columbia River bluff showed the cabbage farmers how to make kimchi as the Koreans do. The taste was challenging for many, but kimchi is one of the healthiest foods known to humanity and in time would become a staple in Corbett.

Several dozen people didn't survive the first winter. Several refused to work with the community by helping on farms or performing other badly needed work. They thought they could make it independently and many failed, starving or freezing during the harshest cold.

On November second, the fuel stored at the Country Market was rationed to farms based on acreage, but the owner cautiously kept 500 gallons in reserve. The Hancock's Happy Berry Farm was allocated 18 gallons. They still had 28 gallons in the Hummer, four in the Toyota and less than one in Joseph's truck meaning they had about 50 gallons to last them forever. The coming crop would be the last one grown with the assistance of internal combustion engines and by the following year all plowing would be performed using human or animal power. One hundred and seventeen scooters and small motorcycles were filled up for the last time in case they were needed for emergencies.

In the middle of next summer Kelly's scooter finally ran out of gas a few blocks from home. She parked it in her family garage and covered it with a white sheet so it wouldn't get dusty. Her prized scooter would never run again.

Law enforcement, or following the rules, as they called it, was backed by a simple system of punishment. Not everyone agreed to this, but all would be subject to it. They voted and it was approved four to one: the ultimate penalty would be banishment. A more severe crime would result in a longer banishment. A less severe crime would grant a shorter banishment. It was a simple system of justice and a removal required a unanimous vote by a jury of seven.

In early October, the Chief found a young man sleeping while on patrol. The punishment was swift and severe: a one-year banishment. Many had argued for the death penalty for such a severe violation, but the people of Corbett had earlier voted to abolish the death penalty, except when applied to outsiders who refused to obey the primary trespassing law, an exception almost everyone agreed upon. A one-year banishment was probably the same since the man was never seen again, but at least the offender had a small chance of survival and it would serve as a very powerful deterrent. For now, the only punishment that would be handed out was banishment with the length of time depending on the severity of the offense. Three months after the collapse it had been imposed only once.

Another man was discovered trying to steal gasoline from a farmhouse garage. The farmer saw him enter the garage, and leave with a full five-gallon gasoline container. He ordered the man to stop and when he ran he shot and killed the thief. The next day a quickly summoned jury exonerated him of any wrongdoing. At least for now, there would be no jails, but a clearer system of justice would eventually evolve. Lawlessness couldn't be allowed so something had to be done to stop harmful behaviors or the town would eventually weaken and constant danger would eventually rise up again. No one wanted that.

The summer session at the high school was cancelled and when classes began once again in the fall few showed up. There were no buses. Students living in far-flung areas either bicycled or they simply didn't travel the distance. Most stayed home gathering food, chopping wood, or hunting. Most teachers lived outside Corbett and were never seen again. Those living in town all showed up. Several parent volunteers asked to teach, but it would soon become apparent that with colder weather settling in, the school would soon be unbearably cold and difficult to operate. Starting in November, the smaller classes were held from noon to four, allowing the rooms time to slightly warm up and giving kids more time to work on farms. The school board voted that only core topics such as math, science, history and English would be taught and the rest of the curriculum would be eliminated. Physical education continued. Football, basketball and baseball games were held, but most organized physical activity involved the mandatory tactical military training for both girls and boys once they reached age 16. If another attack occurred they would be ready.

Books became precious. Once they were worn out they couldn't ever be replaced, therefore they remained inside the growing school library and classrooms where people often sat and read. Pete Roth figured out how to re-charge ereaders with his solar panels, so many of the great classic books people had downloaded continued to be shared.

There were other concerns. After the harvest was over Alison grew deeply troubled about the low amount of food the farms had produced. There would be no bread for at least a year. Meat would remain scarce at least until next year. There were plenty of berries and other fruits, but people needed a wide variety of food to survive and the crops being produced did not provide a full, balanced diet. Alison suspected that the 30 square mile, heavily wooded hillside might not be able to support the number of people currently living there. She was growing more and more uneasy about it. During the month of September she conducted an in-depth sustainability study. She spent nearly 40 hours painstakingly calculating how many calories could be produced on the local farms. She concluded that only 3,000 people could sustainably live on the Corbett bluff and that was only if the harvests went perfectly. She estimated the total number of calories the town could produce and determined that supporting the estimated 4,600 people now living there would be impossible in the long term. Some would starve if the population didn't decline after next summer.

Alison shuddered at what most people were wearing. Many of the high school age kids showed up to work on farms wearing athletic shoes because they didn't own decent work boots. They would be wearing them out soon so a cottage industry of boot making would quickly be needed. She remembered reading in high school that during the Vietnam War people made strong, long-lasting shoes and sandals out of used tires. That might work for a few years, but the supply of tires wouldn't last forever. Plus, younger children would constantly outgrow their shoes. What would they be made from? Leather? Deerskin? Someone would have to master the art of shoemaking and share this skill with others.

Other clothing would eventually wear out and need replacement too. Quite a few of the teenagers only owned one decent pair of jeans. Raids across the river could possibly provide some of their needs but that would only delay the inevitable day when all clothing would need to be made by hand from deerskin, leather and wool. A used clothing store had been set up in a high school classroom where people could donate clothing or take what they needed, but in time it would be depleted. Hunger and clothing would be next year's problems, but for now, with the food saved from before, no one would starve. However, population growth was out of the question and after Alison shared her conclusions with the Chief and he shared it around town everyone was even more thankful they had sealed off the town when the disaster hit. Maybe feeding and clothing even 3,000 people was asking too much, but Alison knew in her heart that for long-term sustainability it was the absolute upper limit.

Nature would take hundreds of lives in Corbett over the next few months and winter would take even more. Hundreds of homes had become vacant and in March the four members of the Lee family moved into one. It was newly constructed and located less than a mile from the Hancock farm. At about 800 well-insulated square feet, it had a small wood-burning stove and would be easy to heat from November to March.

In early October, three months after the disaster, Pete Roth announced that he had finally made contact with someone from the outside. He was spending less and less time on his radio, but he finally found a few hours during their first rainy day and spoke with someone. He had a short conversation with a man claiming to be from the Appalachian Mountains, which is all he would say about his location.

The man said he had made contact over the past several weeks with six others from around the country and it was the same tragic story everywhere: total devastation and unbelievable terror, especially in larger cities. The few he spoke to were in isolated areas: one from Wyoming, two from 'somewhere' outside Los Angeles, two from Eureka, California, and one retired couple from Sweet Home, Oregon. All reported having to defend their homes from marauders on several occasions. They were alive because they were armed, had saved food and had joined with others.

These few people had in turn spoken with others including several from overseas and the conclusion was clear: the disaster struck everywhere. It was a crisis of Biblical proportion resulting in a rapid and historically unprecedented worldwide population crash. The rider of the Black Horse of Famine struck fast, wielding his relentless sword, cutting down hundreds of millions within the first few weeks. Five billion would die by September as the struggle for food intensified and diseases spread unchecked. In city after city across the globe, desperate fighting over the few remaining scraps followed by waves of mass starvation took out the rest. By spring, the world's population had declined to its pre-industrial level. By the following year it would be reduced to half of that. The carnage wasn't televised. Color images would never be shown. With small, desperate bands still lingering, for years it remained far too dangerous to enter most major cities. The survivors living in the countryside had wisely stuck together in heavily armed small groups, most numbering in the tens and hundreds. They eked out a living as best they could in easy to defend isolated rural areas. Corbett was one of the larger colonies. It would be years before they tried to personally contact others, and based on what they saw and learned from the few who passed by they were in no hurry.

Quick exploratory trips across the Columbia or Sandy Rivers for nails, tools, clothing and other valuable supplies would have to wait. Those still alive outside their lifeboat would proclaim their presence to all during the cold months with smoke rising from the fires they would build to keep warm. Few smoke plumes were seen in the distance as winter set in. Some talked of trekking outside but for years none did. No one wanted to leave the safety of Corbett.

Many believed that their survival stemmed from some sort of incomprehensible divine purpose. It was a feeling experienced by nearly everyone. Although regular security patrols continued for months, after summer ended, weeks would pass without anyone from outside wandering in. For the first time since the disaster struck people finally started to feel safe walking around town and working without carrying their weapons.

A sense of security and calm began to envelope Corbett as fall passed. The ever-present fog of fear and uncertainty that had surrounded them for so long was finally lifting. More than a few proclaimed they now felt safer and happier than they ever had in their entire lives. As the warm days of September faded and the days grew shorter and cooler, a comforting sense of peace began to spread throughout the town and a deepening belief that they would succeed began to draw even the darkest among them away from their despair.

Made in the USA
Lexington, KY
08 December 2011